ISBN: 9781090467881

Copyright © 2019 Mike Gould

All rights reserved, including the right to reproduce this book, or portions thereof in any form. No part of this text may be reproduced, transmitted, downloaded, decompiled, reverse engineered or stored, in any form or introduced into any information storage and retrieval system, in any form or by any means, whether electronic or mechanical without the express written permission of the author.

Reluctant Travellers

Set in the early 1940's

The following is a novel, and is not a historical document.

It reflects the people of the time and the world they lived in.

Much of the following actually happened, and has been obtained from over 200 letters, day-to-day diaries, photographs, other memorabilia, stories told, memories and other sources. Some are included.

It is the story of a young couple drawn into War, their life in the British Military services, and that of their family and friends at home in England.

Most names have been changed, due to the Personal Data Protection Act. However, it is intended that most of the facts have been retained in some form.

The Author hopes you enjoy the story about ordinary people enduring the unwelcomed situation of War.

Mike Gould

**THIS BOOK IS DEDICATED TO
THE MEMORY OF
GRACE AND LESLIE.**

CHAPTER 1

It was 37 degrees in the shade. The Sunday afternoon appeared to be far away from the war that had been raging since 1939. It was now the middle of August 1940. The field at the bottom of the garden had been mowed by the farmer, about 10 days earlier. The resulting hay had been recently turned to dry, to ensure that it will be ready to be gathered and stored in ricks, ready for the Winter food for the farm's cows. This ideal situation was just too good an opportunity to miss, so Mum Elsie, and Dad Jim, along with Daughter of nineteen years Grace, and her twenty-year-old long-term boyfriend Leslie, quickly collected some sandwiches and slices of Victoria sponge cake, along with some homemade lemonade, and made their way to the field with the pick-nick and blankets.

Not a cloud in the sky, not a breath of wind and not a sound to be heard, but for the song of a family of sparrows fluttering in a nearby hedgerow.

The blankets were laid on the ground among the soft fluffy dry hay, in the shade of the nearby hedge. The greaseproof paper packages were opened to reveal the sandwiches and cake, and were placed on the blankets. The young couple stretched themselves in the sunshine, on an adjacent blanket, while Mum and Dad sat on another. Grace and Leslie had known each other since they were young, having met at the Chapel Sunday school.

Jim opened the fabric camera case to reveal a Kodak expanding camera. He had previously loaded the camera with a black and white 120 film in the cupboard under the stairs, to avoid light attacking the delicate film.

Jim arranged the group of three, taking particular care of the exposure setting on the camera, and the position of the sun on his subjects. 'Click', and the photograph was taken. He then took a photograph of Grace sitting on the fence.

Elsie was serving china plates containing the white home-made bread and meat sandwiches, when the happy group were interrupted by Leslies Father Charlie, climbing over the fence stile. He was looking very much out of breath, and very hot in his thick collar-less shirt, tucked into his wool trousers and supported by a thick leather belt. He was waving a small brown envelope high above his head.

"I thought I might find you all here, when I couldn't find anybody at home," he spluttered in a broad Somerset accent, as he approached the group. "Had this delivered for Leslie today by that skinny telegram boy from Church Lane. Can't stand his old man. I thought it must be important so I set out to find him. Left Edith at home in a bit of a state, because she thinks that she knows what it's all about."

Handing the envelope to Leslie, Charlie sat down very heavily on a blanket, looking very longingly at the glass bottle containing the lemonade.

The group gathered around Leslie as he held the envelope at almost arm's length to open it. Grace was slightly behind Leslie looking over his shoulder, so as to read the contents as soon as possible.

The enclosed document had a government headed stamp with the date of the previous day, and Leslie's full name and address, with the following message: - "National Service Acts 1939. Dear Sir. In accordance with the National Service Act 1939, you are called up for service in the Royal Air Force and are required to present yourself on 22nd August 1940 between 9am and 12 Noon to: - RAF Halton, Buckinghamshire." The letter contained travel information and was signed by a Regional Controller. Leslie was also instructed to take with him his Gas Mask, Medical Grades Card, National Registration Identity Card and All Ration and Clothing Books.

The emotions of all members of the family group changed as Leslie read the message, so that all could hear the contents of the telegram. Grace put her arms around Leslie and held him tight. Elsie enclosed her face in her hands, and Jim stood up and pushed his hands deep into his pockets. Charlie remained on the blanket and had forgotten all about the bottle of lemonade.

Jim was first to speak. "So here we go again, just finished the last one and now there's this one, damn it can't they just leave us alone. I did my bit in the last lot, so Leslie now it's your turn to try to end this war."

Jim had indeed 'done his bit' in the last war. Somehow, before the 1914-18 war started, he found himself in Wollongong, New South Wales, Australia. working for the Tallawarra electricity power station as an electrical engineer. At the beginning of the First World War he volunteered with the Australian Army, and served for the whole of the war. He never did talk about his time in the Army, for what he saw was so bad, that he just wanted to forget.

__Brighton Beach Wollongong Australia 1914__

Charlie also 'did his bit' in World War One. He joined the Army Royal Engineers, Signals division. He fought in France for four years, and earned the three service medals known as Pip, Squeak and Wilfred. The details of information coming into Britain about the First World War, was very sketchy, for, as many thousands of men were being killed in France and Belgium, life carried on almost as usual in England. But those left behind, had to work very hard to cover for those fighting abroad.

__Charlie's Platoon. Charlie is front right__

Elsie collected the makings of the tea party, and placed each item carefully in the wicker basket. Grace folded the blankets, as Leslie, with hands deep in the pockets of his modern wide legged trousers, just stared across the field at the tufts of golden tossed hay, and wondered if he would ever see this sight again.

A very interesting change of mood occurred, as the family members each climbed over the fence stile, to head for home. From the hot sunny afternoon, black clouds gathered overhead, with a marked chill in the air. The black clouds accumulated very quickly and the atmosphere became very humid. As Grace was the last to enter the back door of the house, the clouds erupted into huge flashes of lightning, making even the dimmest corner glow a yellow white, followed by the thunder that shook the house to its foundations. And then the rain. Huge raindrops crashed to the ground causing reverberating splashes. The rain was intense and went on and on.

Jim filled the large black iron kettle with water, and placed it on the swinging steel arm, and pushed it with his leather soled boot over the low fire, burning in the grate of the combination fire place. The fire was kept burning day and night, summer and Winter, as this was the only means of cooking and heating. The front room and the bedrooms did have a small tile surrounded fire place, for the really cold winters. In winter the small tenement terraced houses were very cold, for regularly the wonderful patterns of ice formed on the inside of the windows, creating some entertainment, in trying to decide what the patterns resembled.

The combination fire place was a very clever piece of Victorian equipment. It was constructed from cast iron, and finished in a black glazed stove enamel. The open fire place was to the right of the unit, with a large oven to the left. An iron door covered the oven. It was heated by the adjacent fire. The temperature of the oven, was controlled by a mechanical damper mechanism. It had a thermometer fixed to the front door, for accurate cooking. Cast iron swinging shelves were mounted on each side of the fire, so that they could support either kettles or saucepans over the fire. The fire place was completed by a dark green tiled surround, and a stone hearth. The fire place was usually the centre of a lot of activities, so had a large brass hearth fender surround, with large brass finials on both front corners, usually polished to high degree. A wooden coal box sat to the right of the hearth. It had brass bindings and a sloping front door, hinged at the top. An array of long brass fire irons, and a wood and leather bellows, completed the outfit.

Leslie and Grace stood by the open back door from the kitchen, watching the rain causing a mini flood on the floor of the back yard. Charlie found an arm chair, not too close to the fire, as the temperature from the heat of the day was still very warm. Elsie had disappeared, but nobody had noticed, as they were all deep in their own thoughts.

Leslie thought that the thunderstorm was very appropriate considering the news he had just received.

Eventually Elsie reappeared, holding a large white handkerchief and sporting two very red eyes, obviously as a result of her weeping. Nobody really noticed the reappearance of Elsie, as they had not noticed her disappearance.

"Must get home soon as the rain eases, as Leslies Mum wants to know what the letter was all about before I came out, but I told her it was addressed to Leslie so only he must open it. She's going to be in a right state when I get home," Charlie said as he cased himself out of the soft arm chair. "Got about a mile to walk home so should take I about aff an hour at my speed."

Charlie had a condition commonly known as bowed legs, caused by a deformation of bones when he was very young, from riding horses. As a young man he wanted to be a horse jockey as he was just the right weight and size. But his father refused, and he was told that it was not a real job, so he must help his Father as an oil delivery man. This being the job that Charlie now holds. The old Bradford Van was packet to the roof with all sorts of soaps, cleaning detergents such as Vim, brushes, pans, heating and lamp oil. Most houses did not have electricity, some had gas lighting, with the majority being illuminated by decorative oil lamps. His condition did not stop him riding horses in the Army.

As Charlie made his departure with the bad news, the kettle over the fire place started to make spitting and popping noises, as everyone had forgotten it was there, and had boiled dry.

Jim removed the hot kettle from the fire and placed it in the ceramic sink in the kitchen, for to put water into it now would cause it to crack. He returned to the living room, and opened the cupboard beside the black combination fire place. He removed a Glass jar wet battery cell, that had previously been charged by one of the shops up the road. He connected the glass battery to a brown wooden cased wireless, with the letters PYE in gold letters on the front. Once connected, using a pair of wires, he turned the wireless on. Nothing happened for some time until a faint hum was heard. Jim moved the tuning knob to the left and then to the right. Several movements had been made by the tuning knob, when the device sprung into life. A very faint and crackly voice said "This is the BBC news from London, read by Alvar Lidell."

By now, the remaining four people gathered around the instrument, and listened intently to the news reader detailing the war information that he was permitted to tell, along with meetings that the King had had with the Prime minister, and certain very odd paragraphs that contained secret codes for certain persons overseas. Very often the strange messages had words or sentences that gave those people specific instructions who were working under-cover among the enemy, such as when and where to expect an aircraft with supplies or arms to arrive, usually under the cover of darkness.

The news reader had now finished, and the happy sound of dance music came drifting into the room from the crackly wireless speaker. Jim did not feel like listening to such happy music at the moment, so he turned the wireless off with a loud klick.

Outside the dark clouds had been replaced by lighter fluffy clouds, whisking across the sky, revealing the blue sky of summer above the clouds.

Charlie eventually arrived home, having walked along the empty Sunday High Street, past the Gas Works large grey coloured coal gas container, and the smelly coal gas conversion building, up a narrow footpath, across two railway lines, through a meadow field, and yet another footpath. Charlie was not a good walker due to his bowed legs, so the excursion did take the half an hour he had expected to walk home. He would have driven the van, but this was a works vehicle, which was not really the right thing to be seen on a Sunday afternoon.

Edith was very pleased to see Charlie home again, for throughout his absence she had been trying to make herself busy by cleaning the gas hob, and occasionally looking out of the front room window, trying to see if Charlie was returning along the opposite footpath.

"So, what did the telegram say, is it his call-up papers, how is he, what did he say?" Edith was almost shouting at Charlie, and not really giving him time to answer, as he was also trying to get breath into his lungs, from his walk home.

Charlie sat in his armed chair, next to the fire place, and replied. "Yes, it is his call-up papers. He has to go to somewhere near Oxford, or somewhere like that, on this Friday. He has to show the letter at the station, and they will give him a free ticket to ride on the train. I think he was expecting it after his brother went last month, but it's still a bit of a shock for him. He has to go into the RAF. I reckon that the RAF will suit him better than the Army or Navy."

Leslie thought it was time he also returned home, so after spending a short time with Grace, with whom he had become engaged to marry a few months earlier, said his goodbyes to Jim and Elsie, recovered his bicycle from the coal shed where he had stored it earlier, tucked the bottom of his trousers into his socks, so as not to get them tangled in the chain, and made has way home.

Monday at 7 o'clock, on a bright sunny morning, the tap on the front door has Grace rushing to open the door. The smiling face of George the baker greeted Grace with the question, "One large white and one small brown, is there anything else I can do today?"

"Yes please. Stop this awful War and let our men stay home where they belong", Grace replied as she pushed past George, and made her way along the front path towards the road where the bakers delivery van and his horse Eddy was standing.

She pushed her hand deep into her apron pocket and drew out a large carrot. After tickling the nose of Eddy, she gave him the carrot which he devoured in seconds.

George appeared beside Grace and said, "Oh dear, has Leslie had the call?" He placed his bread basket into the open rear door of the van, and as he climbed high into the driving seat, he continued. "Not many young men around nowadays. Will his employer hold his job open? Many do now. Don't worry love, he will be all right."

George flicked the reins, and Eddy trotted off up the road to the next customer.

Leslie had a good job. He was an electrician, having completed his apprenticeship for a large local company. After the war the Government bought many large electrical companies including the company he worked for, to install a national network of electrical power to most areas of the country. This company eventually became The Electricity Board. Leslie hoped that they would hold his job open for him when he returned from his National Service. Unfortunately, many jobs remained open after the war as the former job holders never returned.

Moments after Grace had returned home from feeding the horse, and closed the front door, there was another knock at the door. This time Elsie opened the door, and was greeted by Stan the Butcher, holding an aluminium flat tray containing a mixture of uncooked meats.

"Morning Elsie, What's thee fancy smorning? He announced with an accent from the adjacent town. "I got some lovely pork chops today. With the meat shortage, looks like they might be my last."

"Pork Chops will be fine Thank you Stan. Can I have three please," Elsie responded, as she peered past the Butcher to see a cyclist park his bicycle at the end of the front path. It was the skinny telegram boy from Church Lane, who had parked his bicycle, and was now walking briskly up the path behind the Butcher.

"Hello Robert, didn't see you in Chapel yesterday, were you working on Sunday as well?" Elsie said to the boy, ignoring the Butcher for the moment.

"Hello Mrs. 'C'. Yes, I have to work a lot over the weekends at the moment," the telegram boy replied opening the leather pouch on his waist belt. "Is Grace in please? I have to hand this ear letter to her myself, in person, not to anyone else." He was by, now holding a small brown envelope and waving it in air.

Elsie attended Chapel every Sunday morning throughout the year, along with all of the other group meetings for mothers, wives, prayer meetings and the jumble sale group. For many years she had been a Quaker, but with no local meeting house she attended the Methodist Chapel. To make up for the lack of a meeting house, she always read her Bible and the John Bunion Book 'Pilgrims Progress'. She often met Robert and his Mother at the Chapel, and had been aware that she had not seen the boy for quite a few weeks.

As the telegram boy was making his announcement, and continued waving the letter high above his head. Elsie took two wobbly steps backwards, for she was sure she knew what the envelope contained. The Butcher was by now standing aside, allowing the boy to take the foreground. Elsie called for Grace, who appeared from the living room looking very concerned.

"Miss Grace, this is addressed to you," the telegram boy announced as he handed the envelope over. Once the act was completed, he turned quickly, collected his bicycle and was gone.

Grace returned to the living room, holding the letter in front of her with thumb and fore finger, as if it contained a terrible smell. Elsie completed the shopping with the butcher, closed the front door and also returned to the living room, where Grace had placed the letter on the round dining table. She was standing beside the table, staring at the unopened letter.

Jim had very much earlier in the day, left for work in the colliery, at four o'clock that morning. Grace had not gone to work herself that day as a dressmaker, as she had spent all the night crying over the news that Leslie had received the previous day.

"Well open it," Elsie encouraged as she also stared at the letter on the table. "It won't open itself."

Grace opened the letter using a copper opener. with a bullet brass shell case handle, made by her Father during the last War. They were all told that that war was the war to end all wars. That of course was not the case. Grace withdrew the letter from the envelope and opened it to reveille a similar letter to that received by Leslie yesterday. She has to attend an address in Wrexham on Friday at midday. Just like Leslie, she had to take her gas mask and all her coupon books. A travel pass was also in the envelope.

Both Grace and her Mother Elsie, just looked at the letter without moving for some time, reading its contents over and over again. Eventually Grace put her hands over her face, and asker her mother what she should do next.

"You must tell Mrs. Mitchell your boss what has happened, without any further delay. We will walk to your work place together, so that we can tell her, and ask if she will hold open your job. You were doing so well at work, and I know you enjoy it, but you cannot ignore the Army. Oh, my dear I am so sorry this has happened. This evening you must see Leslie and tell him as well, so put your shoes on and let's set off."

The walk to the next village where Grace worked, was mostly uphill from the small mining town in the Somerset Coalfields. Grace's Father Jim, knew that he would not be called-up to fight, as he was a coal miner being a protected job, as the provision of coal is vital for the continuation of the Country.

Eventually Elsie and Grace reached Graces workplace, and spoke at length with Mrs. Mitchell, who told the ladies that she could not guarantee to hold open the job, as there was a War-on. Mrs. Mitchell questioned why Grace did not attend work that morning, as the call-up situation was affecting many other families. Grace collected her belongings from her work area, including a couple of note books, and left Mrs Mitchell, who was still complaining about her high workload, and no staff do to the work.

The journey home was now mostly downhill to the town. In some ways Grace had a feeling of relief, that she did not have to work under a boss who was so demanding. She had, however, learned a very good job to a very high standard, as many of Mrs. Mitchells clients were very wealthy, and very particular about quality. Not knowing about the future in the Army, was very concerning to both of the ladies, as Grace really did not expect to be called to War.

Grace and Elsie had a quiet walk home. The summer that year was very warm. Although the walk home was downhill for most of the way, both of the ladies felt very hot. Half way down the hill was a very conveniently placed bench seat. The rest on the bench was very welcomed. Neither said anything, but just looked at the countryside around them, and enjoyed the quietness. The thunder of a steam lorry trundling up the hill, broke the silence. The smell of steam and burnt embers from the lorry lingered in the air. An elderly man on a bicycle went past, down the hill. Grace thought he was travelling much too fast to be safe. The walk home continued down the long hill, and along the flat road that lead to home. The only other vehicle seen, was an open top charabanc, full of excited ladies waving coloured banners in the air. The charabanc also left a smell behind it, of burnt motor oil, and a cloud of exhaust smoke.

That evening Leslie called on Grace, as he left work, to go home on his bicycle. By now Jim was also home from work, and Elsie was preparing the evening meal with the pork bought from the Butcher earlier that day.

Leslie and Grace walked into the garden, and sat on the bench seat under the honeysuckle, giving shade from the Summer evening sun. They discussed at length the events of Sunday and that day. Leslie told Grace that they would marry after the War, and the he would write to her wherever she was every single day. Leslie did keep his promise to the best of his ability.

As the days went past, Leslie's employer did promise to keep open his job until he returned after the War, which was at least something positive to return too. They did, however, ask him to formally re-apply for the job when he was ready. Qualified electricians were in short supply at that time, and the company knew that there will be even less, when the war is over. The company had sufficient older electricians, who would not be called-up for service, to keep the business going for the time being.

Elsie carried out her daily routine, including the daily shopping in the local shops a little further along the road from the house. Firstly, the newspaper shop, to buy the daily paper, telling of the British and Commonwealth troop advances, as well as the losses, fashion and political news. Then the greengrocer for the fresh produce, and the post office for a supply of statonary, as she felt that she will be doing a lot of letter writing in the future.

Elsie was interrupted from her shopping, as the roar of heavy bombers could be heard in the air, further to the South of the town. She stood still in the street, as the noise became louder. Then they were overhead, eight large bombers heading towards Bristol area. Watching skyward, Elsie saw several fighter aircraft flying above the bombers. By now, other Women had stopped in the street, and were also watching the overhead display. Moments later the sky was alive. Other fighter planes attacked the aircraft with the bombers. Fighters were flying in all directions. The thunder of gunfire sounded as if it were only feet above the watcher's heads. The Bombers flew on, perused by two British planes, firing as they went.

The ariel fight continued, with the aircraft climbing and diving, turning to the right, and then the left. The crosses on the wings of the German planes was clear to see. As were the roundels on the British planes. One German plane flying very high in the sky, had flames coming from one wing. The ground watcher's saw the machine flip up and down rapidly. All of a sudden something came off the plane, and then two more objects came out of the cockpit of the flaming aircraft. Seconds later another object left, and a parachute opened above it. Elsie could not move. She watched as the aircraft dived towards the ground over the adjacent town, less than one mile away. She did not see the pilot and parachute land, as her attention was taken by a second aircraft, on fire, and diving towards the ground upside down, about a mile away to the East. An object fell from that aircraft, but no parachute was seen.

Two towers of thick black smoke, rose from the ground where the crashes had occurred. By now the fighters had moved away to the North. The ariel fight continued, now out of sight, but the sound of the battle was still very clear.

The Women all looked at each other for a moment, as shock overtook all of them. One lady said, putting her shopping basket on the ground, and adjusting her hat. "Well it looks as though our boys got two of um. Shame they didn't get the rest of the sods."

Two days after the ariel battle that had been witnessed by Elsie, Jim came home from work with some news. "Ear," he said sitting in his favourite chair. "You know Sammy who's in the Home Guard? Well, when that fight you saw was going on, he was on duty with is mates. They saw the Gerry land in is Parachute. He got stuck in a tree as he landed. So, they got to un with their guns and arrested un. He said that the Gerry would not give up is pistol too easy, so is mate shoved a rifle up his nostril. They got him in the end, and passed him onto a load of regulars. Apparently, the radio operator got killed on the way down. The second plane you saw blew-up with all lost. Sammy still a bit shook up about it all. The Bombers were going to Yate, but what the outcome of that was, I don't know."

The Air battle was a point of conversation in the area for many a day. The pilot was Lieutenant Koepsell who was sent to a prison camp. The radio operator Schmidt was killed and was found beside an uninflated life raft, with his parachute unopened.

All of the towns people thought that the British Hurricane's did well that day. As far as they knew, there were no British aircraft losses on that occasion. Jim and Elsie hoped that Leslie, who was now going to be in the RAF, was not going to be flying planes, for they now knew how dangerous flying was, and the chances of dying was quite high. Without invitation, the war had reached the small town.

Eventually Friday arrived. After fond farewells to both sets of parents, and Leslies younger Brother Andrew, Leslie and Grace, both arrived at the railway station, each of them with a small suitcase in hand. They had arrived in plenty of time as the train to Bristol was due in ten minutes. The air was warm and the sky was bright blue for five twenty in the morning. The platform was quite busy, with many other young people also carrying small suitcases. Many of the bench seats were already being occupied on the platform, so Grace and Leslie found the edge of a concrete flower planter to sit on.

The Train arrived on time, grinding to a halt, with steam being forced at high pressure from the many valves and pistons. The carriage doors were flung open as a few passengers disembarked. The many people who had been waiting on the platform scrambled into the carriages. Grace and Leslie were very lucky to sit together in one carriage, with Grace next to the window. Leslie leaned forward across, and in front of Grace. He grabbed the leather strap for the window opener and pulled it very hard. The open window rose from its lowered position to close, with a satisfying thud.

This seemed to be appreciated by the other passengers in the carriage, as they nodded in agreement. The window on the other side of the compartment was open, to half way down. Leslie raised his own suitcase, and then Grace's to the high-level storage rack above their heads.

The journey to Bristol Temple Meads station was largely relaxing, as the compartment with eight occupants rocked from side to side, as it trundled along the tracks at a fair speed, stopping at several stations, where other young men with small bags and cases boarded the train.

After thirty-five minutes, the train arrived at Bristol station, where all passengers disembarked taking with them all of their belongings. Leslie and Grace sat on a bench near the end of the platform, as it will be from this station, but different platforms, that they each had to depart to different final locations. They talked for several moments, until a very large green and black locomotive steamed into the station beside the platform, pulling behind it many dark red coaches. The loudspeaker announcement said, it was going to a number of Cities as well as Wrexham.

This was it. Grace and Leslie said their fond farewells, and Grace boarded a compartment that had only two other occupants. Almost as soon as the door was closed, the guard blew his whistle, and waved a green flag high above his head.

And then it was gone. And so was Grace. The last coach rounded the bend and disappeared in a cloud of steam and smoke. Leslie knew he now had to find the correct platform for his destination. This he did easily, and boarded the very crowded train. Many of the other passengers were men of his own age, some in a variety of military uniforms, and others in civilian suits like his own.

Grace found herself in a compartment with plenty of space, and was able to read the book she had brought with her. A tall young lady was sitting in the seat opposite, and an elderly gentleman, who was reading a newspaper, was next to the window. After a while the young lady said to Grace. "Hello, are you going far, you look very contented reading your book?"

"I am going to Wrexham," Grace replied looking up from her book.

"Really. So am I. I've been called-up by the Army and told to go to an address in Wrexham. Have you been called-up as well?"

Grace continued. "I have to go to No. 12 ATS Training Centre at Wrexham, and I have been told that an Army truck will be at the station to collect me."

"Me too," replied the young lady. "Looks like we are both going to the same place. By the way my name is Margaret, but I am known as Peggy. I don't know why Margaret's are called Peggy. But there you are, that's me. What's your name?

"Grace. They say that I am said before and after meals."

"Ha-ha, I like that one. What a lovely name," Peggy replied.

The remainder of the journey was taken up with questions and answers from both parties, including Peggy saying that she was engaged to Jack who was an engineer working for Bristol Council, and Grace telling Peggy about Leslie.

The train eventually drew into Wrexham station, and as promised, several huge Army Lorries were waiting in the road outside the station. Grace stayed close to Peggy as they had created a good relationship on the journey. She noticed that about fifty other young men and women, in civilian clothes boarded the lorries, driven by men soldiers in khaki uniforms, gaiters and big boots. A Sergeant was shouting at everybody and everything, no matter if a man or woman, in or out of uniform. Grace and Peggy climbed into a high lorry.

Each lorry was very high from the ground, and had wooden slatted seats from front to back, on each side, and a row of back-to-back seats in the centre of the lorry. The back wooden tail-gate was slammed shut, and the lorry set off.

Peggy shouted in a very wobbly voice. "It must have square wooden wheels."

A Corporal at the front of the lorry shouted. "Silence. No talking."

Grace looked at Peggy with a smile, hunched her shoulders and winked.

The journey to the Barracks took twenty uncomfortable minutes, as the occupants were thrown from side to side, when the lorry attacked corners at much too fast a speed. The lorries eventually filed through the gates of an Army base.

"Come on then you lot, everybody out, home sweet home," the bossy Sergeant shouted as he opened the tail gate of the lorry. Standing beside the Sergeant was a short burley woman Sergeant, with the peak of her hat pulled down to the bridge of her nose, this was making her having to lift her chin upwards, so that she could see forwards, under the peak. As a result, this made her thrust her well-endowed chest forward, and her shoulders backwards. Grace thought she looked very stern, and hoped that she was just part of the welcoming party, and not to be one of her officers.

All of the occupants in all of the lorries, jumped down from the transport. They were instructed to stand in lines, with their bags and cases on the ground beside them. Grace again stood next to Peggy, with an equally tall woman on her other side.

This time, the woman Sergeant with hands clasped behind her back shouted at the assembly. "For God's sake look tidy there. This is the British Army not a Mothers church meeting. Feet together, shoulders back, arms by your side and no talking."

All of the assembly followed the instructions except one young lady, who was crying uncontrollably, with her face in her hands, and her shoulders shaking with each sob. Grace noticed that the young lady looked either fat or pregnant. The female Sergeant stood beside the crying woman, and shouted into her face at very close quarters. "So, what's the matter with you then. Missing Mummy already?"

The crying young Lady screamed out, with arms and hands outstretched, and stared at the Sergeant. "Can't you see, I'm Pregnant?"

"Get your bag and follow me," the Sergeant commanded. as she turned on her heal and toe, and marched to a building some twenty yards away.

"The other tall women standing next to Grace whispered out of the side of her mouth. "So that's how to get out of this mess?"

By now all of the lorries had moved away, and were parked nearby on a tarmacked area. The drivers were standing near their vehicles, or leaning against them, in a slovenly manor, with most of them smoking cigarettes, but all of them studying the assembly of newly arrived women on 'parade'. Some were pointing to individual women who were responding with a smile and a slight wiggle of hips.

The loudest voice that Grace had ever heard, roared from the male Sergeant, directed at the soldier drivers. "Polish your rubber tires till you can see your face in them. And put those smokes out now, there is fuel about, you are a hopeless lot of layabouts."

The Soldiers scrubbed out their cigarettes, and disappeared behind their vehicles, taking a last glance at the girls as they went.

A Woman Corporal marched towards the assembly, and stamped to attention in front of the Sergeant. The Corporal was followed by six uniformed marching women Soldiers, who halted to attention behind the Corporal.

The Corporal called out the name of each of the newly arrived women, and told them to stand behind a particular woman Soldier in an orderly line. Each group was then led by the woman soldier to a separate corrugated tin building. Inside the buildings were rows of basic beds, a tall and a short cupboard was beside each bed. The women were told to sort out between themselves, who was going to sleep in which bed.

The overpowering woman Sergeant marched into the room, she told the women that they must all meet in a large building, near the edge of the compound at 1700 hours, to be sworn into the Women's Auxiliary Territorial Service.

Most of the new recruits explored the compound of buildings, constructed of curved corrugated iron sheets, and concrete slabs. At five o'clock the group of women found the building concerned. It was a tall two-story building with iron framed windows. As with all the other buildings, the glass windows had diagonal crosses of white tape, to try to prevent shards of glass, in the event of explosion. The entrance to the building had many other women gathering and chatting, before wandering up the two steps to the open door. A very upright male Sergeant, with a stick tucked tightly under his upper armpit, and a flat cap with the peak pulled over his nose, stood at one side of the open door, and bellowed that all should now be already seated, and not being on a Sunday School outing.

Once seated in the large room, with about fifty other women, Grace said to Peggy, who was sitting beside her, that it would be good if her Sunday School did have as many members. To her horror, the Sergeant with the stick, who unknown to Grace, had been standing right behind her, leaned forward between the girls and shouted. "Silence."

The raised stage at the front of the hall, had three chairs facing the audience, with one table in front of the chairs. A door opened to the right of the stage. The thunder of a loud voice, from the rear of the room, shouted the word "STAND." All in the room did indeed stand, as three officers gently marched to the chairs on the stage. The officer in the middle was tall straight and very smart, with lots of gold braid, and a brown leather strap from his shoulder, diagonally down to another strap around his waist

"Please be seated," the officer asked, in a gentle but firm voice. While still standing, he continued to explain that, all new recruits will now be sworn into the Women's Army Auxiliary Corp, and after the ceremony, they will all be members of the British Army, as a result they will abide by the rules as laid down by the War Office. The Officer invited a Priest, in Army uniform, who was standing beside him, to carry out the ceremony. When the official parts had been completed, and all new recruits had been sworn-in, everyone in the room again stood, as the officers and other dignitaries on the stage, left by the same door as they had entered earlier.

The following day started at 6 o'clock in the morning, with the new recruits having medicals, overseen by a lady doctor. Each person was issued with an identification number, a pay book, a small bible and uniforms. The pay book also held vital and personal information regarding each person, including the size of each uniform garment.

An interview was held with each recruit, and they were told which department of the Army that they will serve. As Grace and Peggy were both employed previously in making clothes, they were both told that they will work in the Tailors section. Grace was very pleased about her placement, especially as she was going to be in the same department as her new friend Peggy.

Later that evening, all of the Girls tried on the uniforms issued, consisting of two of each, caps, tunics, skirts, overalls, shoes, corset belt, gloves, jersey, stockings, vests, slacks, plimsolls, pyjamas, and very ruff woolly underclothes. A very heavy great coat, a long-strapped handbag, gas mask in a bag and a fabric kit bag completed the issue. All of the women complained bitterly about the basic uncomfortable underclothes. They were informed by the Woman Sergeant, that they must all muster on the parade ground at 7 o'clock in the morning in full uniform, except for the Great coat.

The morning arrived on a warm sunny day. The group were made to carry out marching. known as 'square bashing', for hour after hour, day after day, for five days. Most were exhausted each evening, as a result all slept very well, with little time for talking or planning escapes from the current situation.

Twelve weeks passed fairly quickly. It was now time for the new recruits to attend the 'passing out' parade, and to be sent to their respective future work places.

Grace in A.T.S. uniform

CHAPTER 2

Elsie and Jim had been delighted to receive several short letters from Grace. The latest letter told them that she will be posted to Coventry, to work in the Tailors department. She also told them of her friendship with Peggy from Bristol and Betty from Swindon. Elsie and Jim had been very worried about Grace. She was not the sort of person, they thought, that would find Army life easy. She had been brought up in a relatively sheltered situation compared to some women. She did have some friends, but they were mostly neighbour's and people from the Chapel. Old school friends had either moved away, or went with their lives in a different direction. She had always been a very determined person, who usually, knew where she was going, and how she was going to achieve her goal. They were very surprised that Grace was getting on so well, and making the best of the situation she now finds herself in.

It was 2nd November 1940, the day of the Annual Chapel bazaar, held as usual in the small Miners Welfare Hall in Rock Road, known as Rock Hall. Elsie had been very busy over the last few months, knitting baby clothes, and making lavender bags. The bags were filled with dried lavender flowers, and sewn into fine small net bags with a silk bow.

The lavender bags, along with baby clothes and other items, made by a variety of Chapel members, were laid out on the fold-away tables, arranged around the edge of the room. The tables were covered with wide white paper, obtained from one of the local printing companies, and coloured crape paper pined to the white paper, that gave a sense of a party feeling. Each table had a wooden frame fixed above it, in the shape of football gaol posts, and covered with the coloured crape paper, giving the impression of a shop window. A tombola was on one table, with small unidentified prizes wrapped in brown paper. Several of the tables had items for sale known as a 'white elephant stall', and a pile of second-hand clothes, as a 'jumble sale'. Each table was decorated with the crape paper.

A small room to the left of the curtained stage, was set aside for the tea making. A few tables and chairs were available to enjoy the tea, and delicious home-made cakes. The Methodist Minister opened the event with a prayer, and a reference to those who could not be there that day, as they were serving King and Country.

In moments the noise was terrific, as the very young male members of the congregation, used the privacy of the hall to make it as a race track. With arms outstretched they imitated a flying aircraft, along with the noise of the engines, and machine guns firing. Most of the boys had short tailored trousers, and Fairisle patterned sleeveless jumpers, long socks and boot style shoes. The young girls generally followed their mothers to the stalls, while trying not to watch the boys playing fighter pilots.

Ladies attended the stalls, with the clothes being strewn in all directions on the jumble-sale stalls. Some ladies were leaning over others to reach the bargain first. Elsie's Brother, Ernest, who was a member of the Salvation Army, played his cornet on the stage, adding to the overall noise of the happy event. The Methodist Minister and his Wife enjoyed the tea and cakes.

Edith, Leslies Mother, found Elsie, and stood beside her behind the table to assist her, as the supply of lavender bags were being sold very quickly. Most of the stalls had ladies serving, each with their best hats pinned to their heads with a variety of elaborate hatpins.

Edith leaned towards Elsie and said. "Have you heard from Grace lately? Leslie tells us he found the training hard, as he had to march for hours at a time in full kit with a rifle and ammunition, and back pack for miles. Apparently, he is being trained in that new stuff they call RADAR. I don't understand it myself, but I do know he is doing well. He asked if you could pass these letters to Grace when you write to her again." She handed Elsie two white envelopes with Grace's name on the front.

"Yes of course I will," Elsie replied very loudly to make herself heard above the noise in the hall, just as her Brother stopped playing his cornet, making her voice heard by everybody in the hall. The boys stopped playing aeroplanes for a moment, looked at the lady who was shouting, and then continued making machine gun sounds, as well as the flying actions. The absence of young men in attendance was very evident.

The time for the bazaar to close was near. All of Elsie's goods had been sold, along with many other items The Minister announced that nineteen pounds, fourteen shillings and eightpence three farthings profit was made for Chapel funds, helping towards the replacement of the coal heating boiler in the boiler room under the Sunday school room. The fold-away tables were stowed away under the stage by the men, and unsold items were placed in boxes for the next bazaar, next year. The boys had by now exhausted themselves, and were quietly playing in the middle of the hall floor.

As the people made their way out of the hall, the evening was well set in, as darkness began to fall. The people leaving the hall looked to the sky, as a deep roar was heard coming from the south, gradually getting louder every moment. A deep winning sound started to hum from the town, increasing to a higher pitched wailing sound. The sound came from a newly installed Air-Raid siren on the roof of the Town hall.

Everybody stopped, and looked upwards, and towards the deep roar. A huge number of very large, dark aircraft flew over the group, heading to the North. There was wave after wave of the intimidating black images, thundering across the sky. The aircraft were flying so low that the black crosses edged with white could clearly be seen on the wings, even in the dim light of the sky. Several minutes after the aircraft had passed, the Air-Raid siren changed to a lower pitch as it slowed down. All of the congregation stopped very still, as the sound of the roar of the aircraft engines, dimmed into the far distance. A few children were running around and between their mother's long skirts, and not really being very sure what they had just heard.

As the people silently, made their way home, the Minister was last to leave the hall, who locked the door, testing the handle several times.

"Look" Jim shouted pointing to the horizon to the North. "Look they got Bristol. See the glow in the sky from the fires, it's only eight miles away." As he said the words a small group of the new fighter aircraft swept across the sky, towards Bristol at high speed.

Jim continued. "When Leslie gets to work on this new RADAR, our Boys will get to them a lot quicker than this. Those poor devils in Bristol, God bless Them."

Life went on normally, in the small town left behind by Grace and Leslie. A river made its way through part of the High Street in the town, with ancient iron railings protecting its banks from the adjacent road. The town shops were mixed, with butchers, grocery stores, haberdashers, building supplies, green-grocers, hatters, post office, dairy shops, dentist, clothes shops' cobblers and shoe makers, statonary and newspapers, and further into the square was a blacksmith.

In the High Street, was also the Army recruitment building, known as the 'drill hall'. Behind the 'drill hall' was the Air Training Cadets hall. Before the War, Leslie was an active member of the ATC. He had the newsagent order the organisations magazine every month. Many youngsters were members of such organizations such as Army cadets, Navy cadets, St John Ambulance cadets, boys brigade and Boy Scouts. At the time before the current conflict with Germany, and the Nazi's, the members of these organisations did not realize how important the basic training, of following rules, and discipline, would help to eventually keep them alive.

Elsie and Edith, every day carried out the daily shopping. Often, they would meet in one shop or another. On this particular day, they met in the grocer's shop, at the end of the High Street, called Welsh's. It was a typical grocery shop, with wooden topped counters running around each side of the shop. Behind the counters men with white aprons tied around the waist, busied themselves with customers. All of the produce was stacked neatly on shelves behind the counters, along with wooden drawers, having names such as 'herbs, nuts, currents, mixed fruit, loose tea and a variety of other things. At each corner of the counters, were boxes of goods stacked to make a presentation tower.

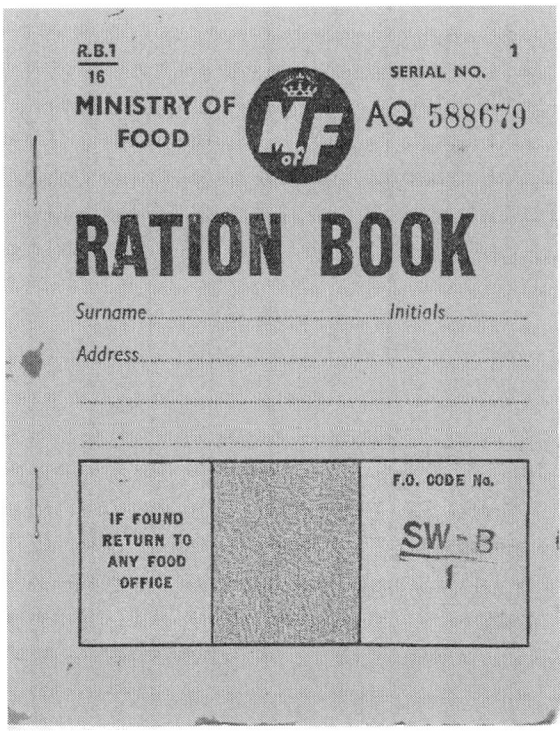

A Ration Book

Elsie ordered her shopping items one by one, as the man serving her selected them from the shelves, and placed them on the counter. Some items were already packaged, while others such as glace' cherries, had to be wrapped in screws of greaseproof paper. The bill was added up on a duplicate pad by hand, item by item. Elsie rummaged in her purse for coin's that was more than the required amount, therefore, in need of some change. The serving man placed the coin's, along with the top copy of the bill, into a small round wooden container, with a threaded brass top rim. He then screwed the container into a circular threaded device above his head. Pulling hard on a cord hanging from the arrangement, the container sped at high speed, along a tight wire near the ceiling, and disappeared into a small room with windows, at high level. A lady could be seen with circular rimmed spectacles. She unscrewed the container, looked at the bill and put some coin's in the container as change, re-fitted the container to the overhead device, and pulled a cord at her end. The device again sped across the wire to the waiting assistant. He unscrewed the container from the device, and handed Elsie here change.

Nobody in the shop took any notice of the flying container, as this method of transaction had been carried out for many years.

Edith was just about to start her shopping, when she saw a poster on a wall near the door. The poster had a picture of a uniformed soldier with a rifle over his shoulder. The poster said: - "Men required 41-55, Home Defence Battalions."

"Look Elsie," Edith said pointing to the poster. "This is just what Charlie wants. He has been so upset that he can't be a regular soldier. Must tell him about this poster when he gets home from work."

The ladies concluded their shopping, after visits to the newspaper shop and the green grocer. On return home, Elsie removed the hat pin from her felt hat, removed her hat and coat, and placed a kettle of water over the fire by means of the swinging arm.

Elsie sat in her favourite chair beside the fire, and gazed out of the living room window, at the large apple tree in the garden, that was beyond the back yard that contained the outside loo, and the coal shed. As it was now late November, only a few leaves remained on the tree. Her mind started to wander to her daughter Grace, wondering where she was, what she was doing, and with who. An image appeared in the back yard. For a moment Elsie thought that her thoughts were playing tricks on her, for wandering towards the back door, was Grace in full Army uniform.

Elsie raced to her feet, and opened the back door, to find Grace standing with arms open wide. Elsie tried to contain her delight, as she threw her arms around Grace very tightly, after a moment releasing the tightness of the hug, for she did not want Grace to think that she had missed her, so much.

"Hello Mum," Grace spluttered, as she tried to contain a few tears rushing to her eyes. "Managed to get a long weekend leave, took me ages to get here by train, so I must be careful to make sure I get back in time. Don't want to be put on a charge for desertion. Leslie has managed to get four days off, before he goes abroad. Has he arrived here yet?"

Elsie stood away from her Daughter for a moment, and just looked at her from a distance. She remarked on how smart Grace looked in her uniform, and on how delighted she was to see her. She moved forwards again, and gave her a long and tight hug.

Releasing Grace from her Motherly arms, Elsie said. "Sorry my dear he hasn't appeared yet. I recon he might be spending a few moments with his Mum and Dad."

Grace came into the living room, throwing herself into the other chair beside the fireplace, usually occupied by her Dad. She threw her hat onto the circular mahogany dining table, making a clatter as the hat badge bounced on the highly polished surface. Undoing her army tunic, she placed her crossed legs on the foot stool, and relaxed into the chair.

"So, my dear, tell me all that has happened to you since we last saw you," Elsie asked, leaning forward in her soft chair, with her for-arms resting on her lap.

Grace leaned forward, and grabbed the long fire poker. Using the poker, she pulled the swinging arm away from the fire, containing an annoying boiling kettle.

Grace spent some time telling her Mother about the training, uniforms, the shouting NCO's, uncomfortable training billets, and her new role in the uniforms department, of the Army Tailors workshops. She explained that when she returns in two days-time, she must report to some Barracks near Coventry.

Grace continued to tell Elsie about her friendship with Peggy, and a few other colleagues. By now the daylight was beginning to fade. It was time to prepare the meal for Jim, Grace's Father, to return from work. As Grace rose from her comfortable seat, the back door opened, and Jim appeared in the kitchen. On this occasion, he did not use the shower baths at the pit, as he often would, therefore he was black from head to foot, except for white circles around his eyes.

"Look who I found," Jim explained, standing aside, to reveal Leslie in full RAF uniform, holding onto the handlebars of his bike.

Grace pushed past her Father, and threw her arms around Leslie, who was trying not to drop his bike. "What a sight for sore eyes," she screamed knocking his side cap from his head.

The early part of the evening was spent with Grace and Leslie in the front room, telling each other about their recent experiences. Jim was in the tin bath, in front of the roaring fire, with hot water being replenished regularly by Elsie, using the water heated by the kettle over the fire. Grace would leave the front room on occasions, to continue preparing the dinner in the kitchen, followed closely by Leslie, as her shadow.

Jim eventually looked cleaner than at his entrance. The round mahogany table was laid for five settings by Elsie. Jim tapped the end of a walking stick on the adjoining wall of the terraced house. Moments later Jim's Brother Bill, appeared wearing a dark blue wool blazer. He saw Grace and Leslie, and grunted an undefined hello. After sitting to the table, Bill tucked the corner of the table cloth under his chin, and proceeded to serve himself, from the array of china dishes containing various vegetables, that had been grown in the garden.

Bill, as they say, had 'done his bit' in the first World War in the trenches, as a result now suffers from the very common 'Shell shock' from which he never recovered. After the war, Bill spent several years, firstly in a general recovery hospital, and then to a Mental health hospital. Jim owned several terraced houses in a row, including the one he lived in. He let them out to tenants. When the house next door became vacant, and Bill had recovered sufficiently, the decision to move him next door was taken. Elsie provided his food, so he usually joined Jim and Elsie for meals, and Elsie cleaned his house. As a result of the 'Shell-shock', Bill had some difficulties in many things, including normal accepted behaviour, therefore, he did act differently, and sometimes abruptly.

Jim had finished his bath. He actually looked like Jim again. "clean as a whistle", as Elsie often said, when he was not covered in coal dust. The tin bath was again hung on a large nail on the outside wall of the back yard, between the kitchen window, and the outside loo door.

Dinner was served. Bill had already started to eat his dinner, as the other four sat to the table. The meal, as usual, was in silence, as all had been told not to talk with your mouth full. Pudding was spotted dick, a suet pudding with sultanas, and boiled in a muslin cloth. After dinner the table was cleared, Bill returned home next door, and the washing-up was completed.

Jim settled into his soft arm chair, next to the fire, he leaned back in the chair, crossed his ankles, and said to Leslie. "So, come on you two. Tell us all about your new adventures."

Leslie explained, that he and his squadron, who deal with a system called RADAR, will be continuing training before being sent to Malta in the Mediterranean Sea, when he returns from the current leave. At the moment the large Island is in British hands, and is in a prime location to monitor the movement of the enemy. It has a native population of around two hundred and twenty thousand, and an Italian military population of sixty thousand. He explained about the training of the meteorological weather and climate work, as well as the basics of RADAR.

Grace was not very happy knowing that Leslie was going to be so far away, however, she knew that the situation had to be accepted, as many thousands of service personnel worked overseas.

Jim asked Leslie what RADAR stood for. He was told it was Radio Detection and Ranging. Leslie explained RADAR a little deeper to Jim, who was very interested, for although he was currently a coal miner, he was a very cleaver electrical engineer, and mathematician.

Edith, Leslies mother, had returned home after her morning shopping with Elsie. She made herself busy with household tasks, until Charlie returned from his day at work, in the oil delivery business, Charlie met many people. On this day, he met a regular customer, Harry Hobbs. Harry provided Charlie with his tin oil can, with the spouted lid, for Charlie to fill from the van. He was wearing the dark blue uniform of the local ARP, Air Raid Precaution organization, and looking very smart.

"I didn't know you were in the ARP," Charlie announced as he filled Harry's oil can from the rear of the Bradford van.

Harry replied. "Oh ah, I've been a member for a while. I'm the boss of our group now. Ever thought of joining yourself Charlie? You could be quite an asset to the organization."

"That's a bit of a thought," Charlie responded handing the filled tin back to Harry. "What do you get up to in the ARP? I've heard of it, but don't know nothin about it."

Harry put the tin can on the floor and said. "We have great fun, although it's a very serious matter. Amongst other things we practice on getting folks out of bombed houses in a very specialist way. We control situations, with the bobbies, if an unexploded bomb turns up. We make sure that light have been put out in houses. We do lots of things, I know you would enjoy it, after all you know most of the folks around here already, and you know your way about. We only recruit very local people. You get to know how many people are usually in each house, cos if it's bombed you know how many to account for."

The thought of joining the ARP. was on Charlie's mind all the way home that evening. In his mind's eye he could see himself in the dark blue uniform with the gold lettering over the shoulder, and the tin hat. He parked the Bradford Van on the drive, in front of the garage, and replenished the stock sold that day, from his supply in the garage. He spent a little extra time in the garage that evening. He sat on an old wooden chair that was covered in paint. He thought about the meeting with Harry. He could do that job easily, and would be contributing to the local community.

Charlie and Edith WW1

Charlie took off his flat cap as he entered the kitchen. Edith was there to welcome him. She wasted no time in telling him about the Home Guard poster she saw while shopping.

"Hear that's a dammed good idea," Charlie agreed. "I was talking to old Arry Obbs today and eh asked I to join the ARP. But I must admit, I think I like the Home Guard better."

Charlie thought a lot about joining either the ARP, or the home guard. At last the decision was made. Charlie decided to join the home guard, with Edith's blessing. He regularly attended the meetings for training in a room at the rear of the Drill Hall. After some basic training, Charlie was issued with his uniform, boots, ammunition belt and pouches, and an Army gas mask. On one training occasion, he was asked to stand up and to tell his comrades why he joined the home guard. Being a deep thinker, he addressed the group. "Without me, and all the other British people, all the Officers, and members of Government, and the Prime Minister, would be useless, just like the last war. So, the British people are more important than any Member of Parliament, the Prime Minister, or any General, but they haven't worked that out yet."

His comrades were astonished at the way he saw the world that they now lived in, so they all stood up and clapped very loudly, with many of them nodding their heads in agreement. Lots of discussion followed Charlies comments. He became well known for giving a sensible answer to sometimes, difficult questions.

Charlie became very involved with the Home Guard. He often attended his station in a concrete defence post, overlooking the town, or carrying out training in the Drill Hall. Regular patrols around the town, usually with another Home Guard soldier, took place. With the Nazi's just the other side of the English Channel, and the occasional German aircraft flying overhead, it was very important to observe, in the event of any enemy invasion.

One evening Charlie's Commanding officer told the whole platoon that "The Yanks are coming." He said that the War Ministry are building new barracks, in a field between the High Street and North Road. It will be used as a training, and a re-deployment base for the American Army. He added that. "British Service people must not communicate with them in any way." He also said that it will be a few weeks before they arrive.

The news about the Americans coming swept through the Town at high speed. Without delay, the Town's Dance hall was smartened up with a coat of paint, The Cinema had new neon strip lighting added to the name 'Palladium'. The tobacconist ensured they had stocks of American Cigarettes and Cigars. The girls in the Town were told by their parents, not to touch.

The War elsewhere carried on. Leslie and Grace returned to their bases, on time. Grace returned to a new base at Bramcote Barracks, Nuneaton near Coventry, and Leslie to RAF Padgate near Warrington.

When Grace arrived at her base, she was directed to here new billet. The billet beds had already been filled by other women, apart from one high level bunk. She took the bed without complaint, as she was very tired from the train journey. She was, however, delighted to find that Peggy was also in the same billet. Grace spent little time in telling Peggy about her time at home with Leslie, and her Mum and Dad. Peggy had a lower bunk near the 'Turtle' heating stove, with a girl named Betty on the bunk above.

Betty, had silently overheard the conversation between Grace and Peggy. She leaned over the side of the bunk, and said to Grace. "You're too nice a girl to have a fella like that. So, if you are engaged where is your ring?"

Grace was so upset at the remark from Betty, she produced a photograph from her bag, and showed it to Betty.

"Nice Boy. How do I know that he's yours?" Came the reply from Betty, who returned to her bunk to read a magazine.

Peggy whispered into Grace's ear "Don't take any notice of her, she has been causing trouble with almost every girl here, before you arrived, she obviously can't get a Man herself."

Grace was still upset when she wrote to Leslie, so she told him about the incident. She also told him about her long journey to Nuneaton, and about the cramped billet. Grace explained that she was very pleased that Peggy was in the same billet. She also confirmed her love for Leslie. At last, she was able to put the incident out of her mind. Grace decided, that she would keep a daily diary of her activities, feelings, and the important events of the day. She found that, by writing down these things, it gave a strange sense of relief, to know that one day, she would look back in the diary, and remember the good, and the bad times. Every day, throughout her life in the Army, she wrote in her diary.

The Army base at Nuneaton, was just a short few miles from Coventry. Since the heavy bombing of the City in November 1940, almost every night the Luftwaffe attacked the City with tons of bombs. The sky was regularly lit by the powerful search lights, picking out the German heavy bombers, and the roar and thunder as the bombs exploded. Sometimes the British fighters, or the Anti-Aircraft guns would be lucky, and a bomber would crash in the surrounding Countryside. The sound of the Rolls-Royce Merlin engines, and the sound of machine gun fire from the British Spitfires, was a very regular occurrence.

It was now May 1941. Grace and her comrades had been working in the Tailors workshops all day. After a good meal in the busy cafeteria, it was Grace's turn to do night Guard Duty. She walked to the Guard Room to receive her orders, to be greeted by a Military Policeman wearing a side-arm, in an enclosed fabric holster, and a tin hat.

"Evening Soldier" The Policeman said in a friendly voice. "your turn again. Only saw you the other night. Can't you sleep? The other fella is already in the Guard house waiting for you."

Women soldiers were never on guard duty on their own. As in this case, a male soldier worked with a woman soldier. Usually allowing one to sleep for an hour, while the other kept vigil.

Grace entered the guard house, to find a very young male soldier, sitting in a chair smoking a cigarette. The Military Policeman followed her into the guard room. From an inner secured room, the policeman issued Grace with her revolver side arm, in a fabric side holster, a torch and a tin hat, he then issued the male with his torch, tin hat, and a 303 rifle. Both soldiers checked their weapons as they were trained, and waited for further instructions.

"You two, are to look after area 'D' delta tonight," the M.P. said looking at a chart on the wall. "You have both done it before, so sign the form, and be off with you."

Both soldiers left the guard house, and marched smartly towards area 'D' of the camp perimeter. Once out of sight of the guard house, they both slowed down, to a more relaxed march. On arrival at area 'D', there was a small wooden hut, of about 12 feet by 6 feet, located about ten feet from the perimeter fence, and the gate in the fence. The hut had a downward facing faint glow, from an electric light, on the outside of the building. The light had been converted, so that no light could be seen above. Inside the hut was a table, oil heating stove and a bed. A small area in the corner, was surrounded by a curtain, hung from the roof. The area contained a tin bucket to be used as a toilet. The inside of the hut was illuminated by one small light bulb. There were not any windows, so the light could not be seen outside. On the table was a methylated spirit cooking device, tea pot, a box containing tea and some matches, and a field telephone, with a winding handle on its front.

Grace told the other soldier, to have his sleep for the first hour, as she was not as tired as the young man had looked. He thanked Grace, telling her that he had a very tiring day and could do with a 'kip'. The perimeter fence was very dark, except for the glow from the half covered shed light. It only took a short time for Grace's eyes to adjust to the low light. She started her duty by taking a short walk to the East, and then to the West, and then returning to sit on a wooden chair, placed outside of the shed.

The night was quite dark, with little clouds, there was a good view of the crescent moon shining, and the stars were bright. Grace looked at the 'Plough' group of stars, and wondered if Leslie was looking at the same group, wherever he was. Her thoughts wandered through many subjects, as the hour progressed. One of her thoughts, took most of her time. Her Mother's Brother, Arthur, and his Wife lived in Birmingham, so, she wondered how she could visit them, as Birmingham was not that far away. Was there a train, or a bus? She felt that she must investigate the possibility.

Grace's thoughts were interrupted, by the roar of aircraft engines overhead from the South. She quickly entered the hut, waking the other soldier, who grumbled, with words that she had not heard before. She lifted the telephone, wound the handle, and reported the sound of aircraft to the South. Immediately the wail of the Air-Raid-Siren sounded in the camp. All lights were extinguished throughout the camp, including the shed. The sound of people running and shouting was plain to hear. Grace realised that the other soldier had disappeared, so she decided that she should find the shelter as well.

Before she could move, a huge explosion shook the whole area. The perimeter fence shook along its length, as though someone had cracked a whip. The sound was accompanied by huge flashes, and the sound of falling trees crashing though the undergrowth, on the outside of the perimeter fence.

Grace dived under the table inside the flimsy shed, hoping that it would give some protection. She pulled her tin hat firmly over her head. Many more explosions and flashes from the bombs occurred, and were accompanied by the loud sound of the Anti-Aircraft guns on the base, trying to bring down the attacking aircraft. One hour passed, with the bombs mostly being dropped further to the North from the base.

At last the sound of the 'All-Clear' came from the siren. An odd smell filled the air. It was a smell that Grace was not familiar with, but made her feel quite sick. Grace stayed where she was, under the table, for a little longer, just in-case.

Eventually, Grace escaped from the shed. She ran as fast as she could to the main buildings of the camp. Many people were now appearing from underground shelters. They looked as if they were well used to the bombing. A woman Sergeant asked Grace if she was all right, she also congratulated Grace for raising the alarm, indicating that many lives may have been saved by her actions. "They have been hitting the town for months now," the Sergeant said as she lit a cigarette.

Grace and her male soldier colleague, were given the rest of the night off-duty. The guard had been replaced by other soldiers. She returned to her billet, to find her welcoming bed waiting for her. As she sat on the edge of her bed, the shock of the situation came over her. Grace was shaking in an uncontrollable way. The reality of what could have happened to her was overwhelming. Betty woke from her sleep, to see Grace sitting on her bed. She was not expecting to see Grace, as she knew that it was her turn to be on Guard Duty.

Betty jumped down from her upper bunk, and sat beside Grace on her bed. "My God Grace. You look as though you have just had a narrow escape. Your shaking like a jelly. We all heard the bombing, so headed for the underground shelters just in time. A billet, two away from here was destroyed completely. As far as we know everyone is safe. But you, my love, were out in the thick of it. Stay there and I will make you a cup of coco."

Betty disappeared into the small kitchen area, and returned a few minutes later with two hot cups of coco. She again sat on the bed, next to the still shaking Grace. "So, come on, tell me what happened out there," Betty insisted holding Graces cup as she drank, to avoid spillage. By this time, several other girls were awake, and had gathered around Graces bed, hoping to give her support.

Grace eventually managed to gather her thoughts, and eased her shaking. She told the others, in some detail, the events at the perimeter fence. She also admitted. that at the time she was not in the least frightened, but later, the shock overtook her. Telling her comrades about her ordeal settled Grace down, as did the coco. Eventually she was able to get a disturbed night's sleep.

The morning light revealed that the perimeter fence had received a bomb hit, destroying the fence and the main guard house. Grace later learned that 131 people were killed in the local town Nuneaton, as a result of that one raid.

Grace regularly received letters from Leslie, sometimes several at a time, with all of them numbered, so that she would read them in the correct order. On many letters, Leslie could only discus things like the weather, and his undying love for her.

RAF Padgate was a training base for RAF trades, along with taking in new recruits. Leslie spent some time learning the trade of meteorologist, Radio and RADAR, before being posted to Blackpool.

Billets in the RAF base in Blackpool were sparse, so himself, and several others, were billeted in a private guest house on the South sea front. Nobody complained very much, as the food and accommodation were much better than the wooden huts that they had been used to. Leslies room was looking over the sea front and promenade. The sight of the sea advancing and retiring up the long flat beach, was calming. From his window he could see the beach in both directions for quite a long way. The South pier was just along the road, and was still very popular for holiday makers, although all lights were extinguished at night. Leslie often watched the people enjoying themselves on the beach and promenade.

Leslies squadron were told that the top of the Blackpool Tower had been removed, and that a RADAR system had been installed, but it was not successful, so it was never used.

12 Met. Squadron, as they were known, had to attend daily training on the Trade. Meteorology, being the study of the weather, Leslie found very interesting, He learned about cloud formations at different levels in the atmosphere, and the resulting weather patterns at ground level. The pressures at higher levels were established using weather balloons on a tether wire, with delicate instruments attached to the underside. The Balloon could be recovered and instruments read. The information was then sent by radio to ships, aircraft, airfields and other establishments. The new system, recently named RADAR was a method of bouncing radio beams off objects far away, and recovering the returned signal. This returned signal, could then be compared with the original signal, and the result shown on a cathode ray tube screen, as a large or small dot. The dot could then have its direction and speed identified, as the dot moved across the screen. As this was a new system, the Ministry decided that the meteorologists would be the best skilled to operate such a system.

Leslie, and his comrades, were able to walk from the 'billet' on the sea front, to a local training area near the end of the promenade. A group of about twenty men found the subjects of instruction fascinating. They also had to identify aircraft from pictures, of both enemy and friendly. This was quite difficult, as many silhouettes of aircraft were quite similar. The practice of using the weather balloons, was carried out on the edge of a local RAF airfield. The system the boys were trained on, was a fixed RADAR unit, with permanent transmitter and receiver stations, and a variety of fixed and rotating aerials. All of the men had extensive training on the use of radio Morse Code, and how to use radio so that the enemy would not detect its transmission locations.

The new system RADAR was to be kept very secret, so when Leslie wrote to Grace every day, as he had promised, he was not permitted to discuss his work or training. Leslie's friend Harry, announced, as they walked along the promenade to the training centre. "Looks like we are going to get a pay rise to ten bob when we qualify. About time, I can't do much on what we get now." Leslie agreed and said, "yep, and we will have letters after our names like RDF, OP, AC2. That sounds grand. Must send some home for savings to be sent, money is a bit tight at the moment. When we get that pay rise, we could send some home instead of scrimping as we do now."

CHAPTER 3

Leslie's elder Brother Donald, was also in the RAF. He was a mechanical instructor at the RAF station at Blackpool. Donald worked on Spitfire engines, and trained others on the craft. Leslie only once, had the opportunity to visit Donald, but he wrote to him often. It was a great shame that their service lives never crossed.

The time had come for Leslie to move again, this time to Haverford West in South Wales. Further training ensued, going over the same subjects learned before. While Leslie was at Haverford West, he, and his comrades, were posted, for a short time to RAF Locking, near Weston-Super-Mare. RAF Locking was, amongst other things, a radio school. After a few months training on the skills of radio, and its electrical components, he returned to Haverford West.

Several months had passed, when Leslie was allowed home leave. This time Grace was not able to get home leave at the same time. Leslie arrived home, to find his younger Brother Andrew, on holiday from the college, where he was training to be a Methodist Minister. It was really good to be home for a short time. He had the time to visit his elderly Grand-parents, who lived close by. For a few days, it almost seemed that the RAF was in a different world. That the war was a figment of his imagination. If only that really was the case.

Leslie visited Grace's Mum and Dad, arriving in time for a cup of tea, mid-afternoon. Graces nineteen-year old Cousin, Albert, was already chatting to Elsie, with Ernest, Albert's father and Elsie's Brother. They were sipping tea, with a new, uncut fruit cake on the table, looking very appetising. Albert was wearing the uniform of the Tank Regiment, looking very smart in the khaki uniform, with his beret resting on the dining table. Ernest also looked smart in the uniform of the Salvation Army. Ernest told Leslie that they were both soldiers. "One working with God, and the other for God."

Albert had completed his training, and was now a tank gunner, with a very happy crew. He hadn't yet seen combat, but he knew that if Hitler invaded, then he would be ready. Leslie spent some time chatting with Grace's parents and their guests. He did enjoy his slice of fruit cake, a little different to the ones usually made by his mother, but just as nice.

Leslie returned to the base at Haverford West, to learn that the station was in 'lock-down'. No leave was permitted and no letters to be sent. The reason was unclear. However, that was the situation, so everybody had to follow the rules.

Three days later, the squadron were informed that they were going overseas. Every person was permitted to send one Telegram only, and that the cost would be covered by the RAF. The destination of their service was not known at the moment. The questions were, will they be in a combat zone? For how long will they be overseas? No-one knew the answer.

Leslie knew that Grace was now on leave at home, so, he sent a Telegram to her saying. "Going o/s don't write, don't worry." He knew that Grace would worry, but there was nothing he could do.

Two days later, Leslie and his crew arrived at Falmouth, after a very uncomfortable long ride in the back of a ten-ton RAF lorry. Two short breaks were permitted on the journey. With kit bags in hand, and rifles over shoulders, they boarded a Royal Navy Destroyer docked in Falmouth Harbour. The Airmen hardly had time to collect their thoughts, as they filed up the gangway. Living conditions were very tight, as Sailors and Airmen had to share almost the same space.

Each Airman were permitted to send one last Telegram, so, as Grace was still on leave, he sent one to her saying that "All is well. I am Good. Tell Mum and Dad Love You. Les."

All again was 'locked down' for several days. Ships were arriving and leaving the dockyard regularly, ranging from stores ships, minesweepers, civilian cargo ships, destroyers and small fast cruisers. British aircraft guarded the sky's overhead with Huracan's and Spitfires, flying out to sea, and returning regularly. Gas air balloons on tethered lines littered the sky, with their height constantly being changed by winches. The Royal Navy's daily life on board went on, with Sailors doing their regular jobs. Leslie and his mates could only watch, as they sat for several days, on wooden fold-away chairs.

The food was not bad. At least it was well cooked on board, and plenty of it.

Twice a day, the RAF commander, along with his NCO's carried out parade's on deck, come rain or shine, usually rain. Every morning and evening, the whole ship took part in the regular raising and lowering of the flag, very similar to that on the RAF bases.

One early morning, the sound of the engines changed, from the regular thud of the generators making electrical and vacuum power for the ship, to the obvious sound of drive engines powering the propellers. Black smoke poured out of the funnel, the tethering mooring ropes were loosened, and the ship eased away from the dockside.

The ship headed due South. Once in open water, the engines noise increased, and full speed was reached. The Airmen still had no idea where they were going, until they were all arranged on deck. Standing to attention, the Airmen looked very smart, as uniforms were all in place, and buttons sparkling. The Commanding Officer, a Squadron Leader, informed them that they are going to Malta. He told them that the Island is in British hands, but with a large contingent of Italian military, who of course, are on our side in the war. This is an ideal place to set up and run a RADAR and Radio communications centre, along with meteorological duties. This now confirmed earlier reports, that Leslie's Squadron had received. However, since those reports, many other destinations had been a possibility.

Leslies friend, Len Beach, leaned towards Leslie and said out of the side of his mouth, so that the Officer would not see. "There you are then, right in the thick of it, going to be blooming hot."

There was then a long silence, for some of the Airmen would have guessed that they were going to Malta.

Two days and nights sailing South, leaving behind a calm Bay of Biscay, and the coast of Portugal on the Port Side. The Ship had been some forty miles off the Portuguese coast, to ensure she was not over the Continental Shelf. The ship turned to the Port, and entered the Straights of Gibraltar. Unusually, this ship did not enter Gibraltar harbour for stores, or fuel replenishment, instead she steamed on, into the Mediterranean Sea, keeping about fifty miles from the coast to the North.

The sea conditions changed to much calmer waters. The wind changed to coming from the South West, bringing with it a warm air current. The North African coast to the South, seemed to be just a few miles away, as the ship steamed on at high speed.

Most of the ship's occupants, by now knew they were heading for the port of Valletta on the East side of Malta, so, the sailors continued with their work, and the Airmen mostly played cards, or just watched the sea go by. It had been six hours from passing through the Straights of Gibraltar, and was now 4.30 in the afternoon. The shrill sound of a siren, signalled 'Action Stations'. The sailors responded, running to their posts throughout the ship. Those who manned the guns, pulled their flash-proof head gear over their heads as they ran. Others put on tin helmets, and gathered some small arms as they entered the armoury. The gun turrets started to swing, and raise to follow targets, directed by headphones.

Other sailors were pointing to the sky. Officers shouted command's using tin speaking trumpets. All were totally engaged and paying full attention.

The frightening sound of dive bombers overhead, ensured that all personnel followed instructions to the letter. Some men were seen to be crossing themselves, and kissing small crucifixes around their necks. The squeal of the aircraft diving increased in seconds, followed by an enormous explosion. Water from the bomb hitting the sea to the port side of the ship, fountained onto the ships deck, and high into the air. Vibration from the explosion made every rivet quake, and every steel plate on the ship creek. The ships guns were firing continuously at the aircraft, following it as it rose steeply into the air after the attack.

Leslie was able to peer through the side of an open door. He recognised the aircraft from the many pictures shown in training. It was Junkers Stuka. As the aircraft climbed, it turned to the right and flew out of sight. Seconds later another bomb exploded on the other side of the ship, preceded by the same screaming sound as before. Again, the ship shuddered, at the same time turning course as tightly as allowed, and heeling over as it went.

A naval Officer in a white uniform, shouted at the frightened Airmen to form a human chain from the ammunition magazine, to the gun deck. The job was to pass the ammunition to the gun crews, as the firing continued.

Two further bombs were dropped, but all missed the ship, as the Stuka pilots weaved their aircraft in the air, to avoid the exploding shells around them, along with the machine gun tracer bullets. Leslie was the last man in line in the chain, handing the rounds of ammunition to sailors on the deck. His location was just inside a door, with steps leading down into the ship. The long line of Airmen were down the steps behind him, and deeper into the ship

"Hurry along there", Came a command from somewhere on deck. The speed of delivery of the ammunition increased along the human chain from the magazine to the deck. "Here he comes again. Keep your heads down chaps, he's only got machine guns left now, all his bombs have gone."

Shure enough, the sound of an aircraft approaching from the side became louder, as he flew towards the ship at quite a low level. The sound of guns was terrific, and could not identify if from the ship or aircraft. The bullets ricocheting off the ships structure, was plain to hear, as well as the structure being punctured. For a moment, the supply of ammunition stopped, as members of the human chain kept their heads down, while the aircraft flew over the ship. Leslie reached behind and to the side, to collect the next supply of ammunition, but it was not there. He turned, to see that the airman behind him slumped in a heap on the step. The next man down the steps announced. "He's cop't it, poor sod, he was only nineteen."

The ammunition started again, being passed over the head of the deceased Airman.

Someone on board shouted. "Here we go again, good luck chaps." The sound of guns almost made eardrums burst, and the smell of explosives was overbearing.

"Got the sod," came a shout from the deck, followed by a cheer that any football team would be proud of. "Here comes the other one," came another shout, again followed by the gunfire. A huge explosion overhead, was followed by another cheer. The aircraft had a direct hit, and exploded in mid-air above the ship. Some fragments landed on the ship causing men to run for deeper shelter. Other components scattered themselves in the sea opposite from the attacking side. No parachute was seen.

All was quiet for a few moments, except for the ship's hooter saying "Whoop, Whoop, Whoop."

The body of the Airman, was moved by his comrades, with great dignity, and taken to the mortuary, beside the doctor's surgery. Several other bodies were already on the floor of the mortuary, as a result of the conflict with the Stuka's.

The sound to 'stand-down' came with relief, from all aboard, as the ship turned again to continue on its designated course. The mood on board changed after the attack. The RAF Commanding officer, spent some time writing a letter, presumably to the fallen Airman's family. The other Airmen realised, just how vulnerable they all were. Some of the men commented on the fact that, any ship could be used as 'target practice' by any enemy aircraft. The loss of the young Airman affected everybody. All now knew, that they were now, very much in the war.

The ship sailed past Sardinia, Sicily, and on to the port of Valletta, Malta, without any further incidence, at the great relief of all on board.

Back in England, Charlie and Edith went about their regular business in the small town, unaware of the experiences that Leslie was going through. Charlie became a very keen member of the home guard, often turning out for duty at weekends, as well as many evenings. One Saturday mid-morning, he was patrolling the High Street with his good friend Burt. Side by side they walked beside the river flowing adjacent to the footpath, with their rifles hung on their shoulders by its straps. As they approached the Town Hall end of the High

Street, they were stopped in their tracks, in amazement. Coming down the hill Silver Street, and approaching the High Street, was an American Army Jeep, containing a driver, and an armed soldier in the front seats, with two officers in the rear seats. One of the officers was smoking the largest cigar that Charlie had ever seen. It was at least eight inches long, he thought. Both officers looked very relaxed, as they motored into the High Street. Following the Jeep were about sixty American solders marching in columns of six abreast.

Burt said. "God don't they look slovenly, they can't even march properly. Hope they can fight better than they can march."

Indeed, the sight was to be behold. Most of the platoon were out of step, looking around themselves, and some were even talking. Some carried their rifles on their shoulder, others carried them by their sides. Most were looking around at the new surroundings. It certainly was a shamble.

As the Officer in the Jeep passed by, he noticed Charlie and Burt in uniform, watching the procession. The Officer raised his right hand to the peak of his cap, and flicked his hand away horizontally.

"Was that a salute or a wave?" Charlie said gazing at the officer. In response, Charlie raised his right arm high and straight in the air. He waved his hand, as if to say goodbye.

"Hear," Burt whispered to Charlie. "They must have come from the railway station. I thought I heard a commotion up there early this morning, but I took nothin of it. They must av bin at it all night. I recon they still got some stuff to come down from the station. Come on Char, let's go un av a look."

As the American platoon moved further up the street, the two Home Guard men left their post in the High Street, and walked very fast up the hill to the Railway station. They ran slowly for a few steps, and then walked fast, both looking like small boys trying not to run, holding their rifles close to their body, but their gas mask bags flying in all directions. They decided to go to the concrete 'pill' box, located just above the station. On reaching the 'pill' box Harry and Hubbert were already peering through the oblong hole in the wall, at the movements in the station below.

"What are you two doing here?" Harry commented, and not taking his eyes of the station below. "I thought you were supposed to be doing the High Street today. Hope the Captain don't find out."

Charlie pushed his way forward, to look through the hole in the concrete bunker. There were Americans everywhere. Most were trying to lift a lorry from a railway flat-truck, parked in a siding, using a large crane. Others were unloading stores from railway box trucks, and some roaming about, doing nothing but chatting and smoking.

"Got to tell the others," Charlie said, as he pushed past to go through the narrow door. "Come on Burt before we get missed."

The two this time, almost ran down the hill to the High Street. Upon arriving at their destination, it seemed as though the whole town had turned out. The American Parade had stopped at the end of the High Street. They had been doing some 'square bashing'. One of the NCO's was shouting commands, but it was a shamble. Most of the soldiers did not know left from right, and could not stand up straight. It appeared that Charlie and Burt had not been missed, as their Captain arrived with the Sergeant, and two more Home Guard soldiers. Charlie and Burt brought themselves smartly to attention, with rifle's on shoulder, trying not to look out of breath. Burt saluted the Captain, as he was the corporal, and most senior of the two. He made very sure that he saluted according to regulations. Just to show the Americans how it should be done. The Captain Saluted very smartly in return, watching the reaction of the American Officer, out of the side of his eye.

The American Officer, at last, realised that they were being watched by the British Army, who were being much smarter than 'his lot'. He brought the proceedings to a halt, as the Home Guard Captain approached the American Officer. Both saluted. The American removed, at last, the cigar from his mouth, spat some tobacco to the ground, and sat on the front mudguard of his Jeep. For several minutes they conversed. They saluted each other again, and the Home Guard Captain left to re-join his Sergeant.

The American parade moved off, led by the Jeep. The Home Guard Captain whispered something to his Sergeant, and they both burst into uncontrollable laughter.

The American parade continued up into the Square, passed the church, and made its way to the temporary billets constructed for them, at the back of the High Street.

The Home Guard Captain, explained to the group of soldiers around him, that, orders have come from 'on-high', that no American personnel were permitted in the Town, under any circumstances. This is due to the previous problems with the American Army in Bristol, concerning the local girls, some of whom had husbands serving away, and the imprisonment of some in Shepton Prison, for unacceptable offences.

Mr. Pearce the Tobacconist, placed himself in front of the Captain, put his hands on his hips, and said in an angry voice, "So what am I supposed to do with all the Yanky Tobacco and fags that I bought in special. Your lot won't smoke it?"

Mr Welsh, the owner of the general store, was standing outside his shop, with a white apron tied around his waist. He looked at the Captain and opened his arms, with the palms of his hands uppermost, and gestured as if in agreement with Mr. Pearce.

"I think you had all better take it up with the Ministry," the Captain said in a loud voice so that all could hear. "I can't do anything about it. Not my fault. Don't blame me." He turned and marched back to the Drill Hall, followed by the Sergeant.

Many of the shop owners, including the Tobacconist, were invited to take their wares into the American Army Base, at regular intervals, to sell them to the men, much to their relief.

CHAPTER 4

Grace spent many hours working in the tailor's department, doing mostly alterations, and enjoying time off with her comrade friends. The billet at Nuneaton was quite comfortable, but very cold in the Winter. Two heating stoves in the centre of the hut, were really insufficient to maintain a comfortable temperature. A very large stack of wood logs was regularly topped-up as fuel, next to the heaters. This caused smelly smoke to poor out of the chimney, both above the roof, and inside the billet. Extra blankets had been provided. These were used not just at night, but also as poncho's during the day, being draped around the girl's shoulders, to assist in keeping them warm.

Both Grace and Peggy, were replying to the many letters they had received from Leslie and Jack. Both were wearing there 'great coats', and huddled around one of the stoves. "I really think the cold up here is a different sort of cold that we get down South," Grace remarked, as she pulled the big collar of the coat around her neck, and draped the blanked over her legs.

"I know," Peggy replied, "There's Jack somewhere in Africa, and your Leslie, God knows where, both of them warmer than us. I recon we ought to find somewhere warm to go of an evening rather than this place."

Grace reached into her handbag, and produced folded a programme. "How about this?" She said, handing the small paper booklet to Peggy. The programme was for the Hippodrome Theatre Coventry, Peggy opened the booklet, to see that a play called 'The Man Who Came to Dinner' was on next Monday, it said that the play was by George Kaufman.

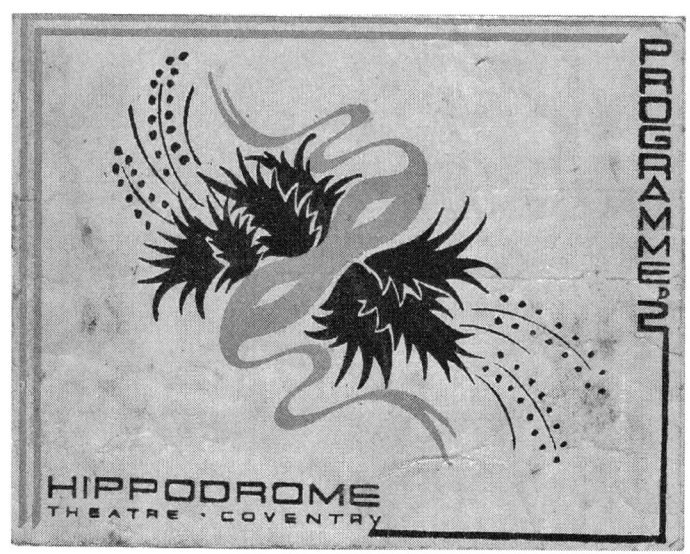

"I've heard of George Kaufman," Peggy replied, looking with interest at the other pages of the programme. "Look, 'Get A Load of This' and 'Floradora' the musical is on in a few weeks. Is the place still standing, after all the bombing that Coventry has had?"

"Yes' I think so," Grace replied taking the booklet back, and looking at it again herself. "Fancy going? There is a bus, I think it's the 88 will take us from here, and get us back before late if you like. I would love to go but not on my own."

"Too true I would," Peggy said excitedly. "Be good to get out of this place for a while. There are a few weeks before we get home leave, so it will stop me going mad. Yes. let's do it."

The Monday evening arrived, it was a cold mid-December evening. The girls waited for the number 88 bus outside the main gates of the camp. As they were going to the theatre, they were able to obtain a pass for the evening. They had only been waiting for a few moments, when an Army truck came out of the camp gates, and stopped beside them. The front passenger Soldier leaned through the open window and shouted. "Going to Coventry Love, want a lift?" The girls looked at each other, and agreed that as they were together, it would be fine.

"Yes please," Peggy said, as she climbed into a seat beside the driver, Grace also climbed into the cab, and squeezed herself between Peggy and the passenger, Both the driver and passenger were in Army uniform.

"Hear this is cosy", the passenger said, as he wriggled to a more comfortable position on the hard seat. "Your both safe with us, because we are both recently married to a pair of twins. So, if I do sumut wrong, then he tells her, and if he does sumut wrong, then I tells her. So Where are you two going this chilly night?"

Peggy, at last moved to a more comfortable part of the seat, and as the driver set off, she said. "We are off to the theatre in Coventry, do you know it."

"If it's the Hippodrome, I recon you could be lucky. Seems like it's the only building still standing in the City Centre. Gerry demolished most of it, including our favourite pub," the driver said, as he peered through the windscreen, and crashing every gear in the gearbox. "We found another though. Fancy a drink after the show?"

"Sorry don't drink," replied Grace. "And who's going to be telling whose Wife?"

"Good Girl," the passenger replied. It's only about 20 minutes, if we don't get bombed to pieces on the way."

The lorry trundled on along the dark road, with the driver still peering through the windscreen, because the headlights had hoods, to protect the light from being seen by enemy aircraft above. This made the illumination of the road limited.

The outskirts of the City appeared to have escaped much of the bombing. As the lorry made its way through the dark streets, a few sections of buildings had been demolished, but most were still very much intact. There was almost no traffic about, except for the lorry. The driver continued to grind his way through the gearbox, causing the few passers-by to turn and look at the noisy vehicle.

Approaching deeper into the City, the sight was very different. Street after street were ruins. An Air-Raid Warden watched the lorry pass by. with his hands on his hips, wondering where it was going.

The lorry came to a shuddering halt. The driver announced. "Here we are then Ladies, Hales Street, and the Hippodrome Theatre, the centre of entertainment for the masses. Return bus stop is opposite the theatre. Sorry about the ride. Must ask the mechanics to put a few more gears in this jalopy, then I might have a chance of finding one. Have a good evening, By."

Grace and Peggy jumped down from the lorry, thanking both of the men. They stood for a moment in the road, just looking at the scene, but had to jump aside quickly, as a black taxi, driven by a man with spectacles, and a large flat hat, thundered towards them, blowing a klaxon type horn as he went by.

The two girls looked up the road, and then down the road, neither of them had ever seen anything like it in their lives. Almost every building was either demolished, or badly damaged in the street. Piles of masonry and wood was strewn across every footpath. Some of the buildings that were still standing, had what was left, of windows at high level. Some people were climbing over the rubble, others sat on the steps of the demolished buildings, and large pieces of masonry. The sight was amazing.

On the corner of the street, opposite from where they were standing, was a large plain building, that appeared to be untouched by the devastation. The wide steps led up to the main entrance, with the word in large letters above the doors, 'Hippodrome'. The building appeared to be closed, except for a glow from an electric light inside the entrance.

"Come on then," Peggy said grabbing Grace's arm and almost dragging her across the street. "As we are here, we might as well go in."

After the initial shock of the devastation around them, the rest of the world came into focus. Lots of other people were heading for the theatre. Most of the men, who were not in uniform, had black evening suits, some waring trilby style hats, some with white silk scarves, and some with overcoats. The ladies mostly were wearing long dresses with shorter coats. Some of the coats were made from real fur. Grace and Peggy did not feel uncomfortable in their uniforms, as lots of other Men and women were also in military uniform.

The area was quite busy. Lots of vehicles, of various sorts, made their way up and down the street, with people walking in the roadway, to avoid the rubble. The strange thing was, that, nobody really took any notice of the devastation around them. They appeared to just got on with their lives, as normal.

Peggy and Grace joined the que, to buy tickets for the performance. Everyone, orderly stayed in the que, chatting to each other as they waited. When the tickets were purchased, the girls followed the signs, and made their way to the 'stalls'.

Electric lighting lit the plush carpeted passageways, and white edged steps, that lead down to the auditorium. Seats 'G' 4 and 5, were seven rows from the proscenium, and almost at the centre stage.

The girls looked around the theatre. It was enormous. The stage curtains were beautifully embroidered with scenes from the 1920's. The words 'Safety Curtain' was in large letters across the centre of the curtain. Grace said to Peggy. "Is the Safety to keep them in, or us out?"

Peggy replied with a whisper. "Neither, it's to stop any fire from the stage coming into this room. Although, with all the fire that's been around here lately, it hardly seems appropriate."

People were filling the seats in all areas of the theatre, very quickly. The six, high level boxes, on each side of the stage, had lots of people in their fine clothes. Some were leaning over the front wall of the box, to see who were in the seats below. One lady, with a hat of very large feathers, shouted to someone in the front row of the stalls, and waving vigorously. It was quite obvious, that the person in the front row, did not want to respond. The man turned away from the waving person, to talk to the woman on his other side. Grace watched the episode with interest, and thought that trouble was brewing between the two ladies, perhaps, over the man in the front row.

The lights dimmed in the auditorium, and a well-dressed gentleman came onto the stage. Addressing the seated audience, he said. "The synopsis of the scenery, is in the home of Mr. and Mrs. Stanley, in a small town in Ohio.

The curtain was raised, and the play commenced. Constance Love was first person on the stage. She took one of the main parts of the play, as Mrs. Earnest W. Stanley. Act 1 scene,1 was 'A December Morning.' A man, in a dress suit, held a large sign above his head, with the title of the scene. The play commenced. Scene 2 was announced by the man in the dinner suit, as "About a week later." The play entered Act 2, and was called "Another week has passed, Christmas Eve." The Play concluded with Act 3 "Christmas Morning." With a cast of twenty-nine, and several scenes, the play lasted for two hours, including a short intermission. The performance concluded, with a piano, somewhere out of sight, playing 'God Save the King'. Everyone in the theatre, including the performers, stood to attention as the tune was played.

People filed out of the theatre in an orderly manner. Taxies seemed to arrive from out of the darkness, and disappeared just as quickly. The occasional horse drawn transport was whisked away, full of theatre goers. Most of the taxies, were motor cars. The front area next to the driver was open, for luggage storage.

Some had the drivers compartment open roofed, and some were fully covered. Most were black coloured, but the occasional vehicle had a dark blue bottom, and a black top.

The return bus ride, back to the camp was uneventful, and very dark. Occasionally, the dimmed lights of a vehicle coming from the other direction, was seen. The seating in the bus, was much more comfortable that the Army lorry, but they did save the bus fare into Coventry.

Grace and Peggy both agreed, that it was a good night out at the theatre, and that they would try to go regularly.

The following evening, Grace managed to reply to two of Leslie's letters, and posted them together, but she numbered them, so that Leslie would read them in the right order. She had a military coded address for Leslie, but she still had no idea where he was in the World. Grace told Leslie about the visit to the Hippodrome theatre in Coventry, and how surprised, both Peggy and herself were to see the devastation of the City. Peggy and Grace often talked about that evening. They marvelled at how resilient the residents must be. How they must live day-to-day, not knowing if their property will be still standing in the morning, or even if they would be alive to see it.

Several weeks later, Grace had seven days home leave. She travelled home on the train, changing at Birmingham and Bristol. Eventually, after a short walk from the station, she arrived home, to very welcoming parents. With a week out of Army uniform, she was at last able to relax. Her Father Jim, was very proud of the recently hatched yellow chicks, that had been brought into the house to keep warm. Thy were housed in a wooden box, and placed near to the fire. Not too close, but just close enough. He joked with Grace that he had already chosen the one to have, for the next Christmas dinner.

While Grace was still on leave, the morning post arrived, with several letters from Leslie arriving together, delivered by the duty postman. As the postman handed the letters over to Grace, he noticed that they were from Malta, and had been censored. "Letters from Hell," the postman announced, having heard that Malta had indeed, been through hell, having almost constantly being bombed by the Germans. Grace opened one of the letters from Leslie. It told her that he was, indeed, now in Malta, but he was not able to give any details or a real location, as the Censor would stop the whole letter. One thing he did say was. "The NAFFI here have got next to nothing in stock. Could you please send me some ciggies and some baccy? I have just bought a new pipe, better than the last one, but it will need burning-in."

Grace arranged for the items requested to be sent to Leslie. She was delighted to know, at last, where he was, and that he was safe. Grace was very good at helping her mother Elsie. She helped with cleaning the house, shopping, cooking and other tasks. She spent some time telling her Mother, all about the things that she had been doing while away in the Army, especially about her friend Peggy. She discussed the evening they had spent in Coventry, and the destruction they had witnessed from the horrendous bombing. Elsie said that she would pray for those people, when she next went to Chapel.

Every evening, Grace would walk down the road to Uncle Earnest's house, to practice on his piano. Her great friend, and Cousin, Albert, Earnest's Son, was also on leave from the Royal armoured Corp. Albert was, as was Grace, a very accomplished piano player. They often sat on the piano stool, side by side and played duets for hours and hours.

One day, while the pair were playing a duet, Earnest said. "Why don't the two of you do a concert in the Town Hall, playing duets? Most people in the town would love to hear you play. At the moment, any light entertainment is welcomed. I can make all of the arrangements, and get it advertised for your next leave."

Reluctantly, Grace and Albert agreed to the proposal. So, Earnest set things in motion. He was a solid member of the Salvation Army in the Town, being the band master of their band, and the towns Silver band. As promised, he arranged a full concert to be held in the Town Hall, with a group of Lady singers, the Town Silver band, and Grace and Albert to play piano duets. The date of the concert, was to be arranged at a later date, due to some of the participants being in the Military.

Two days before Grace had to return to work, Grace and her Mother Elsie, returned home from a morning's shopping. There was a large van parked outside, on the road, with two men dressed in leather waistcoats, and with leather aprons, tied around their waists.

As Elsie put the key in the front door of the house, one of the men said, as they opened the back doors of the van. "Ready when you are missus."

Elsie opened the front door wide, and went into the front room. She spent a moment, making a space along a wall, and shouted. "Ready when you are."

Grace, viewed the proceedings from the living room doorway, wondering what was coming into the house.

The two workmen, gently eased a wonderful piano into the front room, rolling it along the floor on a two wheeled trolley. Grace followed every move of the exercise. Once in place, a form was signed by Elsie, and the men went away.

Grace looked at the instrument. It was an upright piano, with dark mahogany panels, and two brass swinging candle sticks, fixed to the upper panels above the keyboard. To complete the outfit, was a beautiful piano stool with a hinged lift-up padded seat as a lid, giving storage space for music, underneath the lid. Grace thought it was beautiful. She looked at her mother standing beside her. and threw her arms around her mother, thanking her from the bottom of her heart.

"You need to thank your Dad, not me" Elsie explained. "He thought you would need one."

Grace, at once sat on the padded piano stool, and played and played, until her Mother called her to help with the evening meal preparation. That evening, after giving a huge thank-you to her Father, Albert arrived. They played the piano together for hours, until it was time for Albert to go home.

CHAPTER 5

The morning was clear and bright, on board the Royal Navy Destroyer, as it approached the East coast of Malta. Sailors went about their duties, preparing to drop anchor, about half a mile from the coast. The Airmen were told the previous evening, to be ready to disembark at 07.00 hrs the following morning. In some ways, they were glad to arrive, as the attack by the Stuka's had unnerved many of the men, also the conditions for living and sleeping was very cramped. The group had been allotted sleeping and eating areas separate from the sailors, as their duties were different during the voyage. The accommodation areas were below sea level, as there were no portholes, or daylight of any description. As a result, most of the men had spent as much time on deck as possible.

Leslie had found the exercise interesting, except for the Stuka attack. He watched the sailors go about their daily routines. He was fascinated, that even now, ropes were coiled in neat circles on deck, just as they were in the days of sailing ships. The daily tot of rum was always welcomed by most of the ship's occupants, except Leslie, and a few others, who did not drink alcohol. A large Navy launch arrived along-side the ship, crewed by sailors in white uniforms. The sailors had been standing on the deck of the launch, holding wooden grappling spars, horizontally, above their heads, looking very smart and efficient. The launch had been bobbing about on the choppy water, but none of the sailors had to hold onto anything, to support them. It was very impressive to see such skilled sailors.

All of the Airmen boarded the launch, along with lots of boxes containing equipment for their trade. The launch bobbed up and down extensively, compared to the stillness of the large ship. Men and equipment were stowed, and the launch set off for shore.

Five minutes later, the launch pulled along-side a dockside. All of the Airmen and equipment disembarked without incident. It was a very strange feeling for most of the men, for although they were standing on firm ground, they felt as though they were still moving on the sea. Each of the Airmen recovered their own kit bags. The equipment boxes were stacked on the dock, handled expertly by the sailors. Moments later, the launch set off for the ship again, to collect other cargo and men.

The group of Airmen looked around the dock, but saw no means of transport to take them onward from their present position. One of the men, who had been sitting on a box, looked for a long time at a very long box, sitting on the quayside, located away from the other boxes.

"Hey look chaps, its Bob." The Airman stood up, pointing to the box on the quayside. The remainder of the group gathered around the wooden box. It had been constructed by the ships carpenter, from pre-cut plywood panels.

Len, removed his hands from his pockets, and placed them by his side, trying to be rather more reverent. "Corse, as he isn't a sailor, he has to be buried in a cemetery, and not at sea. I wonder if he will ever get home, or if he will be buried here, Poor devil. It was all a bit close to you when it happened Leslie?"

Leslie thought for a moment, What, if it had been him, what would Grace think? It was indeed, a very close thing. The fatal bullet must have missed Leslie by inches to have hit Bob, and killed him. He moved towards the box slowly, for it felt as though his feet just would not move. The memory of that moment, flashed though Leslie's mind. He felt a shiver go down his back, and a tear came to his eye. The sounds and actions of the attack by the Stuka, was all that he could think of.

All of a sudden, the reality of the situation became very real. They were at War, and at any moment, any one of them could be killed. Part of the training at Haverford West, came back into his mind like a flash. They were told, over and over again, that, it is their job to look after the next Man, as the next Man will look after you. For Leslie, the reality of that statement, was one that stayed with him for the rest of his life.

As the men gathered around the long box, two heavy Bedford lorries arrived in RAF blue. What a relief, as several RAF uniformed men approached the group.

"We have a deceased Airman in the box," Len said to one of the Sergeants who had just arrived. "Can we please carry him to the lorry with a Union flag over him. He was only nineteen?"

"Yes, that's fine," replied the Sergeant. "I'm afraid we don't have a Union Flag on the truck, but we do have an RAF Ensign. Will that do?"

The blue Ensign was draped over the coffin, with the RAF roundels, and the small union flag on the Ensign, clear to see. Four Airman of similar height, lifted the coffin to shoulder height, and marched, with a slow march, to the rear of one of the lorries. All of the Airmen, and those who had just arrived in the lorries, stood to attention, as the coffin was loaded onto the lorry, with great dignity.

The Sergeant said, that the coffin would be the only cargo on that lorry, and will go straight to the mortuary in the General hospital, North of Saint Julian's. He would arrange for another truck, to transport the group of men and their equipment.

As the lorry, containing Bob, disappeared behind dockside buildings, the group of Airmen started to load their equipment onto the other lorry. The driver, and his mate, leaned against the side of the lorry, smoking cigarettes, and watched the work being carried out, after all, it wasn't their kit being loaded.

Another lorry arrived at the dockside. Both lorries were boarded by the group of Airmen. Most of the men were feeling very hot, not only from the exertion of loading equipment, but also the fact that they were all wearing long RAF blue wool trousers, in a temperature of 35 degrees. To help to keep the men in the truck cooler, the front canvas flap above the cab was raised, allowing a warm breeze to blow through to the rear of the lorry.

The lorries slowly, made their way through the dockland buildings, passing Chant Street, Kingsway and Mint Street. They left the Town of Valletta, and headed North, passing through the town of Masida. and by-passing the larger

Town of Sliema. They followed the coast road for a while. Passing St Julian's Bay, Leslie noticed that the coastline was very rocky, with small empty, sandy beaches.

Turning inland, the road passed a prison camp, with very high chain-link fences surrounding the camp, and high look-out posts containing armed guards. Next area to pass, was the general military hospital. Again, guarded by armed British soldiers. The Lorry, containing Bob, could clearly be seen from the road. The coffin had been unloaded onto a large wheeled trolley. The RAF Ensign still draped over it.

About three hundred yards further along the road, the lorries stopped at an RAF camp guard post. On a sign outside the base, in colours of RAF blue, was the number 45 in large letters. The gate was raised, and the lorries moved forward, to a large open area. The area was flanked on all sides, by concrete constructed buildings. Some singe story, others with two or three levels.

The Airmen and equipment were unloaded, again by the men themselves. A Squadron Leader smartly marched to meet the newly arrived men. He Saluted to the Sergeant in the group. After instructing the group to follow him. he marched to a two-level building, on a row of buildings, behind those on the square. The group of Airmen, very smartly marched behind the Squadron Leader, led by their Sergeant.

On entering the building, they were led to a large room, with lots of seats facing a stage, just like a theatre.

"Please be seated Gentlemen" The Squadron Leader said, as he walked to the stage area. "You are now at RAF area 45 Fort Magdalena, Malta. You are 12 Squadron Meteorological Ops. If there is anyone who is not in this Squadron please leave now." He waited for a moment, just in case there was someone in the room, who should not have been there, before continuing. "Welcome Gentlemen. You will now carry out your trade as instructed from this base. Home leave is not permitted; however, some time off will be granted, on a limited basis. You will be billeted here on this base, and will be shown your quarters shortly."

The Squadron Leader, continued to instruct the group for another forty-five minutes. He told them about their duties, where they will be carried out, who to report too, the layout of the base, and the importance of absolute top secrecy of their work, equipment and whereabouts. They could write home, but every letter will be censored by the RAF, and those letters not suitable, will not be sent. The return address for post will be provided as a code, and the actual location must remain secret. Parcels are permitted to be received, but they also, will be censored. They were told that the group will be working in Malta for up to three months, on a variety of equipment. At some time in the future, they will be posted to a 'field' location, for important duties.

<u>Fort Magdalene Malta</u>

Life at the base was indeed secret. RADAR, as it became known, was a tool that must be kept away from the enemy, or any person who might have contact, at any level, with the enemy. Photograph's or descriptions of equipment, or locations would put many thousands of lives at risk.

The billets were very comfortable, however as well as heating stoves, there were also large holes in the walls, with fans in the holes, turning very gently. The men of the Squadron, had been given times to work, and specific tasks to carry out. The RADAR room was without windows, it contained large pieces of equipment. Two round Cathode Ray Tubes, that were located on the front panel, with an attached desk, for the operator to fill in forms, from the results obtained from the equipment. High on the equipment front panel were dials, indicating a variety of functions, such as power available, and direction of Ariel's among others technical data. The RADAR operator, sat in front of the tubes for an hour at a time, recording the 'plots' of contacts, and reporting to the radio operator, for transmission to the relative organisation.

One week had passed at base 45 Malta, when local leave was granted to Leslie and five other men. The men had to return each evening to the base. Len was a very resourceful man, who managed to obtain an Austin Champ car for the day, from a contact he had in the Navy. All six men climbed aboard the open top Austin, and set off, out of the base, showing their passes at the gate.

Len, who was driving, said. "Free at last chaps. So where are we going today, Bournemouth?"

The reply came from someone in the back. "Drive on driver. And don't spare the horses."

Len drove on, keeping a close look on the fuel tank, that is currently only one quarter full. The small town of Berchirlara provided the first cross roads. He turned right, going past the village of Balza and on to Attaru. Again, turning right, they found the pretty small town of Rabato. The countryside was generally very dry, with baron areas and rocky outcrops. Roads were generally very good, but occasionally rough in places. Following the road, down a winding hill they came to Dingli where the road ended. The men stood in front of the vehicle, and just looked at the beautiful sea view ahead.

They were on the top of some rugged cliffs, with a gentle slope down to the sea. The water was so clear, that the rocks underwater could clearly be seen. The colour of the sea was a wonderful light aqua blue, as the sun shone brilliantly, making the sea glisten.

"Come on chaps," Leslie shouted, as he started to run down the hill towards the shore. The others followed Leslie, following a ruff path, that may have been formed by rainfall, making its way to the sea. The shore was a mixture of sand and shale, shelving steeply, to cause deep water, very close to the shore.

One of the men stripped off his clothes. He ran at high speed into the warm water. Leslie looked around the area, and could not see anyone, so, stripping his clothes, he followed his friend into the water. The other men were not far behind Leslie. They stripped their clothes at high speed, leaving them strewn over the beach, and also entered the sea.

With warm water and sunshine, the swim was enjoyed by all. A very slight swell, created the smallest of ripple waves, to creep onto the shore. The few men, who were good swimmers, took the advantage, and swam a good way out from the shore, While the others splashed each other, and enjoyed the warm and free environment.

Len was the first to leave the sea. He heading for some rocks at the back of the beach, with a view to drying his body in the sun. He stopped in mid-stride, and dived for his pile of clothes that laid on the beach. Once the clothing was retrieved, he covered himself with the loose clothing, for sitting on the sand, next to his selected rocks, were an elderly lady and gent. They had been enjoying a home-made picknick of bread, dipped into a round metal container, and a fine bottle of wine, buried deep in the sand, to keep it cool. The couple were both dressed in dark, heavy clothing, with well-tanned skin. Unknown to the swimmers, the couple had also enjoyed the swim, but viewed from their current location. They both had large smiles on their faces. The other men had seen Len dive for his clothes, so were now shouting to him to collect their clothes, to protect what dignity there was left, from the watching couple.

Eventually every man was dressed again, although some parts of their bodies were still wet, as the clothes were donned with some speed. The dining couple, continued with the beach picknick, by draining the bottle of wine. They continued watching the men throughout the clothes recovery, and dressing, with great interest. The smile on their faces never diminished.

Len was again driving, as the airmen returned to Rabato, before turning right towards the high-level village of Zebbug. The old village was quite busy. On entering the square, a baker's shop was displaying a variety of bread. Stopping the Austin Champ, Len went into the shop and bought two large loaves of crispy floured bread. Returning to the car he handed them to the men. He asked for some of the bread to be left for him.

All too quickly the day out was over. The RAF base, again became home, and the Austin Champ was returned to its 'owner', almost out of fuel. Most of the men slept very well that night, as did Leslie, after writing a long letter to Grace. He told her about the wonderful swim they all had, but missing out the bit about the elderly couple on the beach.

For many months, Malta had been subjected to many large and consistent bombing raids, from the Luftwaffe. The island was well defended by land-based guns, spitfires of the Royal Air Force, and from ships patrolling the Mediterranean Sea. The use of RADAR, was a vital instrument in advanced warning of attack, and provision of information, to land and sea-based guns. The defence of the island is important, as it is a strategically placed island, in the Mediterranean, being close to Italy and North Africa. 12 Met. Squadron were kept very busy in providing up-to-date information.

Bombing raids by the Germans, was a regular occurrence. The results were devastating. Ordinary people were bombed out of their homes, schools, and places of work. The RAF base, had been attacked on many occasions, but with less damage than other parts of the island at first. The Germans were trying to break the resolve of the population, so that an invasion would be much easier. The fact was, that the opposite effect was achieved. Great support was given to the British Military, and the Allies by the Maltase people.

On several occasions, the 12 Met team left the RADAR bunker, and set up equipment outside, under tents, but still in the confinement of the base. Power was provided by a diesel motor-generator set. The aerials were mounted onto the back of a truck, with a quick fold-away system. The men thought this was not just odd, but very dangerous, as they were open to bombing and attack from the air, and with no protection from a land attack. Little did they know, at the time, that this training would one day save their lives.

The bombing continued on a daily, and nightly basis, with some sections of the base being destroyed. The nearby hospital, had several direct hits, and the prison camp was moved to a safer location. Often the men had to dive into underground shelters from the bombing. The shelters were very cramped, and very hot.

Three months after the men of 12 Met had arrived at base 45, an order was issued to Leslie's Squadron, to move to Tunis in North Africa. Very little notice was given to the men, for any preparation. Leslie was able to send a Telegram to Grace, as a birthday card saying, "Loving birthday greetings, God bless you and keep you safe. My thoughts and Prayers are ever with you." The message had been censored by censor no. 71.

Again, it was time to board a ship. This time heading for Tunis. The sailing took just over twenty hours from Malta. This time the ship was a Royal Navy transport vessel, because the group of men, had to bring not only themselves, but also a large amount of equipment. They were told that the length of the visit was unknown, as it depended upon Government negotiations, with the Country of their next location. All of the men were very concerned about enemy attacks while they were at sea. The events of the voyage earlier, was still very much on their minds.

Arrival in Tunis was chaotic. The locals were everywhere, and getting in the way of everybody. Local men were pushing each other, to present their wares for selling to the newly arrived men. Almost all of the native population at the dock were men. Most had long kaftan style coats, with funny round decorated hats. The items for sale varied from baskets, to cloth and rugs. They were very insistent, and interfered with the disembarkation. The British sailors maned the ships derrick crane's, to unload the equipment onto the dock. But, once the stores were on the dock, a crowd of natives pushed others aside, to load it onto waiting lorries, hoping to be paid for their efforts. The noise was amazing. People were shouting at high level, as the dock became a sea of pandemonium.
The men of 12 Met Squadron, and their equipment, were whisked off to a secret location, surrounded by British Army Military Police. The locals followed, as far as they could, constantly being driven away by the armed escort.

Malta was hot, but this place was steaming hot. Shelter from the burning sun, became an important part of everyone's life. They drove past a huge inland lake, and eventually arrived at a location just outside of the City, called AL 'Attar.

A native of Tunis

Leslie was very surprised at the countryside. He had expected a dry and sandy landscape, instead it was mostly green, with olive trees, plantations of a variety of green fresh bushes, and even some green grass. There was also a lot of sandy soil, that created clouds of dust when the wind blew. The men did notice, that there was rubbish strewn everywhere. Along the roadside, in the ditches, outside of the houses, in fact everywhere they looked was rubbish. Discussions between the men was usually about the amount of rubbish, and its associated smells.

On arrival at the 'secret' location, the sleeping arrangements were poor, with canvas tents for the men, and large tents for meetings and eating. Beds were wooden folding style canvas camp beds, a grey wool blanket, and a pillow with no pillow case. The latrines, as they were called, were constructed from heavy tarpaulins, as was the shower and washing area. All-in-all it was a very temporary affair.

The group, were not allowed to send letters, or any other communications. The work consisted, of constantly cleaning the equipment, to keep the sand out of operating systems. An old Bedford Lorry was provided for the equipment, and a second lorry for transportation, when it was required.

Time went by. The men of 12 Met. became board. Leslie had brought a fold-away Kodak camera from England, he had kept it safely in his kit-bag, along with lots of 120 black and white film. Some of his time, was used to photograph the local population. It showed, the almost Biblical way, that they went about their business. He captured much of the way they lived, their homes, and the countryside. The other men, usually played cards for a few pence. None of the men could leave the base, so could not spend any money. Many evenings, Leslie would pull his camp bed out of the tent, into the fresh cooler air, and would rest on his back, on the bed, just to watch the stars move around the sky. As Grace had done often, it was his turn to wonder, if Grace was looking at the same stars, that he was looking at. His mind was deep in thought about Grace, and remembering every detail of their last time together.

CHAPTER 6

Several letters, from Leslie, had arrived for Grace, at her parent's house, due to the fact that she had not been on leave, at home for some time. Jim, her father, had decided to collect them together, and post them onward, to her Army address. Elsie had gone to Chapel on the quiet Sunday morning, leaving Jim, to find something to do on his one day off work.

Jim squeezed several of Leslie's letters into another larger envelope, and prepared it for the post. As the morning was quiet, he wandered into the garden at the rear of the house. He looked at the vegetable garden, to check the growth of the valuable crop, he then sat on the bench seat, under the honeysuckle roof, provided by the bush. This being the seat also enjoyed by Elsie. Having earlier written the address on the envelope, to be forwarded to Grace, the thoughts of his experiences in the last war flooded into his mind. Over the years, since the last War, he had tried very hard to forget that time. For many men, like Jim, painful thoughts were like physical pain, the mind puts it to the back of memory, as a sort of protection system. But here it was again, tugging at his memory.

Jim was the eldest Son, with eleven Brothers and Sisters. The younger years were busy, helping to bring up his siblings. Born in 1886, Jim was a young man with a thirst for knowledge. He enrolled with the International Correspondence Schools courses. Books were sent regularly to his home, on a variety of subjects, from mathematics, general engineering, electrical engineering and electrical traction. At the end of each course, an exam was set on the subject. He excelled at the learning, and achieved very high scores in the results, with the lowest score being ninety-eight percent, in mechanical engineering.

What then to do with his qualifications? One day, while reading a newspaper, he came across an advertisement for engineers to apply for posts at a new electrical power station, in Wollongong, New-South-Wales, Australia. He applied for a post, and was delighted to be accepted.

In 1912 he boarded a ship in London and sailed to Australia. Many of the prospective passengers, became very worried, as reports of a large passenger ship sinking in the North Atlantic Ocean, reached them. Most people had heard of The Titanic, as she was the largest passenger ship ever built. The news was very sketchy, and details were unconfirmed. The cost of Jim's travel, was assisted by a Government scheme called, "Assistance with Resident status." As a result, he travelled in some comfort, unlike others who had to travel 'Steerage'.

The sea journey was very long, stopping in South Africa, for a short time, for the ship to replenish its stocks, and re-fuel. Eventually they arrived in Sidney Harbour. He disembarked the ship, and made his way to his new post in Tallawarra, Wollongong power station.

He found some accommodation nearby, and settled down into the very rewarding job, making his way up-the-ladder to Assistant Manager.

1914 arrived, as did the War with Germany. Many men volunteered into the Army. For the Commonwealth required, as many men as possible. New men continued to enlist, covering the great losses, of the British and Commonwealth Armies in France. Posters were displayed throughout Australia, showing General Kitchener, asking 'you' to join, and crush the German machine.

The time came, when Jim could wait no longer. He attended the local Army recruitment office and enlisted in the Royal Australian Core of Signals. He filled in the recruitment form as a 'Driver'.

The recruitment Sergeant, scrutinised his application form in great detail, and said in a sarcastic voice. "So, you like horses do you? Driving on the front-line means dragging those poor animals around, and cleaning up behind them. So, sport, I now need to see your qualifications?" Jim showed the Sergeant his qualifications. As a result of seeing Jim's qualifications, the Sergeant crossed out the word 'Driver', and replaced it with 'Engineer Telegraphy'.

Jim recalled his training in the army as a bit of a blur. One thing did stand out, and that was becoming a member of the army band. He was a very competent Brass Euphonium player. Jim did enjoy the time playing in a military band, surrounded by other competent musicians.

Jim tried to remember the journey to France on a Transport ship, but no matter how he tried, the memories, for some reason would not return.

Jim looked towards the sky, watching a pair of crows flying low, and onto a branch of the adjacent apple tree. How peaceful this all seamed, compared to the noise and confusion of the War, that he had tried so desperately to forget.

"Don't make friends with anyone," he was told, you may not keep them very long.

Putting his head in his hands, and resting his elbows on his thighs, Jim recalled the noise, men dying around him, explosions continuous, in all directions, having to install communication cables between the trenches, hiding in bomb creators filled with mud and bodies, the noise, the confusion, the noise, the horses being pulled in directions they did not want to go, the noise, the sight of men blown into pieces, the noise, don't make friends.

Jim's thoughts, were brought to a sudden halt, as Elsie said "Are you all right Jim?"

Jim raised his head to look at Elsie, "Yes, I'm fine, just thinking about the past." Sweat was pouring down his face, as he moved to one end of the seat, allowing Elsie space to sit beside him. Elsie put her arm around him, and held him tight.

"There's time to forget things, and time to remember things. The good things are the most important to remember," Elsie said still holding Jim tightly. "Do you remember when we first met, down at our Earns, you were a bit shy that day?"

Jim did remember the day very well, He had returned to England for good. After the War, he applied for a job as Engineer, in a brand-new power station in South Wales. However, when he arrived to take the job, the power station had not even been built. He returned to his home town, without a job. Work was scarce after the war. Some house building was going on, but not much else.

Jim was in a bit of a fix. He had no job and no income. However, one job was available in the area, coal mining. The area where they lived was in the middle of the Somerset Coalfields, so plenty of underground work was available. He had no choice but to take the job. At that time, it was a booming coal mining area, with no less than dozens of mine shafts within a few square miles, most of the mines were joined together, by underground tunnels. Jim hated the work underground. He wished that he could use his hard-earned qualifications again, but the opportunity never arose. At least he had an income, and could provide for his family.

While Jim was still a bachelor, a few years earlier, on one Sunday afternoon in 1919, when he had just returned from Australia, he visited his good friend

Earnest, to have an enjoyable time playing their brass instruments together. Earn played the trumpet and the cornet, and Jim played the euphonium. They sometimes enjoyed having a 'blow' together, as they called it, and catching up on all the local gossip at the same time. On this occasion a young lady had also visited Earn and his Wife.

"This is my Sister Elsie," Earn said introducing the young lady. Elsie had also just arrived at the house, for she was just removing the long hat-pin, and carefully placing her felt decorated crimson coloured hat, on the dining table.

"Hello," Jim replied, looking a bit 'sheepish', for he had not had much to do with women in the past, except his younger sisters.

Earn and his Wife, Elsie and Jim, spent all afternoon in the rear garden, with Jim just listening to the conversation, and not contributing very much. Jim discovered that Elsie was a Nanny, working for a wealthy family in Porthcawl, South Wales. She was on holiday for four days, as the family were away in London. However, Elsie was soon to finish working for the family, as the children had now become too old for a Nanny.
On leaving Earnest's house, Jim asked Elsie if she would like to go for a walk with him sometime. She agreed without hesitation.

The regular meetings, of Elsie and Jim continued. Country walks were a favourite pastime for them. Jim asked Elsie to marry him, and they were married in 1921.

Married life was wonderful for Jim and Elsie. Jim continued his job as a miner, and Elsie enjoyed her new role as a housewife. Within the year, their first and only child was born. "There you are," Elsie said, holding Jim tightly by the arm. "Now we have a beautiful daughter, so you weren't so shy after all."

Time had now moved on. Jim and Elsie's Daughter Grace, had a wonderful childhood. She was well loved by her parents, grandparents, uncles and aunts. Her young adult years were very happy, especially with her friend Leslie in her life.

"I wish she were here now, and not in that ruddy Army," Jim said, standing up, and thrusting his hands deep into his pockets. "Don't know where she really is, and how safe she is. I've put all those letters for her into one envelope. I will post it tomorrow after work."

The clouds had now covered the sun, so Jim said. "Have you noticed, that, since this war started, even when the sun shines, it still seems dark. I suppose, like the last lot, you could say this is the dark days of the war."

CHAPTER 7

Grace was very happy to receive the letters forwarded to her, by her father Jim. She spent all evening reading them, and writing the replies to Leslie.

Grace's dressmaking skills were second-to-non. The apprenticeship she had completed before the war in dressmaking, gave her the expertise and quality in her work. She was continually asked by her comrades, to help with sewing tasks. Grace acquired an old portable sewing machine, and spent many evenings off, sewing for herself and friends.

One evening, in her billet, Grace was sewing a garment for a friend, using the sewing machine, when she was interrupted by another woman saying. "Are you Grace? Phone call for you."

Grace ran to the phone. It was Leslie. He explained that the call was being censored, and he only had two minutes to talk. He told her that he was in North Africa. He said that as they had been unofficially engaged for some time, could they now make it official? Grace excitedly agreed. Leslie said he will sort it out. The two minutes had now passed, so after telling her, that he would love her until his dying day, the line was cut-off.

Grace returned to her sewing, she did not tell anybody about the phone call. By now she had lost her concentration, due to the excitement of the phone call, so she put away the sewing for the evening, and had an early night. An early or late night made no difference at all. For most of the night, sleep did not come. The feeling of being officially engaged to Leslie was overpowering. She decided that at this stage she would keep the agreement secret. She was sure that her parents would approve of the engagement. Leslie had to keep himself safe, as so did she.

For Grace, life in the camp became a lot more bearable after the phone call, and knowing, that she will be due home leave in a few weeks.

In North Africa, Leslie now had an important task, unrelated to military duties. He now had an official fiancée, so two things had to be done. The first thing was to stay alive and survive the war in one piece, also to obtain a ring. He spent a long time trying to work out the latter. One day, while walking though the local market in AL 'Attar, with his now, very good friend Len, he saw a small cream coloured ring for sale. He picked it up and looked at it with interest. The plain ring was made from some local material, it looked well made, so after bargaining with the native seller to reduce the price by more than half, he bought it. Leslie had previously confided with Len about the engagement. Len was delighted for Leslie, as he was already married to Lillian. Both Len and Lillian had been school teachers before the War. Len had enlisted into the RAF, and Lillian continued as a teacher in Yorkshire, England.

The following day, Leslie wrote to Grace, and enclosed the ring inside the envelope. He said in the letter. "My dearest Wife-to-be. Dear Cuddles, as I cannot buy a proper ring at the moment, will you please wear this ring until I return. In the meantime, would you please choose a ring that you like. Ask my Mother to give you the money from my savings, and buy it. We have been told that home leave might be granted before our next posting. We can then make it official." The letter concluded with the usual loving comments, but did not include anything to annoy the censor.

Leslies Mother, Edith, received several letters from Leslie in one parcel. She had been very worried about his wellbeing, as regular wireless news reported that Malta, had seen some of the worst bombing in the war so far. To hear from Leslie, and that he was safe and well, was a tremendous relief. Edith and Charlie were delighted with the news that Grace and Leslie were engaged to be married, and that he is expecting home leave soon. They also heard regularly from Leslies elder brother Donald. War, being so unstable, was a worrying time for all parents. The sight of telegram boys and girls on their bicycles, always made the heart pound a little faster. Most of the telegrams delivered, were related to the missing or death of servicemen. To have regular letters from their Sons was a great relief, even though they were several days, and sometime, weeks, after being written.

Edith and Charlie listened to the wireless news, every day, hoping that the tyrant Hitler, would surrender. That did not happen, indeed, discussions with the

Italian leader Franco, was not encouraging, that Italy may change allegiance to Hitler. Discussions regarding the politics in Italy was regular, as things seem to change often in the War.

Edith often met with her other sisters, of which she had three, Annie, Florence and Frances. Annie was married to Douglas, who was in the Somerset Light infantry, Frances had just married an American Army officer, but Florence was still very much single. The whole family, along with Edith's parents, lived locally. As it was a small town, many people, and families, knew each other. Events in the town, often brought the families together. Edith's father was a well-known member of the Town. The news of Leslie and Graces engagement was well received by all family members.

Leslie and his Squadron were at last given two weeks home leave. They were told that new orders will be issued upon their return. A Dakota, unarmed passenger aircraft, was made available to transport the airmen to an airfield, in Southern England. The Dakota was supported, at different times by Hurricanes and Spitfires. The most direct route home would be, across the Mediterranean to the North, Italy, and Germany. As this was not practical due to the German occupation, the flight went to Gibraltar, for re-fuelling, along the Portuguese coast, and onward North to the English Channel.

At one point, near Southern Spain, German Messerschmitt's tried to attack the flight. The Spitfire support, attacked with a direct hit on one German fighter, causing flying debris to litter the sky as they flew on. Another ME109 flew close to the Dakota, he must have realised it was an unarmed passenger flight, that was well protected. He waved his wings, and flew off, much to the relief of all. The rest of the flight home, after the attack, became a little frightening. Most of the men spent the remainder of the flight, looking out of the windows. No further enemy aircraft were seen.

Leslie arrived home for his two weeks leave. The War seemed to be in another world. Grace was already on leave at home. The following morning after his arrival, Leslie made his way down the hill, to the town below, where Grace lived. He reached the footpath that crossed the first railway line, when his attention was taken by the sound of screaming aircraft in the sky above. The sound of gunfire was clear to be heard, as a number of Spitfires and Messerschmitt 109's, were fighting an air battle over the town. High above the battle, were several German Junker Bombers, heading North.

Leslie stopped walking, and watched the aerial battle from his vantage point. An aircraft was climbing almost vertical, its engine screaming for the propeller to grab the air. It had others on his tail, firing their guns at the climbing aircraft. The tracer bullets were showing the track of the ammunition as it ripped into the fuselage and wings. Other fighters, of both sides, dived, climbed, turned in tight curves, and looped to arrive behind an opponent. The battle varied from low level, to almost as high as the proceeding bombers. Occasionally, a Spitfire would break-away from the battle, to attack a bomber, being chased by an enemy aircraft, with guns blazing.

An enormous flash came from a fighter, followed by a trail of black smoke coming from the engine area. The fighter, was at a relatively low level, however, the pilot 'bailed out', with his parachute opening, just in time, to slow his fall. The aircraft continued to the Southwest, getting lower, and lower, smoke still pouring from the machine. Leslie watched, as the fighter disappeared over the hill. Moments later, an explosion was clear to hear, followed by a funnel of smoke streaming into the air. as if being dragged up by some invisible ropes.

Leslie lost sight of the position of the parachute, as his attention had been taken by the stricken aircraft. By this time, the air battle had moved much further North, following the track of the bombers. The sounds of the battle continued for some time, but was now, well out of sight.

Later that day, the news in the town, was that the German aircraft, had crashed in the cricket field of a nearby private school, killing nine boys. No news was available regarding the pilot.

Eventually Leslie did arrive at Grace's home. Elsie was delighted to see Leslie, and told him that Grace was in the garden on the seat under the honeysuckle. Leslie appeared in the Garden, He Kissed Grace firmly on the lips, stretched out his arms, and held her tightly in a long embrace. After some time, he released Grace, and said, "Have you got it?" Grace showed him the cream ring on her finger. She held his hand, and pulled him back into the house. Grace disappeared into her bedroom, she returned with a small black box containing a ring. Leslie approved of the ring. It was 24 carat gold, containing three diamonds in a 'swish-over' mount. It was gorgeous.

Without further ado, Leslie removed the cream ring. He replaced it with the 'real' engagement ring. It looked wonderful. Bright and shiny on her finger, as was the sparkle in her eye. The temporary ring, was placed in the box for safe keeping.

Grace pushed her ringed hand towards her Mother, who held it, to view the ring in detail. "Wonderful", Elsie commented. "Your Dad will love it too. Congratulations to you both."

The following day was bright and quiet, so, Leslie again went down the hill to Grace. Hand-in-hand they walked to the High Street in the Town. Grace was wearing a green pleated skirt, and cream knitted, tight fitting jumper. Leslie was very proud of his new wide legged trousers, recently purchased by his Father. Charlie, Leslies Father, had quite a battle on his hands, when he brought the trousers home. Edith said, "Don't want that modern stuff here." But Charlie had his own way, and Leslie was delighted with the trousers, called 'Oxfords'.

The High Street was quite busy. Several people stopped to say hello to the couple, mostly older folks, who hadn't seen them for some time. Jimmy Lynes, one of Leslie's old school friends, came across the road to meet them, struggling on a pair of wooden crutches. He was on one leg, with the other trouser leg, pinned up to the knee, for the leg below that was missing.

"Hello you two", he said, leaning against the steel fence by the river. "Haven't seen you for a while. He was looking at Grace's finger, with the new ring flashing in the daylight. "Been and gone and done it then. Good news. I lost Judy in an air raid in Bristol last month. Looks like I'm going to be a Batcheler boy. Well done, Congratulations. Seen much action Leslie? Must have been hell in Malta, Heard all about it. Must say we all think you lot are brave out there."

"What the devil happened to you Jimmy?" Grace asked, holding Leslies arm tightly.

"Copped it in the Spit. over Kent two months ago," Jimmy replied, waving a crutch in the space where his leg would have been. "Took the 109 down with me though. But lost three mates that day. Those ME's haven't got the power, or turn as a Spit. On my way to the Drill Hall. Got to meet the Wing Commander there for some reason. See you soon, I hope. Oh, and congratulations again. Good show."

Leslie and Grace later learned, that Jimmy had received the Distinguished Flying Cross, from the Wing Commander.

Grace and Leslie continued on their walk. They went up Gas Lane, and past the large grey gasometer storage tank, up the footpath, and across the two railway lines. From this raised location, the whole of the town could be seen below them. It was from here, that Leslie had witnessed the recent air battle. A widen fence protecting the railway line was a convenient place to lean-onto, and view the scene below,

The Parish church was to the left. The High Street, was clear to see. The Methodist church in the High Street was a prominent building, with the primary school half way along the street. Smoke gently rose from many house chimneys. The American base was very busy, with people moving about. In the distance the green fields swept away to the horizon. Also, in the distance, several slag heaps, known as 'the batch', marred the view, This, being the rubbish brought to the surface by the miners. The scene was peaceful. The couple stayed at the viewpoint for some time. It was one of their favourite places to be, for, although lots of things were going on in the town, none of that could be seen from the viewpoint. It was a little bit like looking at a silent movie film, they thought.

The peace of the moment was shattered, as two large green and black steam locomotives roared past them on the other side of the fence. Behind the locomotive, was a second locomotive, and twelve coaches were counted. The train slowed to a stop at the nearby station.

The 'Bournemouth Bell' train, was on its way to the South Coast. At the station, the front locomotive was uncoupled, and sent to a siding. The railway slope from the previous lower village, was one of the steepest inclines in the country, so 'double header' locomotives, as it was known, was used to haul the twelve coaches up the hill. The train moved off, and the single locomotive returned to the previous village, to perform the next 'double header'.

Being now close to Leslies home, they decided to visit his Mum and Dad. Andrew, Leslies younger Brother, was home from university, having recently been ordained into the Methodist Ministry.

Edith had gone to town shopping, and Charlie was 'out on his rounds' delivering paraffine and oil, and all manner of other household items. Andrew had been reading in the living room, and was delighted to see his future Sister-in-law. The group chatted for some time, until it was time for Grace to return home for her evening meal.

Two days later, it was the day for Grace and her Cousin Albert to play their piano duet at the Town Hall. Earnest had done a wonderful job arranging the concert.

The upper floor of the Town Hall, had a large dance floor. One hundred and fifty chairs had been arranged, 'theatre style' for the audience. Two rows of chairs had been placed at the stage end, facing the audience. In front of the chairs, and to the left, was placed, an upright piano, on an angle to the audience. The scene was set.

Grace and her Mother and Father, walked the quarter of a mile from their home, to the Town Hall, at the end of the High Street, known locally as 'The Island'. As they arrived, Leslie and his parents, were waiting outside the main entrance. Moments later Albert also arrived, with his Mother and Father. While the group were talking for a while on the pavement, outside of the hall, they were approached by an American Army Officer. He said, that he had seen the advertisement for the concert, and would it be 'OK', if on this occasion only, that some of his men attended. Earnest pointed to another group, gathering outside the hall. He said that the older man was the Leader of the Town Council, so he would be the person to ask. The Officer had a short discussion with the Councillor, and marched off.

The doors to the hall were opened from the inside, so each group made their way into the building. The performers did not have to pay an entrance fee, but all others were charged sixpence, by a very rotund lady, sitting behind a table, at the bottom of the staircase to the upper floor.

Grace and Leslie went to the front row of seats, a sign on the seats indicated that all were reserved for 'performers only', as was the second row. Grace and Albert sat in the reserved seats to the left, near the piano. All of others sat further back in the hall. Gradually the hall started to fill with people, including the front two rows. Just before ten minutes to eight o'clock, all of the seats in the hall were taken. The noise was quite loud in the hall, as people were chatting to each other.

Grace turned to look behind her. She gasped, as she saw just how many people were sat behind her. Nudging Albert, she said. "Have you seen the crowd? I don't like this at all. I am scared. What do we do now?"

Albert turned around, and also took a large gasp of air. "The Whole American Army have turned up now," he spurted, as he took in a further, large gasp of air.

Indeed, many American Soldiers filed into the room. A very stern Sergeant was directing them to standing spaces, around the side of the room. The doors were closed. The room was full. Not a single other person could squeeze into a space.

The Leader of the Town Council addressed the audience, and also welcomed the American soldiers. He introduced the first act of the evening. The Towns Ladies choir. He said that the ladies were doing a wonderful job, having taken over from the Male Voice Choir, for the time being.

The ladies stood in two rows, to face the audience. Most were older than fifty years, and all wore hats of various types. The pianist, sat at the piano, and started to play. The first song was 'Caravan'. They received a good applause. The choir sang four further songs, each again receiving a supportive applause. The ladies were indeed, in good voice, in tune, in time, and with lots and lots of vibrato. Leslie, almost burst into laughter at one time, for, a young person's voice behind him said. "They are wobbly ladies Grandma." Referring to the level of vibrato, of the voices.

The second act was introduced by the Leader of the Council. It was a pretty young lady, wearing a long flowery frock, and a very flowery large hat. She sang three songs, that seemed very 'high-brow', in a different language. The audience was told, that it was opera. It was very tuneful, and a delight to listen too. The audience clapped very loudly, as the lady curtseyed very low.

For Grace, panic was starting to attack her, as her name, and Albert's were announced by the Councillor. The audience clapped, as Grace and Albert took their places, side-by-side on the long seat, at the piano.

Grace peered past Albert, to glimpse at the audience, through a haze of tobacco smoke. The time was here. The first piece to be played was the 'Queen of Sheba' by George Fredric Handle, followed without a break, by 'Norwegian Dances' by Edward Grieg. The audience were silent, as the pianist's hands flew over the keyboard, without hesitation, but with skill, and control, providing an unmissable performance. As the music stopped, and the pianist's hands rested on laps, the room exploded into applause, combined with shouts of 'more', as every person stood in appreciation.

Grace and Albert, gracefully bowed, and returned to their seats, in the front row of the audience. As they sat, the audience continued standing, and clapping loudly.

"Well how about that then?" The Councillor said, as he clapped vigorously. "So, that's it for tonight, except for one thing." The pianist, who earlier had played for the choir, sat at the piano, raised both hands to the keyboard, and played the usual few notes of the introduction, to the National Anthem. Those who were standing remained standing, as the remainder of the audience stood. The piano continued, as the singing commenced. "God Save our Gracious King," the Anthem progressed, including the second verse.

As the Anthem was being sung, most of the Americans, started to leave the hall, talking very loudly as they went. This upset the audience, most of whom, turned around to watch the commotion, as they sang. Many of the men in the audience were coal miners, who knew each other very well. They were able to communicate to each other, without using words, as the noise underground stopped voices being heard. The message was sent around the room in seconds, so, immediately after the singing stopped, thirty or more men, ran down the stairs to the street below.

Nobody knew what was said, or who said what, but a street fight started, with fists flying in all directions. Many of the remaining audience, watched the proceedings from the safety of the upstairs windows. The miners did not hold back in their aggression. Many of the Americans were running away from the affray. A civil Policeman watched from the side-lines, blowing his whistle, and shaking his truncheon, unable, or unwilling, to do anything. The added shrill of screaming whistles, approached from the American base, as several American Military Policemen, ran to intervein. A shot was fired, 'BANG'. Instantly the commotion stopped. An American Policeman, was still pointing his revolver towards the sky. Another shot rang out, 'BANG'. All was still. Most of the American servicemen, were recovering from the brawl, nursing their injuries. All of the miners stood still, looking at the Americans, as if they wanted to tear them apart. The miners had their shirt sleeves rolled up tight, over their mussel bound upper arms, and just looked on. Without further ado, all Americans gradually walked, or were carried, away to their base.

The American Military Policeman, who had fired the shots, established that his Countrymen had caused the problem, by disrupting the British National

Anthem. He apologised to the Miners, before leaving, and making his weapon secure.

The miners brushed themselves down with their hands, and met with their families, who were now in the street.

Elsie grabbed Jim by the arm, and dragged him away from the area. Charlie and Earnest did not engage in the fight, much to the relief of their Wives.

The townspeople heard, that all the Americans who attended that night, were charged with the affray, and the American Policeman, was charged for discharging a weapon in public. The senior American base officer, was informed by the War Office, that, none of their personnel were permitted into the town, for any reason, except senior staff, reporting to the Drill Hall.

Leslie and Grace, followed the group home, arm-in-arm, with Grace's head, resting on Leslies shoulder. Albert followed his cousin, with hands stuffed deep into the pockets of his 'Oxford' trousers, feeling very proud of himself, and his cousin Grace. Earnest, being in the Salvation Army, told all, that he was disgusted with what he had witnessed that evening.

The American Commanding Officer, was summoned to meet with a British high-ranking officer in the Drill Hall offices. The American made an unreserved apology, stating that most of his men, had never heard the Anthem before, and did not understand how significant the tune was. Never-the -less, all American servicemen were band from the town.

CHAPTER 8

The next Monday morning arrived. Most people went about their daily business in the town. Jim had started his shift as normal at five thirty that morning. Arriving at the Pit-Head office, he signed-in and joined his workmates in the changing room. Each workman had his own small cupboard, Jim hung his coat inside his locker, and collected his hard hat. He attached the lamp to the helmet, and followed others to the Pit Head.

The pit-shaft cage rose in front of the waiting men. Safety gates were opened, by a Gate Warden, raising the gate on rollers, to a high level. Trucks, full of coal, were dragged from the cage, and pushed along railway lines, away from the pit-head. The cage rose again, and again, for more trucks to be unloaded from each of the three levels of the cage. The Gate Warden, then allowed the miners to enter the cages, as it was lowered to each level platform, Bells were rung to identify that the cage was safe to enter. The last cage was full of men, fifteen men to a level cage. A bell sounded three times, and the cage was lowered into the very dark shaft below. In moments, the cage was falling at a terrific rate. The detail in the walls of the shaft, could not be identified, as the cage hurtled towards the centre of the earth at great speed.

At last, a light shone up the shaft from below, as the falling cage slowed. bells again rang as the cage stopped. A very large cavern, lit with huge lamps, greeted the workmen. The first platform of men, disembarked, as the safety gates were opened. The cavern was a sight to see, coal trucks full of coal, were being pulled around by pit-pony's wearing blinkers, being driven along by a man, with a stick. Each pony had several full trucks of coal behind it. Before the scene could be studied further, the bell was rung, and the cage sped deeper into the earth. A full two minutes passed, as the cage hurtled downwards, passing two other illuminated caverns, without stopping. Eventually, the cage stopped, the gate was opened, and the remaining miners, including Jim, walked out of the open cage.

The reception area was very small, with coal trucks on railway lines, that disappeared into several illuminated tunnels. This time the 'tubs', as they were called, had men pushing or pulling them, to the designated locations. Jim, along with other men, collected the tools they required. They walked along a tunnel, as indicated by a foreman. The men walked for about a quarter of a mile, deeper into the earth, passing many other tunnels as they went, each indicated with road names. The area, and section, for the men to work was now in view. The only illumination was from the lamps on each of the miner's helmets. Jim found his area for work. It was further along a low and narrow tunnel, just large enough for Jim, and two men following him, to crawl on their tummies and knees. This area was about another one hundred yards from the last larger tunnel. The coal face had been reached. The narrow coal seam, glistened in the light of Jim's lamp. On his belly, he started to hack away at the coal in front of him, pushing the excavated material behind him, so that the men behind, could pass it behind them, and on to a waiting empty tub.

It was now five minutes to ten in the morning, and Jim, along with his crew, had been at the coal seam for almost four hours, working, almost without stopping, except for a drink of water, from their aluminium flask. The threesome had progressed another nine yards along the new tunnel, that they had created.

The whole town stopped. Everyone looked up towards the coal mine pithead area. A steam whistle blew short loud blasts, over, and over again, without stopping. Everyone knew, that it was the signal, that a 'fall' had occurred underground. Lots of people started to run up the hill. Women with shopping baskets, some dragging children behind them, men in military uniform. Men who were miners, not on shift, and Leslie, who had been in the newspaper shop at the time.

The mine was at the top of a steep hill, on the edge of the town. As Leslie reached the pit-head, a huge commotion was under way. A group of townspeople were watching workmen, running in all directions. The cage was brought to the surface, along with another cage from an adjoining pit shaft. Men with helmets, and rescue materials, boarded both cages. The bells were rung, and the cages disappeared out of sight. The Cables attached to the cages, from the wheels above, sped past, as the cages hurtled downwards. Two and a half minutes passed, when the bell rang again. All on the surface just waited silently.

The 'fall' had trapped Jim, and two of his fellow workers, deep at the coal face. The roof above the men, became dangerous, as debris fell onto the trapped men. The rescue workers, managed to pull Jim's comrades free. Jim. however, was trapped under a very large section of fallen material. He could hear men talking behind him saying. "It's too dangerous. If we move that section above him, the whole lot will come down. The poor sod, is almost dead anyway. I am not going in there and risking my life, got to think of the children. I will wait here while he passes away. Then we can do something with it."

Jim, was passing in and out of being unconscious, as the pain in his back became unbearable, He did, however hear the discussions about him, going on further down the tunnel.

"Sod- you," Jim's mate Burt said. pushing himself into the collapsed tunnel. "Give me that dammed pick, and get out of my way," he shouted, shining his light deep into the tunnel, and pushing the other men out of his way. Burt gently hacked away at the material, trapping Jim. By now Jim had become totally unconscious. Gradually the pressure on Jim's back eased, as the black rock trapping him, was split into smaller sections by Burt.

"Come on, give us a hand back there," Burt shouted. The other men gently eased Jim from his tomb, and onto a waiting stretcher.

On the surface, all was silent, as both of the injured miners were brought up in the cage, to waiting ambulances. The Foreman came to the surface with the first two men. By now, Elsie and Grace had arrived, and joined Leslie. The Foreman approached Elsie, with his chin resting on his chest, and shaking his head.

"Is it Jim?" Elsie said holding Leslie's and Grace's arms very tightly.

"Afraid so," Came the reply from the Foreman. "Sorry couldn't do nothin to save him. Trapped under a gurt big stone. Just can't get near it to move it."

Elsie, burst into floods of tears. She buried her face in Grace's arms. Grace was now also crying uncontrollably, with Leslie trying to support both women. The next cage arrived at the surface. A stretcher was eased onto a large wheeled carriage, and sent to an ambulance. Burt, was holding onto the stretcher, as he walked beside the carriage. Burt looked at Elsie, and beckoned her to come to the stretcher.

"He's alive, but not good," Burt said, as he helped the stretcher into the ambulance. "I'm going with him, are you coming as well?" He said, sitting beside the stretcher in the ambulance. Elsie, Grace and Leslie climbed into the ambulance, and the back doors were closed.

The occupants inside the ambulance, could hear the sound of the ambulance bell, as it tore along the streets. All inside the ambulance, had to hold on to fixed items, as it tried to throw them from side to side. Jim opened his eyes, for a while, to see Elsie. She smiled, and held his black hand tightly. Eventually, the doors were opened, and Jim's stretcher was slid from the vehicle, onto a waiting trolley. The family followed behind the trolley as it was pushed at high speed into a room. The door was closed in front of the family, who stopped abruptly.

Time went by, as people in long white coats, and nurses with white hats and aprons, went in and out of Jim's room. Almost two hours later, a Doctor approached the Family. "He has been very badly injured I am afraid. The severe damage has crushed his back. We are going to have him moved to a hospital at Winford, outside of the City, who specialise in such injuries. He is very much alive, but he may never walk again."

Jim was transferred to Winford hospital, where he received excellent care. The family returned home to a life, at the moment, without Jim.

A few days after the mining disaster, Leslie borrowed a car from a good friend. He was able to take Elsie and Grace to visit Jim in Winford Hospital. Surgery had been carried out on Jim's back, but it was too early to be clear about his level of recovery. Visiting Jim in Hospital was a very strict affair, as only one visitor at a time could be with him. At exactly four o'clock in the afternoon a very stern Sister came into the ward, rang a bell very loudly, and escorted the family from the room. Jim had been very pleased to see his visitors. He was now fully conscious, and totally aware of what had happened to him, and what the prognosis was. He had become fully resigned, that he may never walk again. The severe pain in his back had now eased, but because he had to lay on his side all of the time, he was experiencing a few bed sores.

The family returned home in the Austin 10 car. Leslie parked the vehicle on the road, outside in the front of the house. All felt much happier that Jim was improving, and that, with more treatment, the outlook was much better than earlier expected. At least he is alive.

Elsie prepared tea, with Jim's brother Bill, joining them at the tea table. All was well, until a very loud bang was heard at the front of the house. Everyone ran to the front door. Leslie opened the door, to reveal that the car was gone. He ran to the front gate, and found the car, parked twenty feet along the road. Fifteen feet along the road, in the opposite direction, was another car. The driver was sitting in the driver seat, looking very dazed. It was revealed that, the other driver, had not seen Leslies car, so crashed into the parked vehicle. As the Brass sprung bumpers on both cars, were at the same height, the cars bounced off each other's sprung bumpers, causing no damage to either car.

Leslie retuned the car to his friend, after replenishing the fuel used, without telling him about the bouncing incident, as he may wish to borrow it again.

Grace returned to camp, having travelled all night by train. She arrived at 06.30 hrs, to be given a note by the guardsman on duty at the main gate. She had to report to the training room at 08.00 hrs, for further instructions. Grace returned her bag to the billet, to find the other girls polishing shoes and buttons. They had also received instructions to attend the training room. Grace set-to, and joined in the preparations of the uniform spruce-up.

08.00 hrs arrived. The girls filed into the training room, where they were all told to sit on the chairs provided. An ATS Woman Chief Commander entered the room. She was very smart, Tall, with dark hair tied in a bun, just under the bottom band of her uniform hat.

"How many of you ladies can spell the English Language?" The Commander asked in a very stern manner. All of the women, raised their hands in response. "How many of you can add up and subtract numbers?" The Commander continued. Again, in response, all raised their hands. "Good," the officer said, looking at each of the nine women in the room in turn. "You are to be transferred to A.A.O.D Kidbrook, the RAF base, but also you are changing your trade, to that of Clerk. Please pack-up your equipment, and personal belongings, and report here at 10.00 hour's ready to move."

The Girls looked at each other in amazement. They all had a variety of trades, at the moment, but no reason was given by the Commander for the change. As instructed, the girls prepared for a move. All belongings were pushed into kit-bags and holdalls. Grace made sure the sewing machine was packed safely into its carry box. The women all met again in the training room, at ten o'clock that morning. Grace had her kit-bag over her shoulder, a holdall bag in one hand, and the sewing machine in the other hand. She felt very overloaded. A truck was waiting outside. The Ladies, and their kit, were loaded onto the truck, with the Chief Commander watching the proceedings. She had her arms folded across her chest, with the peak of her cap, over the bridge of her nose, looking as if she was the most important person on the base.

The driver of the truck, sauntered up to the Chief Commander, with a cigarette hanging from his lips. "Got a light governor?" The soldier driver asked, waving the cigarette at the Commander from his lips.

The woman took in a huge, noisy, breath of air. As she did so, her chest appeared to expand by several inches. Her eyes opened extra wide, almost popping out of their sockets. As she stared at the driver, she shouted. "Who the hell do you think you are talking to? Get back to your post immediately, before I put you on a Jankers charge." The huge breath, that the Commander had inhaled earlier, was expelled into the face of the cheeky soldier. As she shouted, the soldier took several steps backwards, almost as if the strength of her breath, had blown him over. He dropped the cigarette from his lips, as he opened his mouth in astonishment, at the massive voice roaring at him. The soldier almost ran to the drivers cab in the lorry, and was not seen again.

The journey to Kidbrook, took them South, through the City of Coventry, through Oxford, and on to London. The lorry was very uncomfortable. It had very hard seats, and even harder suspension, on the vehicle. A short stop was made near Oxford, for refuelling at an Army base. The girls were given ten minutes, for a 'comfort break', Peggy commented, about the small amount of traffic on the roads. There had been a few cars, but mostly it was military vehicles, of various types.

The uncomfortable journey continued. As they approached London, the civilian traffic increased significantly. They went past Watford, and Harrow, heading South West, through the centre of London. Grace felt that London reminded her of Coventry. Many of the buildings had been demolished by the Luftwaffe, and the flying bombs, indiscriminately blowing buildings, and people to be unrecognisable, from that, that God had intended.

Some buildings were still standing, as if in defiance to the bombardment from Germany. The truck wound its way through London City, to Woolwich. It eventually stopped at the gates of RAF Kidbrook. A brief check by the armed guard at the entrance to the camp, and the gate was raised. On the journey to Kidbrook, Grace had time to think. She felt disappointed, that she was never able to visit her Family, in Perry Barr, near Birmingham, but that opportunity had now passed by.

The truck drove slowly to a large tarmacked square, and stopped. An RAF Flight Lieutenant approached, as the women disembarked the lorry. Peggy, who was now a corporal, and the most senior of the group, saluted the Lieutenant smartly. She told him that they were from Nuneaton, and are now reporting for duty. The Flight Lieutenant replied the salute, and asked the ladies to follow him.

The group, following the Lieutenant, had not yet left the tarmac area of the square, when the wallow, of the air raid siren filled the air. Another siren started in a different area of the base. Running to the right, and keeping his head down, the Lieutenant shouted. "Shelter over here." He was obviously a gentleman, for he allowed all of the ladies to enter the shelter first. All kit bags and belongings, were dropped at the entrance to the shelter. The steps went deep underground, and was lit at intervals, by electric lights in the walls. The room at the bottom of the steps, was quite big. It had concrete shelves, at seating height around the walls. The shelves were covered by blankets, some pillows and cushions were strewn about. There were two tables in the middle of the room, with about fifteen wooden chairs around the tables.

"We are a bit of a target here I'm afraid," the Officer said. Grace thought, that he had quite an educated, nice voice. "They target us about every three days, because of our role in the War," the Officer continued, as he made himself comfortable on a wooden seat.

The Lieutenant had just finished the word 'War', when there was a massive explosion outside the entrance to the shelter. Dust and debris flew down the stairs, as the ground shook. By now, most of the girls were under the concrete shelves, with hands over heads. "You are pretty safe in our shelters, you know," the Officer said, brushing dust from his shoulder. "We do insist, that the moment the alarm is sounded ---." He was stopped from completing his sentence for a moment as several more explosions occurred, quite close by. "--- You attend a shelter immediately, as the attack follows very quickly. Don't want to lose any more personal."

The 'all-clear' was sounded by the siren, followed by the bells of fire and rescue vehicles. As the girls climbed the steps leaving the bunker and arriving on the surface they stood quite still. The truck that they had arrived in, was on fire. Black smoke rose from the burning vehicle, as flames leapt high in the sky. An enormous hole in the tarmac was beside the wreckage, with debris strewn around. The image of two burning bodies, beside the truck, told its own story.

Amazingly, all of the girl's kit bags and belongings were untouched. Fire engines raced around at high speed. One arrived near the burning lorry, joined by a military ambulance. The girls, stood next to their belongings, and looked at the scene in front of them. However, most, could not look at the burning lorry, and the soldering remains of the driver and his mate.

The Lieutenant insisted that the women followed him into a building adjacent to the tarmac square, and into a canteen. Hot and very sweet tea was served by the canteen staff, who seemed to be unruffled, by the recent attack.

RAF Kidbrook, is a base very specifically as a store, and for vehicle maintenance. It was also a training base, for the Army, Navy and Airforce. So, indeed, it is a worthy target by the Germans. Most of the billets were constructed in concrete, but due to the large number of personnel on the base, some of the accommodation were 'Nissan Huts'. Nissan Huts were constructed, using curved corrugated sheets of iron, like a gardener's cloche, to cover seedlings. With concrete block walls at each end. The Girls were allotted a 'Nissan Hut'. Inside, it was similar to more substantial buildings, in layout, with latrines and wash rooms at one end, and beds with cupboards, arranged on each side. Vertical windows were fixed in the curved walls, looking like 'gable' style windows. All of the window glass had tape fixed as crosses, to avoid shards of glass flying about if they were blown out. Grace felt that it was not as 'cosy' as she would like, but at least it was a bed. A deep air-raid shelter was close by, this was now an important aspect.

Grace laid on her allotted bed, and wondered how her Father was. The last she saw of him, he was lying on a bed, unable to move. Where was Leslie? He returned to duty at the same time as Grace, so as a result, she had not heard from him. She had written several letters to Leslie, providing her new address. She purposely did not say anything in letters to her Mother, or Leslie, about the bombing, and the vulnerability of her current location.

The girls new work was indeed different. Grace had been given a desk, with a filing cabinet on the floor, next to the desk. A document easel, and a large blotting pad sat on the desk. But, taking dominating position on the desk, was a huge 'Underwood' typewriter. The machine was very complicated, with leavers, springs, arms and other mechanics. Grace pressed a letter key. The machine flew into action, with arms and leavers flying, and the top section of the equipment, moving to the right at the same time. Grace pushed the heavy machine to the back of the desk, and waited for instructions.

A lady RAF officer put a large book on Graces desk. She opened the book, and told Grace that it is called a 'ledger book'. She would receive some paperwork, and must enter the details from the paper, into the ledger book, by hand. All seemed very simple, until the quantity of paperwork arrived by the box full. Training was under way.

Three weeks had passed, when Grace received three letters from Leslie. He did not explain any details, except that, at some time in the future, they will be sent to another overseas post. He also sent his undying love for her.

By this time, the girls had completed their 'training', and were told that they were going to be transferred to North London. "Not another move," one of the women commented. "The moment we get settled into a new job, and surroundings, we get moved on," the girl continued, with her comments being approved by all of the others.

On many occasions, while at Kidbrook, the group had to dive into the shelters for protection. Some bombing attacks were targeted at their base, while others for the surrounding area. One of Grace's friends, Anne, was caught in an attack, and sadly was killed, she was only thirty-one, the oldest in the group. The funeral was somewhere up in the North of England, so it could not be attended by her Army friends.

The time, again was here to move on. Trucks transported women, and their kit, to the new base at Mill Hill, North London. This establishment was much quieter than Kidbrook, with less bombing, although, bombers were often seen passing overhead, with support fighters being pursued by the RAF. Night duty was frequent for Grace, as was home leave, on every fourth weekend.

Grace had a Cousin, who had been married for some time. Her Husband, was a man who was a motor cycle racer, but he also worked as a motor cycle engineer. They had one Son. The family lived very close to Mill Hill, at South Harrow. This for Grace, was fantastic. She was able to visit her cousin regularly. for either twelve, or twenty-four hours off duty. She was very close to her Cousin.

CHAPTER 9

The flight back to North Africa for Leslie, and his group, was largely without incident. The Dakota DC10, flew at about twenty thousand feet, to avoid enemy attacks. However, they were supported by British fighters on several occasions, who flew at a lower height than the DC10. At one point, over the Mediterranean, a naval battle was seen below. Ships could be seen firing at each other. The ownership of each vessel could not be identified, or the outcome, as they were flying too high for detail. What could be clearly seen, was the flashes from the ship's guns, and smoke from the ship's funnels, along with the smoke from direct hits, by the guns rounds. Leslie watched the battle raging, for as long as he was able. The thought, that men were actually dying down there, was very sobering.

The aircraft landed safely at Tunis, along with two hurricane fighters, much to the relief of all concerned.

Arriving back at AL 'Attar base, Leslie and his Squadron were told to report to the canteen, for a briefing. The Wing Commander arranged an Armed Guard outside of the canteen door. In the short time that Leslie had been away, a wooden building had been erected as a mess, and canteen. After closing the door, the Wing Commander told the men, that they will be transferred to the Island of Corsica. The Island is a French Colony, but currently occupied by a large contingent of Italian Military. The occupiers, were mostly made up of eighty-thousand Italian troops, under their operation called 'Anton'.

The Officer, continued to tell Leslie's group, that there were many Corsicans who were collaborators with the Italians, including Corsican Army Officers. The Islands business and politics were still conducted by the French. A very strong Corsican Resistance army exists, and is in contact with Charles de Gaulle in Paris.
The task of 12 Met Squadron, is to establish a RADAR base in the mountains of North West Corsica. To monitor all air and sea traffic in that area, and to report using Radio Morse Code to a specified contact. The Squadron are to remain in hiding, and in total secrecy, as current changes to the political situation is imminent.

The Italian Mussolini is under investigation, so, a German occupation could be expected at any time. The men may meet with the Corsicans, but must not disclose location or intentions. All personnel will be armed at all times. They will live under canvas, as will their equipment. A mobile Rushton generator will also be provided. Food, water, other provisions, and post will be delivered after the camp is set-up.

The Wing Commander continued with his briefing. He gave specific details about technical, security and other matters, for a further thirty minutes. After an any-questions session, the Wing Commander told Leslie, that, as leader of the group, he will now be a Fight Lieutenant for this operation, and that Leonard Beach will be his supporting Flight Sergeant, again for this operation. This was due to the fact, that Senior NCO's and Officers, are currently not available in that area.

After completing the briefing, the Wing Commander left the room. All of the men stood to attention as he left, and Leslie saluted the officer, as he was now in command of the 12 Met Squadron.

All of the men sat down again, and just looked at each other, in amazement. Fifteen men were, for a while, without words.

"Well, well, well. What about that then," Len said, leaning back in the chair, and lighting his pipe. "Well I'm blowed, I didn't expect that. Looks like that we are now in the war proper chaps. Good on you Leslie. Didn't expect that either. Well done skipper."

The following day, orders were provided to Leslie, for the transfer across the sea to the Island of Corsica. Equipment was checked by all of the men, and stowed onto a Navy transport ship. Kit was packed. Weapons and ammunition were drawn from the armourer, and all were ready to go. A package containing final orders were provided to Leslie before boarding.

The crossing to Corsica was only some three hundred miles, passing Sardinia on the Starboard side. No other war machines were seen during the crossing, except British reconnaissance aircraft overhead.

Under the cover of darkness, the ship pulled alongside the dock at Porto. All of the equipment and men disembarked the ship. Three Bedford trucks were unloaded by sailors using the huge on-board derrick cranes. One truck contained the Rushton Generator, mounted just behind the driver's cab, allowing room for tents, stores and some men. Another truck had a portable RADAR mast, RADAR equipment, radio, other technical material. The third truck contained men and their kit, along with a large amount of fuel for trucks and generator.
It was just past Midnight, so the darkness provided good cover for the convoy to travel, by road, North to the town of Lumio.

<u>Lumio Corsica</u>

At this point, they turned right, and headed for the mountains. The road became narrow, sandy, and very rocky, as the convoy, made its way up the gentle slope towards Mount Lumio. As planned, the town had been without people, at that time of night. At one point, in Lumio, a black dog followed the convoy, for a short while, before running back to be lost in the darkness of the town. Daylight started to break, as the convoy reached the position, pre-arranged by the navigator in Tunis. Throughout the three-hour journey, no resident or Italian had been seen. However, the unknown factor was, who might have been peering through windows, at the passing lorries, and wondering what they were doing, and where they were going? Secrecy was paramount for the success of the operation, and the safety of the men.

The pre-arranged location, was near the main ridge of Mount Lumio. It was surrounded by rocky outcrops, with good tree cover to the North. A level area, of about twenty yards by thirty yards, provided a good place to set-up first base camp. A few yards to the East of the selected camp, a steady, but small, waterfall flowed from a group of rocks, into a small stream, that made its way further down the mountain. A small disused stone building was to the North of the area. This was it. This will be the operation position for the Squadron, until further orders are received.

The men set-to, and erected tents for accommodation, just on the edge of the trees. The trucks had been driven under cover of the trees, with tarpaulins draped over them, to avoid detection from aircraft. Toilet and washing facilities were erected from canvas frames. Armed sentries were placed at strategic locations, higher up in the rocks, and around the camp, as the sun was now high in the sky over the Island.

A ruff track led off to the East, just wide enough for a truck. Leslie and two men, walked along the track for about one hundred yards. They found themselves in an area quite suitable for the RADAR mast, and equipment tent. Cables could be run from the generator below, to the upper operating position. This was an ideal location, being away from the living area, in case of attack.

The 12 Met. camp at Mount Lumio

The men set-up the equipment without delay. Very quickly, it was discovered that another RADAR base was operational, somewhere near the South of the Island. Some of the radio signals received, became very concerning, as the political situation on the island was changing. Italy were now supporting Germany. Benito Mussolini had been arrested, and imprisoned. Germany would soon be occupying the other islands, and even Corsica, at some point. So now the Italians on Corsica, were no longer Allies, but were now the Enemy.

Leslie climbed to a good vantage point, further up the mountain. Using his very strong, non-reflective binoculars, he could see clearly the small town of Lille

Rousse, Lumio and the Cove of Calvi below. His viewpoint did not allow a good sight to the North, or South of the Island. The sea was a wonderful colour blue, shimmering under the high sun. The coast of Southern France could just be seen on the horizon. He thought it might have been Marseille. His thoughts wandered to Grace. How worried she would be, if she knew where he was, and what he was doing. At least, there was not a bombing Blitz goin on here. How was her Father Jim? Is he still in hospital after the colliery accident?

Leslies thoughts were interrupted by Len. "Ah, there you are. I've just been thinking about my Lilly, so I bet you have been thinking about Grace. I recon when this show is over, we ought to all get together, after all we get on well, so hopefully, so will the girls." Leslie agreed with the idea with enthusiasm. Leslie continued his recognisance, as Len was lying on his back, on a large flat rock, gazing into the wide blue sky.

The work continued. Aircraft, and shipping were identified by the RADAR, indicating by observation, the height, speed and direction of the detected objects. On several occasions, the mast had to be dismantled quickly, and covered by canvas, due to enemy aircraft getting a bit too close. Many times, the sight of vapour trails was spotted from Bombers, flying at high level, heading for France.

Several weeks had passed by without sightings of any of the enemy, so, Leslie and two Airmen, headed West towards the town of Lumio. The three men found some clothing, that looked similar to those that the local people were wearing, before driving down the mountain in one of the lorries. The Vehicle was unmarked as to its owners. It had been fitted with local licence plates, and it looked very tatty and unkept, as a result they were able to drive to the outskirts of the town. Lumio was about a mile from the sea to the West, and was surrounded by a very old, and substantial, town wall. The men parked the Lorry on the outside of the town wall, alongside other parked dusty vehicles. The town entrance gate was very large. The streets were narrow, with high buildings on either side. This created a cool shadowy place to walk. Groups of Italian Soldiers were drinking in taverna's, where the streets opened out into sunny squares. One larger square was busy with many locals, and Italian military. Leslie and the men, just watched from a distance, as the daily business went on, trying to blend-in with their surroundings.

The three men moved off, along a small street with high, white pained houses on each side. The street opened out into a much larger square. There were some step's that led up to a church on one side, and houses on the other three sides of the square. It was empty of people, and very quiet. The three men, found themselves standing in the middle of the dusty square, looking at the houses and buildings around them, having to partly close their eyes, due to the sun reflecting off the white painted buildings.

As the three men were gazing at the peaceful surroundings, the sound of a vehicle was heard. It was coming down a side road, and was accompanied by loud Italian language, that was clear to hear, above the sound of the vehicle's engine. This instantly changed the focus of the men's thoughts. A door behind the men opened. Standing in the open doorway was a small lady, urgently beckoned them into the open door. The three men, without hesitation, rushed into the house, just as an Italian Jeep style vehicle, entered the square. The door was closed.

One of Leslies fellow Airman, withdrew a hidden pistol, and peered through a net covered window. He watched intently, as the Jeep passed through the square without stopping, and left using a different road.

The jeep had contained four Italian soldiers. They appeared to have been drinking heavily, as their behaviour was very rowdy, in fact, one of the men sitting in the rear seat, had been intoxicated, for he was waving a wine bottle, without control, wildly in the air.

Leslie was very glad that the vehicle was gone, for if the Italians had seen the British Airmen as they were, and not as locals, the outcome would have been very different, especially as the men were quite drunk.

The Airman put his pistol away, much to the relief of the little lady, who by now had been joined by a younger man. Both, the lady and the man were standing in the shadows of the room.

"You Anglaise?" The young man said, moving away from the shadows.

"Yes, we are English," Leslie replied. "Who are you?"

"My name is Pedra, and this my mother Ila. We like Anglaise. We hate Italia. You have refresh with us?" Pedra beckoned to the men to sit at a wooden table, on plain wooden benches.

Pedra and his Mother

The men accepted the invitation without question.

"How did you know we are English?" Leslie asked Pedra, making himself as comfortable as he could on the hard bench.

"You don't look like Corsican, you don't look Italia, and you don't look Deutsche. We hope Anglaise come to help Corsicans," Pedra said, placing several small white cups on the table.

The coffee was carefully poured into the cups by Ila. It was very dark in colour, and very strong. The men had never drunk coffee as strong, so it was sipped slowly, by the Airmen.

Pedra asked, if the British had arrived to save Corsica.

Leslie explained to Pedra and his Mother, that the British have not arrived to take over Corsica, or to save them from the current situation. Pedra explained, that they were part of a very strong underground Resistance organisation. Growing in strength hour by hour. He said that, the native Corsican's were only some 220,00 on the Island. At first, they liked, and helped the Italians, but now they hated them, and will do all in their power to expel them. The fear of all residents, is that Germany will send troops to the Island, to support, or replace the Italians.

The three airmen thanked Pedra and Ila for their hospitality. The taste of the coffee still strong in their mouths. They checked that the coast was clear, and left the house. Not a person was in sight. The square had an earey silence. A black cat ran across the square, and sat beside a stone water trough. The cat raised a rear leg to meet the side of its head, and licked the fur around its tail.

"Did you see that black cat?" One of the men said, pointing at the animal. "It's supposed to be good luck to see a black cat," the man continued.

"That's unless you own a black cat," Leslie returned. "Then you would see it every day. So, it's impossible to have good luck every day. Therefore, it's a myth."

The Airman who had made the comment, shrugged his shoulders, and had to agree with Leslie. The men made their way back along the same route in the town that they followed earlier. By now, the Sun was high in the sky, making the temperature rise to an uncomfortable level. On reaching the lorry, they all climbed into the front seats. Immediately the men scrambled out of the vehicle, with one of the men cursing profusely. The sun had made the hard seats in the lorry so hot that, as the Airman said. "You could fry an egg on those ruddy seats." Leslie retrieved a blanket from the back of the truck, and threw it over the steaming seats.

Eventually the men boarded the lorry, and they set off towards their camp in the mountains. Throughout the journey, much of the discussions centred around the underground Resistance, explained by Pedra. The situation could become very volatile, if the residence started to repel the Italians. Could this jeopardise the camp and the RADAR site? It was decided to report the information to a higher authority, as their mission was secret and undercover.

Back at camp, the radio operator was instructed to convey the information about the formation of Resistance, to Group HQ. Group sent a reply, that they already have good knowledge of the Resistance organisation, and that they were already working closely, with the British authorities. Group HQ also reported, that a

German occupation is expected at any time, due to the imprisonment of the ex-Italian leader Mussolini.

Leslie, Len and Ben had a morning off duty. They took the opportunity, to walk further down the mountain, to an observation ledge, that Leslie had found on a previous occasion. It was a warm, clear morning, with the sun burning the legs, on the exposed area below the short trousers. Len sat on the convenient ledge and spent some time, viewing the coast beyond Lumia, with the non-reflective binoculars. As usual, he saw a few ships on the glistening sea below.

Len, placed the binoculars on his lap, and asked. "How old are you Leslie?"

"Twenty-one, how about you Len?" Leslie responded.

"Same age as you, What about you Ben?" Len continued.

"Twenty last Sunday," Ben replied.

Len continued. "If we ever make it out of here, and we have children, and they have children, will, what we are all doing in this war, make any difference to them? All of this has got to be for a good reason, hasn't it?"

Leslie thought for a moment before replying. "Of course, it's worth it. If we don't stop tyrants like Hitler, then who will? A few hundred thousand have already died trying to stop him, and his cronies. A few more will go before it's all over, so if it isn't worth it, then let's allow Hitler take over the world now."

All agreed, that it is worth doing. What they are doing, as surly, in the future, nobody, would be so stupid, as to have as big a fight as this, just because of one person's opinion.

Len raised the binoculars to his eyes for one last time, before they returned back to the cool shade of the tents. He focussed the binoculars, and sat up very straight. He rested his left arm on Bens Shoulder, to steady the binoculars. "Well I'm dammed, I think you had better look at this Skipper," Len said, passing the binoculars to Leslie.

Leslie rested the binoculars on the horizontal branch of a tree. The sight he saw made his heart beat faster. The few ships sighted earlier, had now increased in number, and were making close to shore. Landing craft were being deployed. Leslie could make out the Nazi flag on one of the ships.

"Come on chaps, looks like we've got trouble on our hands," Leslie shouted, as he turned to leave the observation site. Running towards the group of lads, was the Sergeant, with a paper in his hand, waving it in the air as he approached.

"You'd better come quick Skipper," the Sergeant said, pushing the note under Leslie's nose. "Gerry has arrived. Lots of sea and air activity on RADAR. We have already notified Group HQ. We have been told to observe and report every ten minutes. To keep radio transmission to less than one minute, with big breaks. And to keep our position undercover, and our heads down."

On returning to the camp, Leslie went straight to look at the dots on the RADAR tubes. He then looked at the calculations made by the operator, and signed the report book, adding the date and time.

Things on Corsica could be about to change. Equipment was checked, as was the stock of food and fuel, recently delivered. The camp guards were changed regularly, to ensure that they remained fresh and vigilant.

CHAPTER 10

Grace, had been given sufficient leave to make a home visit. She caught an underground train, from Edgware station, to Paddington station in London, changing at Tottenham Court Road, and Notting Hill Gate. She then caught the main line train to Bristol Temple Meads. It was here that she changed to the branch line, heading South, to her home town. Most of the night was taken up travelling, very often having to stand. Grace had to change trains often, and as she was not able to sit down regularly, prevented her from any sleep.

Grace arrived home at six thirty in the morning. She was very pleased to see that her Father Jim, was now safe in bed at home. For many months, Jim had been in hospital. He had many operations over the time, to repair the damage to his back, caused by the underground roof fall. Due to the nature of his injuries, he was not able to work underground again, so the National Coal Board financially provided for him. Jim was so pleased to see his little girl, at home and safe. He spent most of Grace's first day's leave, in his chair, listening to her tell him about her work. Grace never told either of her parents, about the attacks that she has witnessed, or the bombing, for fear of making them worry about her.

Grace was delighted to receive several letters from Leslie. He always wrote to her home address, as he did not always know where she was. He knew that, if possible, his letters would be forwarded to her by her parents. Leslie never told Grace about the situations that he had been in, or saw. The Censor was always very strict, so most letters told Grace how much he loved her, and missed her, along with weather reports. His location of work was never revealed.

Elsie and Jim, did tell Grace about the ariel battles seen over the adjacent town, as this had now become well talked about in the town. Many versions of the events were going about, some were almost correct, as others were far away from the truth. However, Jim did know the accurate story, and felt that Grace should know the truth.

The following evening, at about seven o'clock, the peace was shattered\ by the whining of the Air Raid siren on the roof of the Town Hall. The dining room table was usually used for a shelter at home, as no other protection was available. Jim, Elsie, and Grace threw cushions under the table, and made themselves as comfortable as possible, in their shelter. The sound of heavy bombers approaching was heard, this time, coming unusually, from the North. An aircraft flew overhead, heading South East. This was the sound that Grace had heard so many times before. The sound of the heavy aircraft continued in the direction of the next Town, about a mile away. Three large explosions were distinctly heard.

"Why are they bombing down there?" Elsie said with her hands over her ears, and her chin resting on her chest "There's nothing down there to bomb except the railway. Why kill helpless people?"

At last, the all-clear was sounded by the siren. Bill, Jim's brother who lived next door, came to the back door. He was shaking badly. Grace, Elsie, and Jim escaped from their shelter under the table. Bill was invited to sit in a chair, while Elsie made some sweet tea. Bill suffered from Shell shock as a result of the last War. His eyes were red, weeping, and wide open, as his whole body shook in the chair. Jim had been lying under the table so as not to further damage his back. He now stood with his back against a wall for support, and to ease the discomfort in his back.

Eventually Bill recovered. He, unusually, thanked Elsie for the tea, and returned to his home next door,

Later that evening, Earnest arrived, with the news that the German bomber had been making a run-for-home, and dumped his unused bombs on the railway sidings area, of the adjacent Town, He missed all of the railway track, but demolishing some railway truck repair sheds, with no injuries reported.

Time at home, for Grace, was wonderful. One morning, Elsie and Grace decided to do some cooking, with a view to replenishing the larder, with cakes and biscuits. The tray of freshly baked shortbread biscuits, had just been taken from the oven, when there was a knock at the front door. Elsie opened the door to reveal George, the co-op baker with his basket full of bread, over his arm.

"Morning George, one white today please. Divvy number 8531. How are you today?" Elsie said, with a smile on her face, as usual.

"I'm Fine thank you Elsie, Do I see Grace in the background? It must be good to have her back for a few days. Did you hear about the bombs the other evening? They demolished three wagon repair sheds, and a privy. Made a bit of a mess of the privy."

Grace appeared at the open door, with the tray of freshly baked biscuits.

"Fancy a biscuit George? I have only just made them, so they are still a bit warm." Grace asked, holding the tray towards George,

"Thank you my lovely," George said taking a biscuit. "Thanks, and see you tomorrow."

George left, munching on the biscuit, to return to his horse-drawn bakers van. He removed the feeding bag attached to the horse's bridal, rose to the driving seat of the van, and gave a friendly wave to Elsie, as he drove away.

The following day, again, the knock at the door, but a little later than usual this time. Elsie opened the door, to find a different baker standing on the doorstep.

"No George today?" Elsie asked, looking past the baker to see if George was behind him, perhaps, showing the new man the ropes.

"No, Sorry," came the reply from the new baker. "George died last night, a bit sudden like," the man replied, bowing his head as he spoke. "What bread today missus?"

Elsie chose the bread, paid the baker and shut the door. She told Grace what had happened to George. The question now remains. Was it the biscuit?

Home leave for Grace was now over, so the return train journey to the camp, once again, took all night. However, this time she did have a seat all of the way. Lighting in the coaches on the train were extinguished, as it would be an excellent target for enemy aircraft. It was bad enough having the glow from the engine's fire box, every time it was opened, for more coal to be added.

Grace arrived at her hut, at six thirty in the morning, just in time for breakfast in the canteen. The day's work was pretty normal, and quiet. After supper she settled down to writing to Leslie, responding to his letter's numbers ninety-nine to one hundred and four. The supply of letters from Leslie, was not as frequent as before, and only had a code name for her to address her letters.

Many of the days at work for Grace, were quite boring, transferring information into the ledger. One day, Grace was asked to work on the telephone switchboard, as two of the girls that normally worked on that shift, had been killed in an air raid while visiting London. Work started to become more interesting. On some occasions, parts of conversations between officers were heard on the telephone system. Because Grace had previously signed the 'Official Secrets Act', she did not divulge any of the information overheard.

Most evenings were spent, either in the hut doing sewing, or knitting. Every fourth evening, a film was shown in the hall on the base. One of the films of the week, was 'Irish Eyes Are Smiling'. The girls all agreed it was very good.

Betty, one of the girls, was getting married very soon, so Grace and Peggy arranged a collection from the other girls. They were very surprised to collect four pounds, seventeen shillings and sixpence.

Grace's trips to Harrow to visit her Cousin, was very easy, by catching the number thirty-eight bus from outside the camp gates. Twenty-four-hours leave, and short week-ends, were often spent at Harrow.

"Let's go into London one day and have fun," Peggy announced, one boring evening. "We could go and see a show, and perhaps, have tea somewhere special." Grace thought that Peggy's idea was wonderful, as long as they weren't killed, like the other girls who went to London.

The day arrived for the visit into London Town. Three of the girls, Peggy, Grace and Lilly, had twenty-four hours leave. The underground train journey to Oxford Street station, was a new experience for Lilly. Grace and Peggy had used this route often, when going, and returning, for home leave. What was different this time for Grace, was to leave the train at this station and climb the stairs upwards to the surface. The streets were very busy. People were going about their daily business as though there had never been a War. Gents with brief cases, and bowler hats. Ladies with handbags clutched under their arms, wearing hats placed at different angles upon their heads. British uniformed service men and women. American soldiers, Men smoking cigarettes watching everything going on around them. Policemen and Wardens wearing tin helmets. Newspaper sellers with large orderly queues of people, waiting for the day's news. There were very long lines of people at the many bus stops. And traffic everywhere.

Double decker buses by the dozen, were bursting with as many people, as the bus would hold. Lorries, cars, vans, and some military vehicles, trundled along the road. At one point a very large lorry went past carrying an enormous army tank, however, nobody even noticed it.

Some of the buildings had been bomb damaged, with gaping holes in the line of shops and buildings. Many of the buildings were shored-up with timber beams to prevent further structural falls. They had huge timbers, some reaching onto the road. The bombed John Lewis Store was a sad sight to see. Advertising hoardings had been placed around the building to hide the unfortunate sight.

The girls walked up and down Oxford Street gazing into the shop windows as they went. At one-point, Grace caught sight of themselves in the reflection of a window. How smart they all were she thought, in ATS uniform, with shoulder handbags and gas-mask bags. She stopped for a moment and watched the other people in the reflection of the window glass.

With the window shopping completed, there was plenty of time available for other activities. The girls decided not to go into the shops as most items were very expensive, and they did not want to be disappointed as Army pay is adequate for the basics in life, but not for luxury items.

Peggy found a cinema advertising the film 'Mrs Parkington'. The bill-board advertising the film looked interesting. The entrance fee to the cinema was only sixpence each, so the decision was made to go inside. The film had not yet started as the screen was showing an advertisement for Pears soap. Somewhere near the screen, a piano was being played, but could not be seen from the seats occupied by the girls. The film at last started. It was a black and white talking film. The accompanying piano player ceased playing when the film started.

The girls did enjoy the film. The actors Greer Garson and Walter Pidgeon made a very good story.

"Lunch," Peggy said as they left the cinema. "Why don't we have lunch at Lyons Corner House? It's only just at the end of this street. I saw it earlier as we passed by."

The decision was made very easily, J. Lyon's Corner House it was. The outside of the restaurant was very beautiful. Large curved glass windows with ornate wood work at street level, and a wonderful lattes-work of wood and glass adorned the top of the windows. The glow of the electric lights from the inside of the windows, made the rooms look warm and welcoming. As the name Corner House conveyed, the windows swept around the building into the next road, therefore, going around the corner. The girls stood for a moment looking at the splendour of the building.

"Come on then," Grace said, grabbing the other girl's arms to make a line of three, with Grace in the centre. She pulled themselves into the open door. They were instantly welcomed, and found a table, by a very well-dressed gentleman waiter. The waiter had a white apron, tied around his waist, that almost reached the floor. He looked very neat and tidy, with dark hair combed close to his head. A large dark, well-trimmed moustache, completed his look. Most of the other waiting staff were ladies known as 'Nippies'.

The splendour of the room was almost overpowering for the girls. They spent the first few moments looking in all directions, and taking-in the atmosphere of the establishment. The ceiling was supported by several large round highly embellished marble columns, rising from the floor to the ceiling. At ceiling level, the columns opened out like large petals. Lights shone upwards from behind the petals, illuminating the very ornately plastered ceiling. Tables were arranged with plenty of room between each of them. Each table had a long white table cloth, supporting silver cutlery. The chairs had wooden arch-backs, with very plush seats.

Lunch was served by the 'Nippy' waitresses in long black dresses, white starched hats and white pinafore aprons. Cod, with new potatoes, and small peas were served on plates, with the J. Lyons crest, placed at the furthest point, away from the customer. The sweet, was a Knickerbocker Glory, of Lyons Corner

House renown. Fifteen shillings and threepence each was expensive, but worth every penny.

After leaving the Corner House, and the wonderful and very filling lunch, the Girls walked to Marble Arch, very slowly, as the Knickerbocker Glories were already taking their toll. On arriving at Marble Arch, they were overwhelmed by the size of the building. They walked through the Arch, to find themselves at the famous, Speakers Corner. A very overweight man, in a long black coat was holding a book above his head. He was shouting about freedom of the people. The man was being watched by several American soldiers, who were laughing at him. The girls thought it would be much safer to wander on.

Time was moving on. Lilly thought that it should be time to make their way back to camp. She thought, that the trains would start to get busy near the end of the working day. The train ride back to camp was uneventful, as all of the girls fell asleep throughout most of the journey.

One week after the visit to London, Grace was given the job to accompany a driver in a very large Army truck, down to Sutcliff Park, in South East London. The task, was to deliver and collect stores. The RAF driver was very quiet, as he drove through the centre of London. The previous evening many incendiary bombs had been dropped by the Luftwaffe. The sight was horrendous. Some buildings were still on fire. The smell of the smoke was almost overpowering. Rubble from the demolished buildings littered the streets. Some uniformed people were climbing over the rubble, peering into the piles of masonry. On one occasion the driver had to reverse down a street and choose a different route, as the street was blocked by wardens. Fire engine bells rang out, and ambulances raced around the streets. As they passed the end of Tottenham Court Road, Grace looked up the adjacent Oxford Street. The road they had walked along a few days ago was a mess. The cinema visited the other morning, no longer existed. A pile of smouldering rubble replaced the building. A shiver ran down Grace's back as the thought occurred to her, that the bombing could have easily occurred while they were in the building. She wondered if the people who worked in the cinema were safe.

Arriving in the area of South East of London, was very upsetting for Grace. Street after Street of houses, had been demolished by the flying bombs, Doodlebugs as they were known. People were crawling over the remains of bombed houses, trying to find, perhaps, some possessions. Children, in ragged clothes, played amongst the rubble. The driver shook his head as they passed many streets with very few houses standing.

The base at Sutcliffe Park was a temporary 'Hutted Camp'. The lorry was directed to the stores. Grace had some tea in the canteen as she waited for the soldiers to move the goods from the lorry, and re-load with boxes for the return journey.

"Good job you weren't here last night," the girl behind the canteen counter said, with a large teapot in her hands, and a cigarette bobbing about in her lips as she talked. "Had some Bugs here last night. Made an ell of a mess round here." The ash from her bobbing cigarette dropped onto the counter, so she wiped it away with the back of her hand. "Bet you don't see much of the War where you come from," she continued. "Gerry seems to like London for some reason. You got a fella? Nice girl like you. Not a care in the world I dare say."

"I'm from North London, sorry to say, but we get a good deal of bombing as well. I have lost a few good friends already," Grace replied, trying not to be degrading of the situation here. "Yes, I do have a brave fella, he is doing his bit overseas, but they won't tell us where he is."

"Must be somewhere dangerous, if they won't tell you where he is," the lady continued, lighting another Wills Whiff cigarette. "Never mind lovey, he'll be home safe soon enough."

The conversation un-nerved Grace, for the man she is supposed to be marrying is somewhere in the World unknown, and may be in danger. If only she knew where he was?

The driver decided to take a longer route back to the base. He drove further to the East, away from the centre of London. There were still lots of places that had been bombed, but also areas that appeared to be normal, and untouched by the demolishing aerial attacks. Grace thought that the residence in these areas would not think it was normal, without the threat of death at any moment.

The camp gates at RAF Kidbrook was a welcomed sight. When the lorry entered the camp, the evening had well set-in, so both the driver and Grace went straight to the canteen for supper. An early night was decided for Grace, but sleep would not come as she was now very worried about Leslie, and the comments made by the canteen lady.

CHAPTER 11

Life at the RADAR station on Corsica, had now become tense. Movement of large numbers of shipping had been identified around Lille- Rousse, Ajaccio bay, Calvi bay and Propriano, further to the South of the Island. Aircraft movements had also been detected, most of the aircraft movement was on the East side of the island.

One of the Engineers had found an overhead electric power line nearby, as it made its way from the towns below, to further up the mountain. He was able to run electric cables, and connect them to the overhead power cables, by hooking-on. This meant, that the Rushton generator, could remain silent, so not giving their position away to the enemy by the noisy engine.

The work became intense as every small identification of movement on the screens was noted, and logged, in great detail. The radio was used as little as possible to Group HQ, The Morse code, was also sent as a coded message. Equipment and tents, were moved to a more discreet location under the trees, to be hidden from above and general sight. The RADAR mast had undergrowth wrapped around it, as camouflage. All of the men remained constantly vigilant, as something big was definitely happening.

News coming through, regarding the political situation with Italy and Germany, was very confusing. The decision was made to stay under cover for the time being.

The Summer was very hot, as the camps store of water was becoming of some concern due to the extra dry weather conditions, the supply of water from the rock, became less and less every day. Showers for washing were banned, and other water for washing was restricted. Food stock was good for the moment. The next supply of food and fuel could be weeks away.

A shrill whistle signal from a sentry, was passed down the line of men, indicating, that the enemy had been seen, and were close by. Emergency action in the camp was put swiftly into place. All personnel stopped work. All of the men drew additional weapons, and ammunition from the armoury tent. The camp was surrounded by the armed Airman. A machine gun position was set-up above the camp, hidden by undergrowth. All was still. All eyes were watching the sentry hidden on a ridge above the camp. The sound of a vehicle engine was identified about eighty feet away, this brought all of the men to top alert. Rifles were loaded, and pistols were cocked. The machine gunner silently, checked his weapon. The sentry indicated, that the enemy was very local. The vehicle was heard to changed down a gear, as it climbed the hill towards the entrance of the camp.

There it was. A German Staff car coming up the track, about forty feet away.

At the location where the car was first seen, the track had a turning to the right, or straight ahead, into the camp. All of the men held their breath. Rifles were aimed at the driver, guard, and the two rear seated officers. The Staff car stopped at the junction in the tracks.

The two officers in the rear seats of the open topped car, appeared to be drawing a map on a large board. Moments later, one of the officers got out of the car. He placed a compass on the front mudguard of the vehicle, and looked in the direction of the North. Had the German been more observant, he would have seen two of Leslies men, hidden behind bushes. Thank goodness that he was more interested in his task, than looking for snipers. The officer climbed back into the Staff car. He indicated with his arm to the right, and relaxed into the back seat of the car.

The Staff car moved off, it turned right, and with a judder of the clutch, started to climb the right-hand track, leading further up the mountain. Leslie hoped that the power cables installed by the Engineer, was sufficiently hidden in the undergrowth, for the Germans not to see them.

The sound of the staff car engine disappeared up into Mount Lumio. Leslie instructed his men to 'stand-down', much to the relief of all concerned.

Len was the first to talk. "I reckon that Gerry is trying to identify a route from the West side of the Island, to the East, as there it's just across the water from Italy. Did you see that Gerry officer making a map? I think that they are worried about the political situation. If things go wrong, they can also get to France easy, they just have to cross over the hill from Bastia, and they are there."

"You could be right Len," Leslie replied. "We now have to be aware, that the car might come back this way, or try to find an easier way, to get across the Island. I think we need to change sentries, and keep alert."

For two months, all remained quiet. A lot of activity was monitored at sea, and in the air. The political situation was changing between Germany, Italy and France. Most of the shipping monitored previously, had disappeared.

A radio message was received, that the Allies were on their way. Within hours from receiving the intelligence, a large amount of shipping was monitored on the West and South side of the Island. Again, the sentries indicated, that the enemy was close-by. The camp was on full alert. Parts of Italy had been invaded by the Allies, so the Germans could not escape to the East. The Allied occupation was coming from the West and South of the Island. The sentry indicated, that a large number of Germans were seen taking a more Northerly crossing from the camp, to the area North of Bastia.

Leslie and his men again 'stood-down' from the high-level camp protection. Frequent gunfire was heard, mostly from small arms. The RADAR, monitored large quantities of Allied shipping, and aircraft. Day and night, the rattle of gunfire was heard, some very close-by.

Whistles and sounds from sentries, once again brought the camp to full alert. All Airmen were armed, and loaded. Each man was hidden in the undergrowth, and behind huge flat cacti, that grew throughout the area.

A sentry made the sound, that the camp was to be invaded. A group of about twenty local men, found themselves in the clearing, looking at the camp. In a fraction of a second, the locals were surrounded by armed Airmen, guns pointing at them from every direction. The locals, all raised their arms above their heads, each holding a weapon. Some of the Airmen, relieved the men of their weapons, while others kept aim on the invading group.

One man stepped forward, wearing an open necked shirt, and dirty flannel trousers. A bag containing spare ammunition clips, hung around his chest.

"We did not know the British were here," the man said with a very strong local accent. "We are Corsican Resistance. We have been following the Deutshlander's past this place, to chase them away. We have killed many and want to kill them all."

Leslie instantly recognised Pedra in the group. He looked dirty, and very tired. "I know this man," Leslie announced. "I believe him to be a member of the Resistance."

Leslie stood right in front of Pedra, and said. "Is this true Pedra. Is this man telling the truth? my men can still kill you all, if this is not true."

"It is true Leslie, we have driven the Deutsch, and the Italia, out of our towns. The British soldiers, and the French soldiers, are all over the Island. The Deutshlander's are running like pigs. We have killed many, and need to protect our Country. A submarine, has been supplying our Resistance with arms, for a long time now. We believe freedom is here, and we want to protect it."

Leslie realised, that Pedra was probably telling the truth. He instructed his men to 'stand-down', and to return the weapons to the men, who were standing with Pedra. He did understand that he was taking a very large chance, for if Pedra was not telling the truth, then both him, and his men would be in danger. He did have some back-up, as the sentries still had their weapons trained on the invading group, and the machine gunner, still had them in his sights.

The current situation became much more relaxed. The Corsicans, stowed their guns over their shoulders, or into leather holsters. Most of the weapons, were British, mark two nine-millimetre Sten guns. Some of the men, also had British service pistols, similar to the one issued to Leslie.

The leader of the Corsicans was a very tall, stocky, man called Alex. He was wearing a dirty, broad flat cap, covering a head of thick black hair. His shirt, was a striped open neck, collar-less style, with part of his last meal, spread over his front. His trousers were of grey flannel, slightly too short for him, and was supported by a very substantial leather belt. His shoes, had scrapes and cuts, and was made in a very old leather, the colour of which could not be determined.

"What you do here?" Alex announced, in a deep voice, with a distinct French accent. As he spoke, he was looking around the area where he, and his men now found themselves. The other Corsicans, were by now peering into the area beyond the clearing, trying to see detail. However, all they could see were tents. The Airmen had made quite sure that, at all times, the RADAR equipment, and mast truck was hidden from view.

"Watching. Just watching," Leslie replied, in a very uninteresting sort of way. "We watch the Italians. We watch the Germans. We just watch everybody. We are just watchers."

"So are you the only Englander here. Or is there more of you," Alex said, now seeing the armed sentries, at a higher level, above them.

"Can't tell you that," Leslie said, as he beckoned to another Airman, to supply the Corsicans with water. Trying to change the conversation. "Come-on chaps, you all look very thirsty. Have some spring water before you go on your way."

The Corsicans accepted the water. Some drank it, others splashed it around their heads and necks. After thanking Leslie, the group moved off, further up into the mountains. But not before they promised not to divulge the camp to anybody. Leslie told Alex, that one day, they will be able to help the Resistance, but only if their camp is kept secret. This was agreed.

Leslie and Len discussed the Corsican Resistance men at length. It was agreed, that Group HQ should be informed of the discovery of the camp by the locals, and await further instructions.

The daily work continued, but all were still confined to camp. One Airman called Rob, continually confronted Leslie, not agreeing with his decision, to let the Corsicans go. He felt that their camp location had been compromised, and their safety was now at risk. This became an annoyance to Leslie, as this man was always questioning everything. He annoyed most of the other men, and became very unpopular. Len said several times, that there is always one that causes problems, wherever you go in life. Leslie tried to put the man's comments out of his mind, but this was very difficult, for what if he was wrong, what if the camp location had been compromised, what if the Corsicans were lying?

Two weeks had passed from the Corsican invasion of the camp, when a Morse radio message was received. It said that a senior British Army officer, will visit the camp. All of the men made themselves busy, ensuring that the camp and equipment was put in top order for the Officer to arrive. The equipment was checked, tents were checked, kit was checked, sentries posted, and camp cleaned.

Sentries, indicated in the usual way, that an approach was imminent. A British black car arrived with driver, an armed guard, and two Officers. The most senior Officer was a Major. Leslie, Len, and the Corporal, smartly marched to meet the Major, as he climbed out of his vehicle. Leslie Saluted smartly, and all stood to attention.

The Major repaid the salute. "Good morning Gentlemen," the Major said in a very English, well-educated voice. "Can we please speak somewhere privately?" Leslie led the small group, to a part of the camp away from others. The only tents were for accommodation, so a tent for meetings was not available. The Major continued. "The Island of Corsica has now been occupied by the Allies. Mostly British, with some French and others. As far as we know, all of the enemy have run to Southern France, where they have been met with very strong Resistance. As from now, the situation has changed for the better, Corsica has become the first enemy occupied Island to be Liberated. And you, Gentlemen, have contributed greatly to this Liberation. We all congratulate you, for your fine efforts under enemy occupation. The information received from you has been of such importance, that without it Liberation would not have been possible. You no longer have to operate under cover, but operate you must. The post remains active. Your commanding Officer of Met 12 Squadron, section Q, will be in touch soon. Post and supplies for you all are imminent. Thank you all for your assistance. Written orders will follow. God save the King."

Without further ado, the Major Saluted, returned to the car, and was gone.

Shortly afterwards, the camp burst into celebration. The thoughts, that they do not have to be continually undercover is a relief. Post arriving would be wonderful, as none had been received for several weeks.

At the first opportunity Leslie found the privacy, and the time, to write to Grace. He knew that all letters are censored, so his location, and the political situation, was not discussed in his letter. He was only able to tell Grace how much he missed her, and the weather. He was able to ask her, where she was at the moment, he also said that he had written to his parents.

The post arrived in the camp. Several letters came from Grace, along with two letters from Leslies Mum. This was a very welcomed receipt. Stores arrived, with a few luxury additions, such as corned beef in tins. Fuel was provided for the trucks, and the Rushton Generator. Instructions had been given that the electrical connections onto the overhead supply cables, had to be disconnected, and the generator was to be the power supply. Tents were moved to a more open aspect, allowing some warmth from the sun. This was good, as the winter was approaching, and temperatures began to drop, especially at night.

The occasional trip to the coast was made in a truck. Swimming trips made a welcome break from the previous confinements of the camp. Pedra had returned to his home. He was recovering from a bullet wound to the leg, but his new Wife, and his Mother, looked after him very well. He had received the injury, when the Corsican Resistance group, attacked some German infantry in the mountains above Bastia in the North. Alex, and three other fighters, were killed in the exchange.

Life seamed good. The RAF Group Captain, had visited the camp on several occasions, and was very happy with the current arrangements. Orders were given, that Met 12 had to concentrate on monitoring the sea, as well as air movements, as very frequent sea battles were still going on in the Mediterranean, not far from the Island.

The swimming party

CHAPTER 12

Grace, was again at home, on a forty-eight-hour leave. Sunday morning was chilly. Ice had formed on the inside of the bedroom window glass. She could hear her Father re-lighting the fire in the combination fire place, in the living room below. The sound of a kettle being filled with water, brought thoughts into Graces head.

Back at the camp, two days previously, Betty had been making tea, at about seven o'clock in the morning. The post arrived. A registered letter for Betty. Moments later, the kettle was dropped. A scream from Betty, several women came running to the kitchen. On arrival in the kitchen, Betty was on her knees with her head buried in her hands, screaming loudly. Peggy had arrived first. She manged to prise the letter from Betty's grasp, as she continued to sob loudly. Peggy read the letter, then handed it to Grace. The wedding that Betty was expecting a few months ago, for which present's had been bought, has to be put off, as her fiancé had been posted overseas. To where, she did not know. The letter was from Rodger's Mother.

Grace read the letter. The letter had a separate telegram attached to it. The telegram said, that Rodger, her fiancé, has been killed on active duty.

The girls, who were now with Betty, comforted her as best they could, but their efforts were in vain. The Commanding Officer, permitted instant home leave for Betty.

Now at home, Grace recalled the news that Betty had received with tears in her eyes. What terrible news to receive? One letter telling her that Rodger was posted overseas, with an attached Telegram telling her that he was dead. Grace knew that Betty's Mother lived on her own, since the recent death of her Father from lung cancer. How on earth could her Mother cope with such tragic news.

Where is Leslie, what is he doing, where are you my darling? These thoughts were most prominent in Grace's mind, and would not go away. So many servicemen and civilians were dying, and for what?

After breakfast, Grace and her Mother attended Chapel. Tears were not far away from Grace, as the Minister's Sermon was about helping others. Elsie, was not told about the sadness that Betty was going through, for fear of making her Mother worry about Grace. In fact, Grace never told her parents about any of the atrocities that she has witnessed. After lunch, the Chapel was visited again by Grace. This time to help with the Sunday School. Grace found this time very rewarding, spending time with the Children. who had very little concept of the War, and what it meant?

The Sunday School, was a small room to the side of the Chapel. It had long wooden hard bench seats. The back rests of the seats were supported at each end on steel supports. The steel supports were hinged at the bottom, and protruded through a slot in the seat, so that the backs could be swung through the slots in the seat. This allowed the sitter to sit on either side of the bench, and have the luxury of a back rest.

Children will be Children, concentration on the task in hand for most Children, will depend upon the interest of the subject. A scream from Billy certainly did concentrate Graces mind. Billy had been playing with the swinging seat back. His hand was jammed between the steel arm, and the slot in the wooden seat. With very careful manoeuvring of the device, eventually, released Billy's hand. It was very blue, from the bruising he received.

Billy, never played with the seat ever again. He did, however, concentrate on the subject being taught. Grace retuned home unhappy to think that Billy was hurting so much.

On returning home after Sunday School, Grace found her Father and Mother in their favourite arm chairs, in front of the roaring fire. Her Father was listening to a Brass band concert, on the PYE wireless. Her Mother was reading from her favourite book 'Pilgrims Progress'. The book is the story of a devoted Christian, making his way through life. Elsie was a devoted Christian, and a Quaker. She had not been able to visit her designated meeting House near Wantage, since the start of the War. Her very good friend, and fellow Quaker, contacted Elsie regularly by letter. Elsie's friend, was also a very good artist. On one occasion, when Elsie visited her friend, she sat for a portrait. The picture was a pencil drawing that was currently mounted in a glass frame, and sitting on the living room sideboard.

Jim Loved to listen to the brass band concerts. He is a very accomplished Euphonium player, and a member, not only of the Town Silver band, but also an occasional player in the Salvation Army band, conducted by Elsie's Brother.

The peace and tranquillity within the room was good. Black clouds had gathered outside, as the late Winter afternoon became colder. Jim stoked the dimming fire, with a long brass poker, and added more coal to the fire. The wireless was turned off, as the Band concert had concluded. Elsie closed her book for the day. Grace went to the kitchen, to prepare the tea time meal of jam sandwiches, and cherry cake. Grace, peered out of the kitchen window. She saw some flurries of snow blowing in the wind. She started to become a little concerned, for she had planned to catch the six forty train, back to the Base that evening.

Tea was served on the round mahogany dining table. The flurries of snow, increased significantly, to became a steady, silent, flow. After tea, Grace helped with the washing-up. She returned to her room to change into her Army Uniform.

Grace left the house, thirty minutes earlier than usual, so as not to miss the train. The last thing she wants is to be put on a charge for being late at the barracks. It was now quite dark, as she made her way to the railway station, about half a mile away from the house. The snow, was now accompanied by a strong wind, causing a mini blizzard in her face. She pulled her great coat collar further up around her head, and pulled her hat down to meet the collar. A quarter of a mile to go to the station. The snow is now above Graces service shoes as she walked. Her stockings were getting wet. The snow was sticking to the wool of the army great coat. She sometimes had to close her eyes against the blowing snow. At last, the shelter of the station waiting room. Someone had kindly lit a fire in the waiting room fire grate. This was very welcoming. As Grace was the only waiting passenger, she sat in a chair near to the fire, and stretched out her legs to the warming fire, hoping to dry her wet stockings. Ten minutes to wait.

The waiting room door opened, and a male Soldier came in rubbing his hands together as he made his way closer to the fire. Like Grace, he had his great coat around his face, and his hat just above his ears.

"Bit cold outside Miss," The Soldier said, as he turned his collar down.

"Albert, is that you, Albert?" Grace almost shouted at the man.

The Soldier, turned to see who knew him. "Grace," came the reply. "What the devil are you doing here?"

"Just finished leave. What about you?" Grace said, as she threw her arms around the Soldier's neck, realising that the Soldier, was her much lover Cousin.

"Same here," Albert replied.

Both of the Great coats, were so thick and heavy, that Grace's arms could hardly reach Albert.

Albert managed to become detached from Grace's grasp, to tell her. "Got to get back to Bodmin before dawn. Been on twenty-four-hours. Something big going to happen soon, so we had leave before we get down to it. We have been told that when we return, our tank regiment will be moved to Plymouth, but nobody knows what it's all about."

The train arrived at the station on time. Grace, and Albert had the luxury of an empty carriage to themselves, all the way to Bristol. The conversation between them was continuous. They talked about the concert at the Town Hall. They were now able to laugh about the behaviour of the American Soldiers. Grace had received the newspaper cuttings of the concert from her Mother, and Albert, had the same cuttings sent to him by his Mother.

After leaving the train at Bristol, Grace caught the next train to London, leaving Albert on the platform, waving wildly, as the train left. Grace thought that he looked lonely, on the cold station platform. He was the only person on the platform at that time, with his hand waving, as Grace's train disappeared around the bend.

The journey to London Paddington was as tedious as ever, although Grace did have a seat all of the way. She had to change to the underground, and on to the base at Mill Hill, North London.

Grace arrived at the base a little later than usual, due to the snow, but still in time for work. She had not had any sleep on the journey, thinking about the chance meeting with Albert. Her curiosity got her wondering what the 'big show' was that Albert was talking about.

Work for Grace, was again very normal, except that some correspondence, requiring typing was marked 'secret', with the same word 'Overlord' coming up time and time again.

Christmas 1943 arrived, but work continued as if Christmas did not exist. Grace and her Army friends, took every opportunity available to leave the camp behind. Grace was lucky that this Christmas Day, she was able to spend on a twenty-four-hour pass, with her Cousin, and her family, in Harrow.

On the evenings that the women had to stay in the camp, they found other things to do, including, watching lots of films, such as, Madonna of the Moors, Man in Half Moon Street, and Woman in the Window. The camp was very good at providing the films for camp personnel. Usually, a film was shown every other evening. Grace was not always able to go to watch a film, as she had to do her turn on night duty.

Betty did not return to her duties for several months. She became very ill from the shock of losing Roger, before she was even married to him. Roger's Mother never recovered from her news, and died a few months after Roger's death.

New Year 1944. The R.E.M.E. at Kidbrook, put on a Pantomime. Several Army trucks, took about twenty girls, to the camp at Kidbrook. The Pantomime was great fun. Most of the off-duty girls attended. The Pantomime was called 'Aladdin at Kidbrook'. It was presented by 3AA WKSP. COY. R.E.M.E. The all-male cast, except for Aladdin, who was played by a girl called Doris, was hilarious. Men dressed as Women, and men dressed in silly costumes, was a welcomed relief from the War work. The Major Commanding Officer, congratulated the cast and crew.

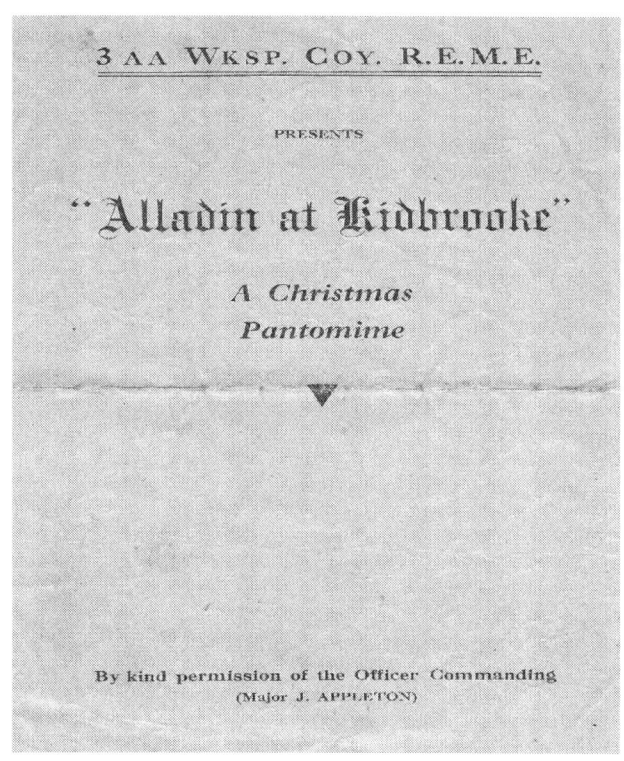

Some of the friends that the girls had made at Kidbrook were still at the base. They invited the Girls from Mill Hill, to coco in the canteen after the performance. It was great fun. There had to be a lot of catching-up to do. Grace had been updating Margaret with the recent news, and asked where Mary and Charlie were, as they were both very good friends in the past?

Margaret, turned away from Grace. She put her hands to her face, and told Grace that they had both been killed in a bombing attack two weeks earlier. Margaret composed herself, and continued to tell Grace, that, they were both returning to the base from a day out. They had passed through the front gates, and were walking across the parade ground, when the attack started. They were both too far away from a shelter to reach one in time. They received a direct hit by the shrapnel of the bomb that exploded right next to them. Their identity discs were the only means of knowing who they were.

Margaret excused herself from the party, and left, shaking uncontrollably.

The Camp at Mill Hill, Inglis Barracks, is not the best place in the world to work. Grace had to change jobs quite often, from typing, to stores accounts, telephone operator, to post clerk. Her original job of Tailor, seemed to be years ago by now. Many of the women who started work with Grace, followed her, as their jobs changed as well. The current tasks are typing confidential letters, and reports, along with staffing the Post Room.

By the Summer of 1943, the activity in the Barracks seemed to have changed. Stores were being moved at a much higher rate than normal. Men and equipment were being despatched, to many different areas on the South Coast of England. These additional movements did not go un-noticed by the A.T.S. Girls. Grace, had continued to type reports, indicating, that something big was going to happen soon.

A twenty-four-hour pass had been granted to four of the Girls, including Peggy and Grace. Information had been received, that a 'Special Show' was to happen at the Stage Door Café, in Webber Street, in City of London. The underground train was boarded at Mill Hill station by the girls. One section of the journey had to be carried out by bus, as the rail track had been damaged by bombs. At long last the girls arrived at the venue. Outside a sign indicated that "All are welcome to the Workers Playtime. A rare opportunity for the City of London. A live British Broadcasting Corporation Wireless program."

Workers Playtime was always a live Wireless broadcast, usually from a factory, somewhere in England. It was originally devised as a morale-booster for the workers of Britain. On this occasion, the broadcast was for the workers of Central London, so the Stage Door Café was chosen by the BBC as the venue for this broadcast. The programs usually lasted for an hour, this being the lunch time break in factories. Often it came from the canteens, and was organised by the 'outside broadcast' section of the BBC.

The Stage Door Café is very large, and is attached to one of London's theatres. The girls found a table where all of them could sit together. Tea, and little fairy cakes, were provided free of charge before the program was due to be broadcast. Engineers were very busy running cables, and microphones, at different locations in the room. One area had been set aside for the performers, with a raised platform. The platform did look a bit rickety and unstable, but the girls thought that the wonderful BBC would not let people perform on an unsafe surface. Several microphones on stands were on the platform, with large mesh discs attached to them.

The room was now full of people. A general chatter of voices made it difficult for the girls to talk to each other across the table. A man stepped onto the platform. He instructed the gathering to react to certain arm movements, made by himself. One movement meant, clap loudly, another, for silence, along with several more, with their appropriate responses by the audience.

The presenter, Norman Wooland announced the start of the program, followed by music played on a music machine. The audience reacted to the arm movements as instructed. The program was hilarious. Elsie and Doris Walters did a very funny sketch. There were lots and lots of community singing. The Announcer introduced Jack Warner, who was wonderful. He told lots of funny stories about things that happen in normal life. It was certainly interesting to look at life in that way.

The program ended with a very hearty sing-song, Norman Wooland closed the program in his usual way, and the show was over. Jack Warner spent some time chatting to people in the audience. It seemed that he gathered some of his presentation material, by talking to people that he meets. He grabbed an empty chair, and joined the four Army girls.

"Did you enjoy the performance?" He asked. The girls were so shocked at meeting the real Jack Warner, that they all nodded heads in agreement.

"Where are you based?" Came the next question from Mr. Warner.

"Mill Hill," Peggy managed to say, looking at the man in an overwhelming way. "We all work at Mill Hill at the moment Sir, but we have worked in many other places as well," she continued, but then, as her mouth dried-up, she had to stop her reply.

Lilly managed to add. "We very much enjoyed your performance Mr. Warner. It is a big relief to see such humour in these awful times. Thank you very much.

"You are all very welcome," Jack Warner said, as he stood up, and returned the chair to its proper position. He moved to a different table to chat to some ladies, who looked as if they worked in an office, as their clothes were of 'office type'.

After leaving the Café, the evening was yet young, so off to the Phoenix Theatre at Charring Cross, to see the six-thirty performance of the play, 'Pink String and Sealing Wax'. The play was very entertaining. It had three acts, and was set in 1880 in Brighton.

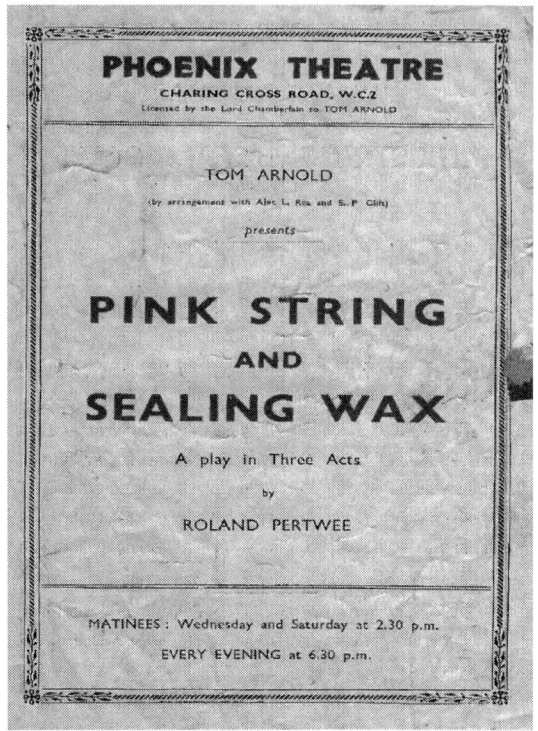

As the girls left the Theatre at the end of the performance, the streets were very busy with people rushing in all direction. Grace wondered where they were all going? Busses were full of people, with some hanging onto the rear flat deck by the grab poles. One man was seen running after a bus, with the lady Conductor waving him away as the bus increased speed. The man threw his arms in the air in despair, as the bus mingled with the other traffic.

Charring Cross underground station, was also very busy. Two trains thundered into the station, and on to destinations not required by the girls. At last the correct train arrived, with the hiss of compressed air, as the doors slid open. Grace was first to board the carriage, however, a well-dressed gent, with a bowler hat, brief case, and umbrella dashed in front of Grace, without a care for anyone else but himself. She tripped over the man's trailing umbrella and fell down. Her head and shoulders were on the train, and the bottom half of Grace was still on the platform. The other girls ran immediately to Grace's aid. The train Guard also ran to help the fallen female Soldier. The only thing that was damaged, apart from her stockings, was Grace's pride. The City gent made no attempt to apologise for his jumping the que, and causing the incident. When all were seated on the train, one of the girls, whispered in the ear of the gent. He approached Grace, apologised for his behaviour, and sat in another part of the carriage.

The rest of the journey back to camp was dark, and again partly by bus. The girls were quite tired, so an early night for all.

CHAPTER 13

The late Summer of 1943 was very hot on the Island of Corsica. As the Allied occupation on the Island was settling in, the 12 Met Squadron had to resume meteorological duties, as well as their other work. As much of the technical meteorological equipment previously issued, had been either damaged or misplaced, new equipment arrived from the stores department at Ajaccio.

New weather balloons, and associated equipment arrived, along with wind speed indicators, and rainfall indicators. The previous rainfall indicator, had been dismantled and used for part of a catapult and sling, for catching a pheasant type bird, adding to a usually tasteless diet.

Leslie took the opportunity to obtain from the stores, photographic developer fluid, acid stopper and photo fixer, along with 120 black and white film. This was used to print photos at work, and also for his individual use. Leslie still had his Kodak fold-away camera, which he used on many occasions, however, not having a decent dark room was a major setback. In the past he carried out contact printing in a dark tent, so a new dark room must be found. Leslie had sent many pictures taken with his trusty camera, to his parents and Grace. Occasionally the photos did not turn out very well, and sometimes not even at all.

The weather balloons were loosely inflated with the Helium gas provided. Instruments were attached to the lower tags of the balloon, along with a very long, lightweight, tether rope. After carefully checking the RADAR, that all was clear, the balloon was allowed to climb to its lofty height into the atmosphere.

As the Helium filled balloon rose into the air, it increased in size, as the gas expanded in the air with less atmospheric pressure. When the balloon had reached its desired height, it was lowered back to earth, using a hand wound winch. The balloons instruments results were entered onto a chart, known as the THUM chart. This was the Thermal Upper Air Measurement. Wind speed, and direction were recorded. The rainfall measuring vessel had not been unpacked, due to the fact that no rainfall had occurred for about three months.

Work became fairly regular, with different shifts of men, watching the cathode ray tube of the RADAR unit, on a continuous basis. Radio communication was much easier, than when the Italians and Germans were on the island. Trips out of camp was now a regular occurrence. Leslie wrote to Grace most days, every time, telling her how much he missed her, and sending the occasional photograph.

Leslie took his camera wherever he went, taking pictures of the countryside, local life, the coastline, mountains, and the men of his Squadron. The beach at Calvi Bay was a regular and favourite place to be, when off duty. The sea was always so clear, that one could see the tiny fish wriggling about, just above the sandy bottom. The colour was always a wonderful clear mid blue, known as Mediterranean Blue. The water was usually very calm, with the smallest of waves turning themselves onto the beach, of golden soft sand.

<u>Calvi Bay Corsica</u>

One particular morning, the sun was warm, and the sea was just right for a swim. Len and Leslie had become particularly strong swimmers, regularly swimming two or three miles at a time. The previous evening Len had suggested, that as they had the day off the following day, that a very long swim would be good exercise for them both. They could swim from Calvi Bay, right up to Lille-Rousse and back, this being about twelve miles. A boat was arranged, by some of the other chaps, to act as a safety boat. The boat was about ten feet long, with a small inboard motor. It was skippered by Ben and Bob. The swimming pair left Calvi beach at nine o'clock that morning. It was decided, that the boat would lead the way, and that every-so-often. a hand grenade was dropped into the water ahead of the swimmers, just to make sure that there was not anything nasty in the water.

What a wonderful swim the two men were having. A steady pace of a crawl stroke was quite easy in the calm warm water. The small beach of Lille-Rousse was reached at eleven thirty in the morning. Without stopping, the swimmers turned and set off back to Calvi. Things were starting to get tougher, fatigue was beginning to set in. Calvi Bay was in sight. Every stroke was becoming heavy.

The boat slowed down, and drew behind the swimmers. Calvi Beach was reached at last. The swimmers walked out of the sea to a tremendous reception from many of the locals, including Pedra and his family, along with eight of the Airmen. A few British soldiers were also in the group. It seemed as though the beach was full of people welcoming the swimmer's home.

Leslie thought that he would feel tired after such a long swim, but instead, he felt on top of the World. Arms and legs did ache a bit, when he thought about it. Many of the locals had brought food and drink to the reception. Great fun was had by all. Somebody was playing music on a violin, and another on a piano accordion. Any excuse for a jolly party, Leslie thought. It was really good to see the locals enjoying the occasion, considering how depressed they had been for so long. A small island with only two-hundred-and twenty-thousand native inhabitants, had been under strict rule, firstly by the Italians, and then further depressed by the Germans. Spirits needed lifting, and parties was one of the best ways to do just that.

Back at camp Leslie was able to tell Grace, in a letter, how Len and himself swam in the sea for miles. He did not tell her where it was, as the Censor would probably stop the entire letter being sent. He also wrote to his Mother and Father, telling them about his epic swim. He knew that his Mother would be very worried, as they did not know were Leslie was in the World. What she did know, was that both Leslie and Grace were very much reluctant travellers. If the Army and Air Force, hadn't made them go to wherever they were, they would not have gone by choice. Leslie could never have imagined that he would ever have travelled to North Africa, or Corsica, or that Grace would have spent time in cold, wooden huts, so far away from home.

<u>Leslie at Corsica camp</u>

Edith was delighted to receive any letters from either of her three sons. At least she knew that Don was in England, working on Spitfire Aircraft, at different locations in the Midlands and the North of the Country. Andrew was at home most of the time, as a Lay Preacher in the Methodist Ministry. Leslie, however, she had no idea where he was in the World. Even the letters that she did receive from Leslie very often had sections obliterated by the censor.

Charlie, Leslies Father, was very proud of all of his sons, but he also, would love to know where Leslie was, and what he was doing. At this particular time, there was excitement at home. The house was to have electric lighting and power installed. Currently lighting was from oil filled decorative lamps, standing on the sideboard in the living room, an oil lamp in the kitchen, and candles everywhere else. Edith did not like the thought of gas lighting in the house. She had heard of so many accidents with the open flame. The Local

Council were offering a scheme, where eight electric lights, and four power points, could be installed in the house for thirty pounds, the rest of the installation cost, would be paid by the Council. This became a very popular scheme. The thought of no more oil lamps in the house was very exciting for Edith. The oil lamps needed very regular cleaning, and always seemed to need filling-up with oil. The smoke from the lamps caused the ceilings to become black. Picture frames needed cleaning on a regular basis, as did the windows and curtains. It was always advised that a supply of free air was available when using oil lamps, so the top of the sliding transom windows were often open, even in winter.

The electricians arrived on bicycles. Wooden drums, of lead covered cable were suspended on the handlebars of the bicycles, with tool bags tied behind the saddles. The work started in the attic. Beds were covered with old sheets, as cables were pulled in all directions. Then the work moved to the first floor. Floorboards were lifted, and cables were installed all over the place.

While the work went on, Charlie spent his days on the delivery van, and then every evening on duty with the Home Guard, just to keep out of the way.

At last the work was completed. What a difference electric lighting made to the house. The oil lamps and candles were stored away, not too far, just in case the electricity failed. Every room was now illuminated. Charlie bought a new two bar electric fire to keep the bedrooms warm, before going to bed. The difference was amazing. Edith was able to carry out sewing late in the evening, without having to move her work close to the hot oil lamp. The loss of smoke from the dirty lamps was very welcomed. When a wall or ceiling was cleaned, it remained clean. Charlie was able to read his newspaper in the evenings. He often had complained, in the past, that by the time he arrived home from work in the winter, it was too dark to properly read the newspaper.

Edith, spent some time telling Grace's Mother Elsie, about the wonderful difference electric lights made to their lives.

One Saturday morning Charlie was on Home Guard duty, again in the High Street of the Town. Both Charlie and another Home Guard soldier took a few moments, to sit on a bench at the end of the High Street. Lots of people were going about their weekend business, shopping, and talking to friends. A few Soldiers in uniform, possibly on-leave, made their way into the Drill Hall. Some workmen were erecting a banner on the Town Hall, advertising a future event. All was normal for a Saturday morning. The peace was shattered, by the thunder of large military vehicles. American trucks were trundling out of the area from behind the High Street, where the American Army were billeted.

Truck after truck left the High Street. They made their way up the hill to the railway station. Charlie and his mate watched the exercise with interest from the bench seat. Moments later Joe, the owner of the dance hall, joined the two men on the bench.

"So they'm leaving then. I heard that, from the Town Clerk tother day," Joe announced, in his usual deep Somerset accent, as he lit his pipe, and watched the American exodus. "Didn't see a dammed one of those Yank's in the dance hall, all the time they were here. I spent loads of money doing the dammed place up before they came. Now they 'r goin, and I ant made a penny out of um."

Most of the townspeople stopped their business, to watch the trucks, and other vehicles, make their way up the hill to the railway station. And then they were gone. The High Street again became silent, apart from the coal merchant's Sentinel Steam lorry puffing along the High Street.

"Let's go and see if they have really gone," Charlie said standing to his feet, and swinging his rifle over his shoulder. "Come on you two, let's have a look." Charlie led the way, followed by the other Soldier, and Joe. Up into the Church Square, past the Parish Church, and into the old Orchard where the American Billets were located. The wire gates were closed but not locked. One good push and the gate swung open.

Like naughty little boys the three men crept through the open gate. A wide path led to an open gravel surface square of land. The square was surrounded by the curved roofs of cream painted Nissan huts. Behind the huts, at one end of the plot, was two larger single-story buildings. The three men peered through the windows of the Nissan huts. The windows were covered on the inside by a brown netting material, similar to a gauze. The camp appeared to be completely empty. Charlie thought that the Americans must have left in quite a hurry, for, leaving the gate unlocked was, in his view, reckless. Nobody could be seen anywhere on the base. The feeling was quite spooky. A silence seemed to overcome the site. Even the sound from the very close Town could not be heard. Charlies boots made a crunching sound as he walked around the deserted gravel pathways.

Joe tried a door handle to one of the huts. "Here look, this one's unlocked," he whispered, but his whisper sounded like a soft shout, in this eerie place. "Come on you lot, let's have a look inside," Joe continued, as he opened the door wide.

Charlie and his mate stood behind Joe to view the inside of the hut. It appeared to be empty, except, that all of the beds were stacked on their sides, with some bedside cupboards piled upon one another, beside the beds. The men stepped cautiously into the room. The smell of burnt tobacco was still very strong in the air. An iron 'Turtle' heating stove was standing in the centre of the room, with a chimney flue pipe rising from the stove and through the ceiling. The heating stove still had some warmth to the ironwork. Pinned on the walls around the room were a variety of articles, including, newspaper cuttings of pictures, calendars, pictures of American country views, and 'pin-up' pictures of girls, in various poses. Joe spent some time looking at the 'pin-up' pictures.

At the furthest end of the hut from the door was a corridor. It led to washing facilities to the left, and toilets on the right. Charlie's mate asked, what a sign over the wash basins meant. It said "Turn off all faucets after use." Charlie explained that a faucet is American for a tap.

"Why can't they call a tap a tap?" Joe asked. "I thought the American language was English, but it isn't is it?"

The men took some time looking around the billet with interest. Charlie found a discarded half smoked cigar on a windowsill. He tipped his Army cap to the back of his head, threw his chest forward, and pushed the Cigar into his mouth. "The name is Churchill, Winston Churchill," he said, trying to create a double chin as he spoke. "You men are doing a wonderful job, keep it up, and we will send Hitler to his grave." The other men laughed and clapped their hands, watching Charlie's interpretation of the Prime Minister. "Sh," said Charlie, as he returned the cigar to its windowsill. "Don't want to wake any Yanky's left about."

The group left the hut, and closed the door behind them. Two other doors to huts were found to be open, to find the same contents and arrangements, as the first hut, in both of them.

"Strange that nothing is locked," Charlie's mate said, closing the last door behind him.

"Let's have a butcher's in here," Joe said, opening a door to one of the larger buildings.

"Hello, anybody home?" Joe shouted, as he stepped through the door.

No reply came. All was silent. Again, the strange spooky feeling filled the building.

The door led to a long passageway stretching to the other end of the building. Along the passage were doors on both sides. Some of the doors were open. Joe entered the first open door on the right of the passage. The stale smell of burnt cigar tobacco was again overwhelming. A wooden desk was pushed against a wall with a swivelling leather covered chair, standing on top of the table. Three filing drawer cabinets stood beside the table. Joe opened the top drawer of one of the cabinets.

"Here look at this?" Joe said in a loud whisper. "Look what I found." The others peered into the open drawer. Three empty bottles of American Bourbon, and four cut-glass whisky glasses sat in the front of the drawer.

"I recon this was the Boss's office," Joe said taking a glass out, and polishing it on his sleeve. He held the glass at eye level so that he could see the quality of the fine cut glass.

'BANG'. All of the men jumped, as the door closed its self.

The glass left Joe's hand, and flew high into the air. On the way down Joe tried to catch the flying glass. The glass bounced off his extended fingers, flew to the left, and careered towards the floor. Joe, by reflex, extended his leather booted foot in an endeavour to save the flying glass. All was in vain. The glass exploded into tiny fragments as it hit the floor.

"Damn. I could have done with a set of four in my bar at home" Joe said, pushing his hands deep into his trouser pockets, and pouting like a small boy who has just lost a favourite toy.

Charlie left the room in some disgust. Thinking that Joe was going to steel the glasses. Each room was investigated, only to find a similar arrangement in each, except for the omission of whisky bottles and glasses.

Having explored the first large building, the group moved on to the second large building. Again, the door was unlocked. When the door was opened, it reviled a similar arrangement to that of the first building. Each room was investigated by all three men. Charlies rifle hanging by its web strap over his shoulder, was beginning to get in the way as the investigation continued. The group reached the end of the passageway, with only two doors left to investigate, Charlie stood his rifle against the wall adjacent to a door.

The penultimate door was opened, to reveal a very big surprise. Dozens of dark green steel ammunition style boxes, were stacked on one another.

"Coo, Look at these chaps?" Joe said taking several steps backwards. "This surly aint right. Who the devil left this lot? Is there anything in them Charlie?"

Charlie carefully opened the first box to reveal a full box of live bullets. Point three calibre ammunition, in magazines packed the box. Several of the other similar boxes were examined, to find similar ammunition. Some larger boxes were then opened to find them full of sixty-millimetre mortars. Two final boxes reviled point four-five calibre, side-arm ammunition.

"Now that is just clumsy," Charlie said, as he sat on one of the closed boxes.

The three men just looked at the boxes, wondering what to do next. Charlie said that they ought to report the matter to his C.O. in the Home Guard. After a great deal of discussion, that idea was put aside, as the men should not have been in the camp in the first place, and that by telling the C.O. would show their unlawful entry into the camp.

Joe opened his mouth as if to make a suggestion on the subject, when the distinct sound of a rifle being 'cocked', and loaded was heard behind the men.

All three men froze absolutely still. Charlie's mate, still had his rifle hanging on his shoulder, but he did not move a muscle.

In a very deep American accent, the person, who was presumably holding the rifle said. "What the hell is goin on here. Who are you gentlemen, and how did you get in?"

Charlie turned around very slowly, to see the American Officer, who had saluted to him many months earlier, pointing Charlie's Rifle at Charlie. By this time the other two men had also turned around. Without a second's delay, Charlie and his mate came stiffly to attention, and Charlie saluted very smartly.

The Officer became very confused, while trying to continue pointing the rifle at Charlie, he tried to respond a salute. As he did so, he knocked the long, smouldering cigar from his lips, with his arm. The Officer tried to catch the flying cigar, but in vain. The rifle barrel pointed skywards as he lost control of the weapons direction. The cigar hit the floor and hot ash shot out in all directions, from its burning end.

"OK, relax. Just answer my questions if you please," the Officer said as he placed, the now loaded, rifle against the wall.

Charlie spoke first. "Sir. We were on patrol, and saw, what we thought was intruders. On entering the property, we tried to find the intruder, without success. But we did find this ammunition, in an unlocked, and unsecure state. Sir."

The Officer thought for a moment while retrieving his cigar, before saying. "Well done men. Looks like my crowd have messed up. This ammo should have gone with the rest. The camp and buildings should have been locked and made secure. You have done well. I can take over from here. Thanks."

The Officer picked up Charlies rifle to pass it to him, as he did so he inadvertently touched the trigger. The loaded weapon exploded into life as a round of ammunition went through the ceiling. All three men threw themselves onto the floor, as the rifle also crashed to the floor beside Joe.

Charlie recovered his now discharged weapon, applied the safety catch, and all three men walked briskly out of the building, and through the open main gate. As they walked past the Church Charlie thought, that at the very least, he taught the Officer how to salute properly.

Edith and Elsie had met again in the General store while the American base situation had been developing. Elsie was very interested to hear about the new electrification of Edith's house. She said, that she would discuss having their house wired with Jim, when she gets home. The ladies had no idea that Charlie had been involved in an altercation, with an American Officer, and that his rifle had discharged a live round.

Charlie and the other two men appeared in the High Street, having come from the Church Square. All three had big smiles on their faces. The two Soldiers smartly marched into the High Street, with their rifles supported by webbing, hanging on their shoulders. Joe sauntered behind the marching men, with his hands stuffed deep into his trouser pockets. Before they reached the Church Square, discussions between the men had already taken place, to explain why Charlie had a bullet round missing from the magazine, when he had to return his weapon. The decision was agreed by all that a very large rat appeared, so Charlie shot it. The excuse was a bit weak, but at least it was an excuse.

The ladies, having left the general store, watched the men approaching the High Street. Elsie waited for Charlie to arrive before asking him how to go about getting the help from the Council, to have electric lights installed in her house. Charlie sat on the bench seat at the end of the High Street, and explained all of the Council application detail to Elsie.

Elsie also asked, if there was any news as to the whereabouts of Leslie, as they had not had any letters for Grace for several months.

Charlie and Edith explained, that they had only just had several letters from Leslie, and that they had been written on different occasions, but delivered together. This gave Elsie new hope that letters for Grace should arrive soon.

Jim, arranged with the electrician's company for new wiring to be installed as soon as possible. He contacted the District Council, who agreed to provide some financial assistance as he was currently not working, due to a mining accident.

Jim's recovery from his injury was well under way. He was able to move quite easily, without too much pain. He busied himself with his garden, and the chickens. A large area near the bottom of the garden was put aside for chicken runs, and egg laying sheds. All of the eggs used in the house were provided by the chickens. The cockerel frequently carried out his duties, so a new supply of chicks replenished those chickens used for the table. Sometimes, some of the hens were reluctant to lay eggs. A ceramic artificial egg was placed in the nest. This often worked to encourage laying.

Elsie and Jim's house had the electric wiring installed, with seven lights, and four electric power points, over a five-day period. The difference was amazing. Elsie was able to do her knitting and sewing well into the evening. Jim, bought a new wireless that ran off mains electricity. Gone were the days when the glass battery ran out of power. Jim said to Elsie, that he hoped that when Leslie returns home, that he would be able to extend the system, to include even more lights and power points. The house did previously have gas lighting. The Electricians removed the redundant lead gas pipes. A new gas pipe was installed from the gas meter to a new position in the kitchen. Jim thought that a gas cooker might be as asset, at some time in the future.

Grace arrived home for a forty-eight-hour leave. She had, as usual, travelled all night by train, after earlier completing a full day's work. She was delighted to find electric lighting at home at last. She was also very happy to receive fourteen letters from Leslie. Every letter was numbered, so that Grace would read them in order.

Grace spent a long-time reading Leslie's letters, over and over again. Some of the letters had sections cut from the paper, with others having words blotted out, by the Censor. None of the letters gave Grace any indication where in the World Leslie was stationed. Neither did they explain what he was doing, or what he had seen. The return address was, 12 Met. Squadron, Q Group, followed by a letter and a code number. The front of each envelope had been written by hand. "On active service."

Grace replied to each letter in turn, indicating to which of Leslies letter it referred.

Saturday morning arrived. It was really cold, so Jim replenished the fire with some fresh coal. After breakfast, Earnest, Elsie's Brother arrived with his brother Arthur. Both men were in Salvation Army Uniform, and carrying instrument boxes.

"Coming for a blow Jim?" Arthur asked, as he warmed his back against the roaring fire. "We are going up to the Army Hall to practice for the Christmas do. Thought you might be well enough to come and join in."

Arthur played the trumpet, and Earnest played the cornet. Jim loved to be in amongst a live band, and being part of a special community. To hear the sound of other instruments being played all around him was a delight. Jim had played his brass instrument for many years in the Town Silver band. The Town band uniform was a dark blue tunic, with strips of gold horizontal braid across the chest. However, Jim had not played since his accident, as sitting for a long time was very uncomfortable, but his health was improving every day.

"Give me five minutes and I'll be there," Jim responded to his brother-in-law. Arthur was the Uncle who lived in Birmingham, that Grace would have visited, if she had continued to be posted near Coventry. She was delighted to see him after such a long time. Jim disappeared upstairs to collect his jacket. He felt that the chance to play with Arthur, was a rare opportunity, not to be missed. The Brass and Silver bands in the Town, were very competitive, with both of them having won many national competitions in the past. Jim retrieved his instrument case from the cupboard under the stairs, put on his old Australian Army, great-coat, and followed his Brother-in-laws out of the back door.

It was indeed cold. A bitter wind, cut right through the walking men. The Salvation Army hall was about half a mile from the house, just off the High Street. The few people they passed on their way, were as well wrapped-up from the cold as the three men. Mrs Brown was making her way home from her daily shopping excursion. She had her silk scarf tied over her head, with the 1920's blond curl of hair, rolling around the outside of the scarf. Today's lipstick was a very bright red, and for some reason her eye lashes were very black.

"Hello, you three nice gentlemen," Mrs Brown said as she stopped in front of the three walking men, blocking their way forward. "Off for a tinkle on the valves I see? As its usually very cold in that Salvation Hall, you are all very welcome, to drop in, and have some nice warm tea, on your way home."

Mrs Brown loved all men. However, all men knew that was the case, so tried to avoid her, at all costs. "Thank you for the invitation Mrs. Brown," Arthur said, as he squeezed the other two men past the rotund lady. "Sorry, but we are going to be late for practice, and then home to the ladies."

"Hear, that was a close one," Earnest said, as they hurried along the pavement, in an effort to leave as many yards between them, and Mrs, Brown, as they could.

The warmth from the heating stove in the Salvation Army hall, was very welcomed. Chairs had been arranged in three circles around the heater. About twenty other people were already seated, with their instruments. One seat was left in the front for Earnest, as he played the Cornet. Coats and instrument boxes were discarded.

"Brought my Brother-in-Laws to join us today. Arthur has come down from Birmingham, to stay until after Christmas, and our Jim needs to use his lungs a bit," Earnest said. Both of the extra men were made very welcome, and two additional seats were found for the Euphonium section. All of the instruments were tuned to the sound of an upright piano.

<u>Some of the band. Arthur far left, Earnest second from left standing.</u>

The paper music was arranged onto stands, and all was set. The Conductor, a relative of Leslie's, tapped his music stand with his stick.

"Once in Royal, please gents. From the top. Oh! Nice to see you Jim. If you want to have a walk about, please do so. One-two-three-four." The Conductor waved his batten, and the music started. The soft tones, of finely tuned brass instruments, warmed the atmosphere in the room, as "Once in Royal David's City" was played with great expertise.

Jim enjoyed the 'blowing' session, as the rehearsal was referred to. The walk home for one-o'clock dinner, was just as cold as the walk earlier that day. Mrs. Brown's house was passed by very quickly. Jim did not have to walk about during the rehearsal, so, he was now beginning to feel a bit stiff.

The Salvation Hall was in the High Street of the Town. Some men were starting to make their way to the football field, located in the road next to the High Street. Most of the football team, were made up of Miners, and other Army exempt men, like Farmers, a Policeman and a Baker.

At the end of the High Street a dray horse and cart, had just made a delivery at the pub on the cross roads. This was unusual for a Saturday. The reason for the Weekend delivery was unclear.

The driver drove the dray cart across the Cross-roads, very close to the Pub, with the pair of blinkered shire horses trotting away, pulling their cart full of beer barrels. The driver was wearing a long leather apron, and cracking a long whip in the air, above the horses. Without warning, a pair of fighting dogs, rolled in front of the trotting horses, with teeth and claws flying in all directions. First one horse bucked his front legs high in the air, followed immediately by the other.

Jim and his Brother-in-laws, stopped, to watch the experience. As the horse's front feet came down from the bucking, to meet the road with the crashing of horse shoes, they ran at high speed, down the High Street. The dray cart, followed the attached horses as it careered down the road. The poor driver, was pulling on the rains as hard as he could, this caused the horses heads, to raise higher in the air. The driver's mate, held tightly onto the dray cart's seat as his bottom bounced up and down, and his legs flew in all directions. Wooden beer barrels became dislodged in the cart. They rolled about dangerously as the wagon bounced along the road at high speed. People ran in every direction for cover, as beer barrels left the wagon, and exploded into wooden and steel fragments, as they hit the road. The liquid, that had been in the barrels, showered into the air like fountains as the containers exploded.

Further down the High Street, near the Salvation Army hall, the coal merchant was driving his noisy Sentinel steam lorry, in the opposite direction to that of the speeding dray. He saw the charge of horses coming towards him. A pull on the lorries whistle cord created a long and very loud screeching whistle. The horse's ears pricked-up as they heard the whistle ahead, and to the delight of the dray's driver, the horses slowed down, to a stop. The horse's shoes scrapped on the road, with grit flying, as they stopped, right in front of the screeching lorry. Steam poured from the vehicle, as it did from the horses.

The driver of the dray, sat in his seat, holding loose rains. The driver's mate, was hanging onto the outside of the drays seat, with his feet dangling, six inches from the road. Broken beer barrels were strewn across the wet road. One barrel had survived the fall, and was quickly being rolled away by several very young men.

The three Brother-in-laws continued their walk home, laughing and singing. "Away, away with rum-by-gum, with rum-by-gum, with rum-by-gum, that's the song of the Salvation Army." The three men enjoyed seeing beer being spilt, as, like all Salvation Army and Methodist members, they were absolute 'tea totalers'. The abuse of alcohol, had been a major problem for many working men in the past. After wages had been collected, the first visit was to the pub. Many families went short of money because most of the earnings was spent on beer. Since the late eighteen-eighties, many organisations were set-up to try to protect this situation. The Temperance Society, started the song sung by the three men, but later became a well-known verse for the Salvation Army.

Earnest and Arthur made their way further down the hill to home, leaving Jim at his back door, still singing the song of the Salvation Army. The Saturday Lunch was served on the round mahogany table, Uncle Bill from next door arrived to join the table. Jim told the story of the experience that he and his Brother-in-Laws had witnessed, with the dray wagon. He purposely omitted to talk about the meeting with Mrs. Brown. The hilarity lasted throughout the meal time.

CHAPTER 14

The journey back to Mill Hill barracks for Grace, was a cold one. The rain had set-in, with the temperature at about minus 2 degrees, just below freezing. As usual, Grace arrived at the billet at about six-thirty in the morning.

Most of the train journey was spent curled up on a railway carriage seat, with the collar of her Great Coat, pulled right up around her ears. She reflected on the letters she had received from Leslie. She still had no idea where he was, or at this stage, if he was still alive. Wireless and newspaper reports had explained heavy fighting on different fronts, around the World. She knew, that he was in a Squadron, that worked with RADAR, so she guessed, that he might be on an airfield somewhere overseas. The reports from all over the World was bleak, for it appeared that the Germans, were moving closer to invading England.

That morning in the billet hut, Grace prepared for work. The water in the wash sinks was frozen, so basic hygiene was very difficult. Someone had lit a Valor floor standing oil heater, and had placed it next to the frozen cold-water pipe. Grace warmed her hands above the heater, and left the billet for work.

The work today was in the telephone exchange, the exchange was located in a concrete building, about twenty yards from Grace's hut. The telephones were quite quiet today. Betty had returned after her compassionate leave, and was also working on the telephones. She would often stop work, put her hands over her face, and weep uncontrollably. The loss of her Fiancé, was still a major factor in her life.

The tea trolley arrived, pushed by a lady from the canteen. Any speech, or listening, was impossible when the trolley is being pushed into the room. Tea cups crashed together, due to one of the wheels having a mind of its own, and wanting to go in the opposite direction to the other three.

Coffee time was cut very short. The sound of the rotary fire bell, on the wall outside of the exchange, was deafening. Both girls disconnected all telephone call leads, and left their station, without question. Was this a practice, or the real thing? On leaving the exchange the question was answered.

Smoke was pouring from a window in a billet hut. To Grace's horror, it was coming from her hut. She raced to the billet door, only to be stopped by a Military Policeman, holding his arm outstretched, preventing her from passing.

The camp's fire engine came roaring around a corner. Men jumped off the machine, and started pulling fire hoses in all directions. The brass nozzle, held by two men, fired a fast jet of water into the now broken window of the billet. Flames could clearly be seen inside the hut. Grace thought the incident was at the toilet end of the hut. A fireman entered the building using the front door, He was dragging a fire hose behind him, followed by two other firemen.

A few minutes later the fireman walked out of the hut, carrying the remains of a smouldering towel. After investigations, it was found that a plumber, had been called to unfreeze the water pipes. He had moved the Valor heater away from the pipe, so that he could carry out his work. The heater was relocated next to a pile of dry towels. The towels overheated and ignited.

Grace, and the other women checked their property and beds. No fire damage had occurred, but the stench of smoke, and water, filled the atmosphere.

The camp Commander told the girls from Graces hut, that they will be relocated until repairs could be carried out. Two huts were currently empty, so the girls quickly moved all equipment into the spare hut, including the new electric kettle. New, clean sheets, pillows, and towels were provided, however the smell of smoke on the girl's kit bags, and spare uniforms, stayed for many days.

Grace thought that Leslie, would be much warmer, wherever he was overseas, for she thought, that almost everywhere overseas was warm.

Indeed, it was anything but warm where Leslie was, on the island of Corsica. A heavy fall of snow had occurred overnight. The tent containing the radio equipment had partly collapsed with the weight of the snow. A team of four men quickly cleared the offending snow, and checked equipment for damage. All was well. The generator was started, and power to the equipment made the instruments jump into life. A small gash in the tent canvas, was quickly repaired, and made good.

Leslie thought, that although it was colder, and had been snowing, that it was a different cold to that he remembered in England. It was Leslie's turn on the RADAR Cathode Ray tubes. He watched the screen, as the dots and slashes on the screen, moved to a different place, every time the RADAR ariel, rotated a full turn. He could see greenish slashes, indicating ships at sea, that generally stayed still on the screen. His mind reflected on the hot sunny day in the hay field in England, when he received his call-up notice. He remembered the last sight of the fields, and the hills beyond. Will he ever see that sight again?

His mind was sharply brought back into focus. Several dots appeared on the screen, moving towards the Island. "Confirmation please," Leslie shouted. In seconds, another Airman was looking over Leslie's shoulder. He pointed to the moving dots with his pencil.

"Contact confirmed," the other man shouted towards the rear of the tent. Two sentries with binoculars, scoured the horizon to the North East of the Island. One of the sentries shouted from his higher view point "Sighting Confirmed. Twenty plus heavy aircraft taking this heading, Friend or foe not determined."

Leslie, and another Airman followed the aircraft group on the tube. The centre of the screen was the RADAR Ariel, and therefore the location of the camp. The group was definitely heading for the Ariel. A quick count of dots confirmed twenty-eight aircraft, flying at a height of seven thousand feet.

"Please radio and inform Group that, twenty-eight---." Leslie was interrupted by a shout that the aircraft had been identified, as enemy, possibly JU 52's. Leslie continued. "Enemy heavy aircraft, heading overhead and South-South West, two-one-two degrees, Estimated speed of two hundred and twenty miles per hour. Height seven thousand feet. Get confirmation please."

The message was sent, and the confirmation received. The roar of multiple aircraft engines throbbed, as the aircraft flew directly overhead, heading for North Africa. At seven thousand feet high, this was very low, compared to other contacts. The flight crews could be seen, with binoculars, in the aircraft as they passed overhead. It was at that point, that the fighters flying above the bombers were seen.

Leslie, and two other men, returned to the RADAR tube. At first the large dots of the bombers obliterated the fighters. But there they were. About six, were flying above the bombers, at about nine thousand feet.

"Send to group. Enemy formation supported by six fighters at nine thousand feet. Same trajectory. Get confirmation," Leslie shouted to the radio operator.

Again, the message was sent, and confirmation received.

Leslie said to Len. "why are they flying so low? Ack-Ack guns could pick them out of the sky so easily. Where are those devils heading? Looks like North Africa. Oh well we have done our bit. We aren't payed enough to work out the rest. Would someone watch this screen please?" Leslic left the RADAR screen to watch the disappearing aircraft into the horizon.

The sight of snow on the mountain roads, and surrounding hills, provided a very good opportunity for Leslie to photograph the area. Some of the 120 film he brought with him, was becoming quite old, so several pictures were taken, of the hills and mountains, the valley, the camp, and his comrades. The problem he now had, was where to find a new dark-room, suitable to develop and print photographs.

The track up to their camp, from the larger road below, had a number of disused, stone built, buildings. It was assumed they were used, in the past, as shelter for shepherds. One of the small buildings, was only about fifty feet from the camp. There was another building on the edge of the camp, but its condition was very poor, with half of the roof missing. Leslie investigated the other premises, and decided, that with a small amount of work to the door, it would make an excellent dark room. During his time off work, he carried out repairs, and set-up the room for photographic work. Electricity was not available, so all pictures had to be contact prints. He was able to develop the films easily with the developer fluid obtained, however, the fixer fluid was a week mixture. After many attempts, by using larger quantities of fluid, he was able to produce good prints. On occasions, the other airmen used his camera, to take photos of him, and his chums. Some of the pictures were sent to Grace, who cherished them greatly.

Spring on Corsica came very early in 1944. Time off work, gave the men many opportunities for leisure activities. Country walks was a pleasure, along the winding roads through the mountains. The roads were very dusty, and many of them had been cut into the hillside, with deep cliffs to one side, and steep mountains to the other. An occasional local native was met. One was pushing a very old and rusty bicycle, loaded with bags of wool, another with a bullock pulling a cart. As the men wandered through the villages, the locals made them very welcome. Frequent visits were made into the villages, and friendships began, with some of the locals.

The village of Montemageior, was just a short walk over Mount Lumio. The village seemed to be attached to the Mountain by glue. Narrow streets lined with ancient white buildings, topped with terracotta tiled roofs, opened out into a square. On one side of the square stood a very tall square church tower, that dominated the village from wherever it was viewed. The men spent some time in the village. A small taverna occupied one building in the square, always occupied by several elderly local men. The drinking of the local wine, and smoking was the usual pastime, along with the playing of a game, similar to dominos. The forty-five minuet walk back to the camp often took at least double that time, for most of the returning men, after the consumption of local wine.

<u>On the mountain road, Corsica</u>

The new friends from the village often embarked on Boar hunts. One day, Leslie, and six other men, were invited to join their village friends, on a Boar hunt. The animals often damaged the valuable crops that had been carefully grown by the villagers. The group moved off further up into the mountains. Leslie, had his trusty service revolver, as the other Airman brought their rifles. One particular Wild Boar had been causing a lot of crop damage. The locals, had previously identified the probable whereabouts of the animal.

The group of men quietly trudged along the mountain tracks. Over rock outcrops, and across open ground, the party progressed. The Corsican leader, raised a hand. All members of the hunt party stopped walking, and lowered to the ground where they stood. The animal could clearly be seen near some bushes, twenty feet ahead, and to the right. The leader indicated to an Airman, who had a rifle, to take a shot. He carefully took aim, using a convenient rock to steady the weapon.

'Bang'. The sound of the single shot seemed to bounce off the surrounding hills, as the echo continued for some time. The animal immediately fell. The shot was clean and accurate. Some of the local men provided a long almost straight, strong leafless branch. The carcass was tied to the pole by its feet, and was carried triumphantly back to the village. Two of the Airmen were given the honour of carrying the pole over their shoulders. Leslie took a photograph as the party stopped for a moments rest along the dusty road. The party posed for the important picture to be taken. Leslie printed several images of that particular photograph. Some of the pictures were given to the locals, on a later occasion.

The Boar hunt.

The carcass of the Boar provided the locals with meat for a long time. That evening the Boar was prepared for roasting, by the Corsicans. The Airmen, who were not working were invited to attend the roasting of the beast. The aroma from the roasting was wonderful. Pork style fat, was basted over the meat, as the steam rose from the spitting carcass. A long table had been erected in the Town Square, and laid with other local food and drink delights. An additional table was placed to join the long table. Seating arrived from almost every home in the vicinity.

The meal was delicious. The Airmen sat amongst the locals, and not as a group, showing a true feeling of joining-in. A local man with only one tooth protruding his lips from his upper jaw, played a violin, with gipsy like tunes. After the meal, and oceans of wine, many of the locals danced with their women to the tunes of the violin. Some of the men, both Airmen, and locals, continued to enjoy the home brewed red wine. The time had arrived to return to camp. Len, had enjoyed a small amount of wine, while Leslie had washed the meat down with a copious amount of local, fresh orange juice. Several of the Airmen, found the road home to have more bends in it, than when they had arrived earlier, as they swayed from side to side across the road.

Back at camp the work continued unhindered. On several occasions vapour trails, from very high aircraft was seen heading to the South of France. The aircraft were flying much too high for the RADAR to detect. Every time Leslie saw the trails he wondered where they were heading, and who was about to die from the deadly cargo carried.

Mid May 1944. The Squadron knew that something was going to happen, somewhere. Extra military activity was going on. Was Germany going to invade England? The rumours were, that Britain, and its Allies were losing the war. The Prime Minister Mr. Churchill, had made many supportive statements. Eventually English newspapers reached Corsica, several weeks later than published. Leslie wondered if Grace was worried about the current political situation.

Grace was also aware that something big was on the cards. Activity in the telephone exchange, and the clerk's office, was sometimes frantic. The same word 'Overlord' appeared over-and-over again. What was 'Overlord'? The girls, often talked about the word that they heard, between themselves.

On a recent visit home, Grace had received a pencil written letter from her Cousin Albert. It had been written, he said, on scrounged paper. Albert said in his letter, that he was delighted to have met Grace by chance on the train to Bristol, some months earlier. He explained that his Regiment was moving from Bodmin, to Plymouth the next day. He told Grace to keep safe, and he would be looking forward to another meeting in the future. Like all letters received, Grace treasured them all.

<u>Albert</u>

Late May in 1944. Activity, generally increased in all of the Army and Air Force bases throughout Britain. Men, and equipment, were moved to the South coast in great numbers. The Mill Hill Camp became almost deserted. The Telephone exchange now only had two operators, as opposed to the four that usually sat at the exchange equipment. Clerical duties came almost to a standstill. The base felt almost earey, with only a few personnel left on site.

7th June 1944, the newspapers arrived in the post room of Mill Hill Barracks. Grace cut the string holding the papers in a bundle. As she cut the string, the announcement was clear on the front pages. Mr. Churchill the Prime Minister, had announced in the House of Commons yesterday, that, Northern beaches of France has been invaded by a massive force of British, American and other Allied troops. They had been met with substantial opposition from German positions. Many of the troops had broken through the German lines, and were progressing further inland into Normandy. No other reports are yet available.

Grace collected one newspaper from the bundle. Leaving her station, she rushed into the Clerks typing room, where Peggy was working. Peggy's man Jack, had volunteered into the Army. The last she had heard from him, he told her that he was with Field Marshal Montgomery in Africa.

Grace pushed the paper in front of Peggy. "Look Peg, this is what all of the fuss has been about. This is the 'Overlord' that we have been hearing about for the last few months. Is Jack still in Africa?"

"The last I heard, Jack was in the tank regiment in Africa," Peggy replied, staring at the front page of the paper. "I don't know about any of his movements. Just like Leslie, I only get the occasional letter, and even then, he can't say where he is."

An A.T.S. lady officer entered the clerk's room. She was walking very smartly, with a file of papers in her hand. "What do you ladies think you're doing? This is not a Mothers meeting you know," the officer barked at the girls.

Grace sternly pushed the front page of the paper in front of the scowling woman. The woman caught sight of the headlines. Grabbing the paper from Grace, she spent a few moments reading the report.

"I see," the officer said, now in a much softer voice. "Well now that is a turn-up for the books. Do either of you have anybody involved?"

"No Mam," Peggy replied. "Both of our men are already somewhere overseas."

"Then get about your work, and stop worrying about something that does not concern you," the Officer replied, in a much sterner way. Taking the newspaper with her, she left the file of papers on Peggy's desk, and walked stiffly out of the room.

Grace returned to her duties in the post room. She looked again, at the report in the paper. It said that, "They had been met with substantial opposition from German positions." What did that mean? Was it a success or not? It said that, "Some had broken through the German lines." That surly meant, that the Germans must have been waiting for them, she thought. Did somebody tell the Germans that we were coming? After all, the only thing that Grace and her colleagues knew, was a code name 'Overlord'. There was never any detail, or to what 'Overlord' meant. This thought troubled Grace. She knew that other typists, and Clerks, on other bases had seen the same words, and all were, as they were, sworn to secrecy under the Official Secrets Act. What could have gone so terribly wrong? Someone in a high authority must have informed the Germans of Churchills intentions. The thoughts would not leave Graces mind.

For Grace, the time for a long weekend at home had arrived, one week after the Normandy Invasion. The newspapers on the station platforms in London, was full of it. The same questions were asked by Government officials, that Grace had been asking herself. Talk on the train to Bristol, amongst the other passengers, was constantly about the invasion, and the losses of Allied lives.

Six thirty in the morning, Grace arrived home. She spent a few hours sleeping in her bed before reading three letters from Leslie. Elven thirty that morning, Earnest came to the back door of the house. He handed Elsie a letter, on buff coloured Paper. Elsie sat in her chair, and put on her glasses. The moment she started to read the letter, all was explained. It said. "It is with regret, that we have to inform you that, Albert was killed in action on the 6th June 1944." An attachment note, to the official letter, was from Albert's Commanding Officer. It said, that Albert and his crew, were killed in the tank, as it landed on the beach at Normandy. That he had been a very respected Trouper by his comrades and his Officers. He showed courage, and willingness, to perform his duty without question. Further information will be provided when available.

The room fell silent.

Earnest, also reported that his Wife, who, upon reading the letter, received a heart attack, and had died. Being her only beloved Child, the shock had been just too much.

Grace could not believe her ears. Her world had fallen apart. Earnest was comforted by his weeping Sister, and Jim gave Grace, as much support as he could. Grace remembered the chance meeting with Albert on the train, unaware, that this would be the last time she would see him. The pencil written letter was, again, the last one she would ever receive from him. Her heart was severely broken, and would remain so for the rest of her long life.

CHAPTER 15

Leslie, and this Squadron, had received information about the invasion of France, from the BBC World Service. The Airmen in Corsica, could do nothing about the invasion, but to wonder about its success or failure. The German war machine must have been upset by it, Leslie thought. The mood among the men, was quite good, knowing that, at last, the Allied forces were working together to crush the Nazi Party. Perhaps an invasion of Britain by Germany, was now not as possible.

The BBC was always very positive, about the reporting of the Normandy invasion, so as to boost morale.

Time off, for Leslie, and a few of his men, meant an opportunity to, once again, visit the coast. Sam, one of the Airmen, had found a disused boat, apparently, abandoned. The large rowing boat was a wooden clinker-built hull. It had three plank seats, and one and a half oars. One of the oars had a broken shaft, leaving just the paddle end. Sam, had stowed the boat in a different location, from where he had found it, under a thick evergreen bush, just inland from the beach.

Sam had very skilfully repaired the broken oar with some reclaimed timber. It worked well, but made the repaired oar, very heavy, compared to the other.

<u>The rowing boat</u>

The boat was recovered from it hiding place under the bushes. The men carried it across the beach. It was put to sea near the South end of Calvi Bay. The sea, as usual, was very calm. Summer had arrived. The sun was very hot. Leslie allowed his hand to brush the surface of the warm water. Sam was in charge of the rowing, due to the fact that he had found the boat, and had repaired the oar. They made their way out to sea leaving the beach far away. Sam, Leslie, Len and Bob, enjoyed the freedom of the open sea. Sam had stowed the oars inboard, and had allowed himself the pleasure of relaxing in the bottom of the boat, with his legs outstretched under the other seats. The other men relaxed against the side of the boat, as they gently drifted in and out of dozing, in the warm sunshine.

The stillness was abruptly brought-to-a close, by the sound of a large motor Launch very close to the boat.

Sam rushed to recover himself from under the seats, as he did so he crashed his head under one seat, and bashed his knee under another. The other men, were now very much awake, and staring at the approaching boat. The Launch, was a Royal Navy Vessel. A Sailor shouted using a metal tapered horn. "Hello there, can you speak English?"

The reply came from Len, who was peering over the gunwale of the boat, "Non-Monsieur." He then ducked-down, and disappeared behind the side gunwale of the boat, leaving the others to answer any further questions.

"Thank you, sir," the sailor replied, as the Launch's engines roared into life. The boat disappeared out of view around an outcrop of rocks.

"I wonder what he wanted," Bob said in a very unconcerned way, as he relaxed back into the boat.

The most important thing to achieve at the moment was relaxation. All the men in the boat, took full advantage of the calm and sunny conditions. Len raised his head above the gunwale of the boat, to discover that the wind was a little brisker than previously. He also noticed, that during their time of relaxation, the boat had drifted further to the South of Calvi Bay.

Len and his colleague's concentration, was urgently brought into very sharp focus. The deep thud of big engines, was accompanied by the sound of the sea being churned-up. All shipmates stared in the direction of the sound. Within moments, the bow of a huge Royal Navy Destroyer emerged from behind the Southern headland. The men instantly realised, that the wake from the big ship would be hazardous to their little boat. They knew that their boat, being so small, compared to the Destroyer, that maybe the huge ship may not have seen them.

The Airmen recovered themselves, and the oars, instantly. Without a second to lose the little boat was being propelled away from the Destroyers trajectory. Len was rowing with every ounce of strength in his body. The Ship was gaining quickly upon the little boat.

The entire length of the big ship was now in full view, from the little boat. The huge bow was now less than one hundred and fifty feet away.

"Whoop. Whoop. Whoop. Whoop." The ships sirens were so loud, that it felt as though the sea was shaking. Len continued to row with all his strength, as he knew that all of their lives depended on him.

The Destroyer was a wide ship, so even if the bow missed the boat, would the side of the ship miss the little boat? Sailors appeared on the deck of the Destroyer, waving arms, as if to shoo the little boat away. The direction of the ship seemed to be going slightly out to sea, as it progressed.

The high bow was now alongside the little boat, and some thirty feet to seaward. Waves from the bow created a white bow-wave. Had Len done enough?

Within seconds the bow-wave lifted the small boat, and almost threw it aside, as the ship ploughed through the water. The movement from the bow-wave must have done the trick, as the high side of the grey ship, thundered past, and above the tiny boat.

All was not yet over. As the stern of the ship approached, the turbulence from the propeller's was churning the water into a frenzy behind the ship. Len continued to row as if the Devil was after him, away from the Destroyer. The little boat, was now being tossed about like a toy, by the remains of the bow-wake.

"Whoop. Whoop. Whoop." The ship again blew its sirens. Sailors on board leaned over the side, to watch the excitement. And then it was all over.

Calmness returned in the small boat. Len had done enough. He laid down the oars, as he collapsed into the bottom of the boat, exhausted. The Destroyer continued on its way, heading out to sea.

All of the Airmen clapped wildly as Len laid still, trying desperately to breath.

"So that's what that launch wanted to tell us," Sam announced, in a relatively calm way.

Len could not now row a single stroke. He was truly exhausted, and shaking from head to toe from the terrifying experience he had just encountered. Sam took the oars, and navigated the boat back to the beach at Calvi. Almost without a word, the boats crew dragged it from the sea, and stowed it again in the shelter of the undergrowth. All of the men collapsed onto the warm sand of the beach.

"That was dammed close," Sam said, lying on his back, with hands behind his head, looking into the cloudless blue sky. "Nearly copped it chaps. I recon Len is a Hero. Thanks mate."

The journey to return to camp was without discussion. All of the men knew just how close to drowning they all were. The Bedford truck, driven by Leslie, made its way to Lumio. Heading East, it followed the road, as it rounded the winding mountain roads. The truck turned off the mountain road, and progressed up the uneven track to the camp. As Leslie approached the camp entrance. He stopped the truck. Walking up the track towards the camp was Joe, one of the Engineers. Joe was dragging a donkey behind him. It had a halter and lead made from course rope.

Joe said. "Hello Boss. Found this tangled in a thorn bush, so I thought it was now the camp pet. Hope that's all right?"

Len, who was in the front passenger seat of the truck, leaned across Leslie and asked Joe. "Can you get Milk or eggs from it?"

"No," replied Joe. "Just fertilizer."

Leslie parked the truck in the usual place in the camp. The men jumped down from the truck, feeling some relief that they were all still alive after the day's excitement. Rob had been RADAR operator for the morning shift, and after being relieved by another man, he joined the shipmates, for a welcomed cup of tea in the canteen tent.

"I say Skipper," Rob said. "We knew where you chaps were heading this morning. Did you by any chance see a large ship? We saw it on the screen, and wondered if you might have seen it?"

"May have seen a British Destroyer at some point this morning," Leslie replied, but he did not elaborate.

Information from the occasional newspaper and wireless, confirmed that good progress was being made by British and Allied Troup's, deeper into German occupied France. Heavy losses were reported, mostly by the Americans and British.

Leslie continued to write to Grace, always sending his letters to her home address. At this time, he was totally unaware of the tragedy to Earnest's family. Grace did not inform Leslie by letter, of the loss of Albert, for she was sure that the news would make Leslie unhappy.

Grace was always delighted to continue to receive Leslies letters, at least she knew that he was certainly alive when he wrote them.

Bombing in London seemed to be less since the attack of the Normandy beaches. Returning to Mill Hill Barracks after the terrible news about Albert, was one of the hardest things that Grace had ever had to do. Her relationship with him was very close. She treated him, almost like a Brother. Tears would often overtake her emotions, usually at times when it was the most inconvenient.

War is an awful thing, Grace thought. It brought misery to so many people. How could one man in Germany, control so many ordinary people, that all they want to do is to kill anyone who does not believe in the same things, that they believe in? Hundreds of thousands of people have died, just because of one man. Grace, and her work friends often discussed what would happen if Hitler invaded England. What sort of freedom would they have, if any? Would it be a military run Country? Would people be able to talk and do what they want? Thank goodness that hasn't happened yet. Perhaps the invasion of Normandy might push the Germans back?

Another tragic event for Grace, was to receive news of an A.T.S. Soldier who she had befriended, had gone home for a short leave. Hazel lived in Portsmouth. An air raid over Portsmouth, had not only caused devastating damage to the docks, but had also killed Hazel, her family and several other families in the same street. Portsmouth, being an important Naval Town and dockyard, had already been devastated by bombing attacks on a regular basis.

Leslie had often said in his letters to Grace, that when he gets home leave again, that they should get married. This created great excitement for Grace. The main problem was, that she had no idea when he would be home again.

A seven-day home leave for Grace was again a very welcome break. The mood was still very unhappy at home, due to the loss of Albert. Grace had lost all interest in playing the piano, so the instruments lid stayed firmly closed.

Elsie suggested that Grace should prepare for the Wedding. She said that Leslie could be home at any time without warning, so she must be prepared.

Grace walked to a different railway station than usual, at the top of the hill, with her very good friend Valery. The train from that station, would take them into the centre of the City of Bath. Shopping for Wedding dress material, was the task in hand. On arrival at Green Park Station Bath, the walk into town only took ten minutes. Grace often visited Bath, when the leave time permitted. Today for some reason, the City was very busy. Shoppers rushed about from shop-to-shop. The City before the War, was very popular with visitors from many parts of the World, as well as from all over from England. It's Architecture and culture, was known Worldwide. Visitors to the City was now almost non-existent. The City had some bomb damage over the years, but mostly the buildings were intact. A number of bombs destroyed some buildings in 1942, when the Nazi's wanted to destroy the cultural world of Britain. One of the most sensible things Hitler did, was to stop bombing Britain's cultural centres. This was not totally successful, as many City's lost many treasures, never to be replaced.

Grace and Valery visited almost every material shop in the City, only to return to the first shop to buy the merchandise. A purchase was made of white satin, and buttons that could be covered with the material.

On the train journey home, the girls discussed how frequently they used the train service. It wasn't always on time, but it was convenient. Grace said that she could not imagine how difficult life would be without the local trains.

The following day Grace visited her former dressmaker employer, in the next village. Their last meeting had not been the best, as Mrs. Mitchell did not fully understand the significance of Grace having to be called-up into the Army. The reason for today's visit was to try to obtain a pattern for a Wedding Dress. Mrs Mitchell was very obliging, and by way of a forgiveness, she gave the pattern to Grace, free of charge.

Work on the dress started without delay. The sewing machine whizzed along, as Grace peddled the mechanical machine almost without stopping. In three days, the dress was mostly complete. The long dress with long sleeves, fitted in at the waist, and flowing over the hips, fitted perfectly. The first part of the preparations was complete. Each of the buttons had to be covered using the satin material. This was expertly carried out by Grace's Mother. The button covering was a good form of therapy for Elsie. The loss of her Sister-in Law, and young Nephew played heavy on her mind. Elsie, had always enjoyed embroidery, but, for some reason recently she had not been able to enjoy the pastime.

Another visit to Bath for Grace resulted in the purchase of the material for two Bridesmaid dresses. The task in hand now was to assemble the dresses, in double quick time. Again, the sewing machine whizzed along, as her feet peddled the machine at full speed.

The weeks home leave was all too quickly over. Back to camp on the overnight train. This time the journey was a little different. Bombs had destroyed part of the railway lines into London Paddington station. The last part of that section of the journey was made on a red London Bus. Paddington Station did have some damage, but the underground station was still working. Very often the deep underground stations were littered with the effects of people, who had previously used them as bomb shelters. Usually the deep stations near the inner City, where Grace had to change trains, were used as shelters. Grace often felt very sorry for the shelter users. Sometimes every night the underground was used as shelters, as the bombs and Doodlebugs, dropped indiscriminately on the streets above, blowing the City to pieces, and killing innocent people.

Work again became very boring. The post sorting was carried out within the first hour after delivery. Typing was almost non-existent. Other clerical duties consisted of orders for food, drink and equipment. The telephone exchange duties had now been reduced, down to two girls on the switchboard. The time dragged. For three evenings a week entertainment was very good. The engineer who operated the cinematograph equipment was still on camp. He was very resourceful in obtaining the up-to-the-minute films. The Games room, that doubled-up as the cinema was very popular with the girls.

The wireless in the billet was a very popular means of entertainment on the evenings that that films were not shown. One evening, a discussion on the wireless provided the girls with a wonderful idea. In three days-time, the Royal Albert Hall in London, was to be the venue for the Proms Concert. Six of the Women agreed to go to the concert evening, including Grace.

On the evening of the concert work finished on time. The underground train was caught by the girls to South Kensington station. The main discussion on the train was, are they safe on the train? Peggy said that they could be killed by bombs, anywhere in London, even in their beds at Mill Hill. It was agreed, that if a bombing raid occurred, the Royal Albert Hall would be evacuated to the masses of underground rooms, under the hall. All of the girls felt a little happier, about their safety.

The Royal Albert Hall was a short walk from the South Kensington station. As the girls approached the building its size and grandeur was overpowering. It was a very imposing building. Long steps led up to the ticket office. The outside walls were very ornate, and the domed red covered roof was plane to see. Once inside the Hall the cheapest tickets were purchased. The price of the tickets guided the group to the less costly upper gallery. They marvelled at the vast size of the domed ceiling, being totally unsupported, except by the circular high walls.

Alost every seat was occupied. The 'stalls' surrounded a carpeted circular floor that was full of standing audiences. At the far end of the hall, a large number of seats rose from a raise stage, to a tiered higher level. These seats surrounded the most wonderfully decorated multi-manual theatre organ, that Grace had ever seen. High in the walls of the building, above the 'stalls', were many audience boxes, full of people. Considering the large number of people in the hall, all who were talking to each other, the girls found that they could talk to each other easily, without shouting. The acoustics in the building was almost perfect. The view from the girl's high location was overwhelming. As was the size of the inside of the hall.

The orchestra arrived on stage at the far end of the hall, with the huge concert organ located high above the stage, almost appearing to look down on the orchestra. The arrival of the conductor was accompanied by a rapturous applause, from the very large audience. The concert began. The main problem was that neither of the girls had a program, so the name of the pieces played, the soloists names, and the name of the conductor, was not known, but all enjoyed the evening.

After the concert a program had been left on a seat, so Grace collected the document and stowed it safely in her handbag.

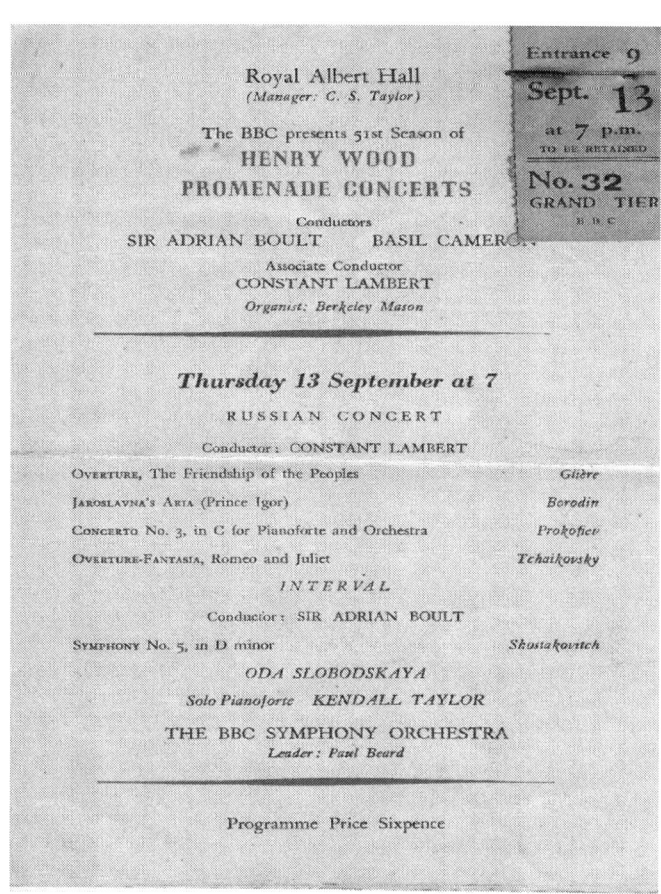

After the concert, the journey back to base started at South Kensington Underground station. The group had just missed a train to Charring Cross. This is the station where they will have to change trains to take them North to Edgware, this being a local station to their barracks.

The girls waited on the platform for the next train to arrive. Without warning the lights on the platform went out, and then, in moments a few of the lights came back on again. Most people made their way down the now stationary, moving staircase. In moments the platform, and corridors, were full of people. Many of the people were carrying big bags, bedding, food, bottles of beer, children in arms, and other youngsters, running around as if it were a playground.

One of the girls, asked a lady who was carrying a baby, what was going on.

"Air-raid luvvy. If you thought you were going to catch a train tonight that aint going to happen. All shut down now till morning. If you go outside the station now it might be the last thing you do," the woman replied, with a cigarette bobbing up and down in her lips as she spoke.

Grace thought that this situation all seemed to be very normal to the people in the station.

"We had better find somewhere to sleep for the night," Peggy said looking around trying to find any space against a wall to rest. The station was packed with people, so they were very unlucky, and could not find any space to rest. At the far end of the platform near the tunnel to, God knows where, a space was found just large enough for all six girls to sit together. The draught of air, coming from the tunnel entrance was quite cold, and was accompanied by lots of rumbling noises from deep inside the tunnel. The group of women made the best of a bad job. Most of the girls managed to doze for a few moments at a time.

It must have been that three hours had passed when people on the platform, started to move away. One lady with a sleeping youngster slung around her hips said. "All clear now dearie."

The girls did not know what to do. Did they wait until morning for the trains to start running again? Or do they go up to the surface, and try to return to barracks that way? The decision was made to try to get back onto the surface.

The group of girls followed the other people up the stationary wooden slatted, non-moving staircase, to the surface. The people seemed to just melt into the City streets, leaving the girls to wonder what to do next. The sounds of either fire engines, or ambulance bells, were ringing in every direction.

A bus would have been very welcome at this moment. But none were in sight.

Grace had a map of the underground stations in her shoulder bag. The map reviled that if they walked to the North, it may take them to Oxford Street. Surly a bus would be working in Oxford Street. One of the girls commented that it was only three o'clock in the morning, so a bus might be difficult to find. Nevertheless, they started to walk to the North.

The walk North affected everybody in the group. The illumination of the streets came from the buildings on fire in almost every street, for the first quarter of a mile of their walk. Debris was strewn across the roads, and in many cases had to be walked over for the girls to progress. The level of devastation was too much for the firemen and the wardens to attend.

A pile of smouldering rubble blocked the way forward for the girls.

Peggy, who was leading the group stopped, as did the others.

A hand, and part of an arm, was protruding from under a large wooden beam, that was partly buried in the smouldering rubble. The hand was moving. Nobody, apart from the girls were in the area. One of the girls shouted for help. This made the hand move more vigorously. A decision was made without question. The girls grabbed at the debris above the waving arm. A leather handbag appeared under the rubble. More furious digging continued by hand. Vigorous pulling at large and small items of rubbish. A head appeared, followed by a torso. The face of the buried woman was bloodied and in obvious pain. A few gentle pulls by the girls, and the woman emerged from her tomb. Her left leg was obviously broken, for it was at an angle that was not normal.

One of the women left the scene, to return soon after with a Warden and a Policeman carrying a rolled-up stretcher. Several other rescuers arrived at the scene. The A.T.S. ladies allowed the skilled team of people, to take over the situation. They all rested on the debris feeling exhausted, brushing dust and dirt from their uniforms. It was somewhat fascinating to watch the members of the Civil Defence organisation, carry out their work. They knew exactly how to identify if other people were trapped under the rubble.

A Warden in a black tin helmet shouted. "Everybody, move right away please. Now. Gas is present."

This was a serious situation, for the adjacent building had a jet of flame, shooting high into the sky. An ignited gas leak was clear to see.

Without a second warning everybody moved to the other side of the street. As daylight was now breaking the darkness, the group of girls decided to try to continue walking to the North. Surly a bus might appear at some time, to take them back to camp.

Oxford Street was very quiet. Only a few people were going about their early morning business. Grace looked at her wrist watch. It was seven o'clock. Two big red London busses appeared, and stopped at bus-stops on the opposite side of the road, going East. One of the busses was a number 83, with the destination 'Hendon' displayed.

They all jumped onto the back open deck of the bus. The lady conductor was asked, if it was going anywhere near Mill Hill.

"Only going to Hendon," the conductor replied. "I recon it's only about half a mile on to the Mill Hill camp. Quite a lot of service people get off there and walk the rest of the way. You all look as if you got caught up in that lot last night. You look knackered. I'll tell you what. I will let you have six free tickets. You look as if you need a bit of good luck."

The conductor allowed the girls to sit down. She took a wider standing stance, to balance herself, and as she pressed the bell, the bus moved off. Winding her ticket machine six times, six tickets were generated in a long line.

The group of girls knew that the bus would stop at Hendon, that being the last stop. Exhaustion overtook all of them. So, the view of the journey did not exist for any of them, as sleep overtook them all.

The group arrived at the camp guard house at nine fifteen in the morning. The duty guard made them sign-in, and allowed them to proceed. The lady Chief Commander of the A.T.S. met the girls at their billet, and demanded an explanation as to their lateness in returning to camp. A full explanation of the nights experience was sufficient for the Commander to grant a day off work for all of the girls, due to exceptional circumstances.

CHAPTER 16

The news of the progress of the War reaching Leslie and his Squadron, was very good. British and Allied forces had pushed the German lines back to such an extent that some German troops, were almost running away. Late in April 1945, news came that Hitler might soon surrender.

Then it happened. At sixteen minutes past midnight, on the eighth of May 1945. The Instrument of Surrender was signed in Berlin, Germany. The war in Europe was over.

News reached Leslies Squadron almost immediately by the BBC World Service, on the Wireless.

The same news was given to Grace and her colleagues at breakfast, later that morning. Twenty-four hours leave was granted to all A.T.S. members.

Betty found a union Flag, and draped it over her shoulders like a wrap. Six of the girls who were good friends, including Grace. headed to Trafalgar Square in London. The atmosphere was electric. Hundreds of thousands of people overtook the City. Grace had never seen so many people. They were singing, dancing, kissing, shouting, drinking, and overwhelming excitement was everywhere. The girls were being pushed around the square by the huge throng of crowds.

The crowds started to move away from Trafalgar Square, and flooded down the Mall towards Buckingham Palace. One of the girls had brought a camera. She arranged that the other five women would hold the Union Flag, with all of them behind it. The background of the photograph, was a bronze lion at the base of Nelson's Column. Two of the tall girls stood either side of Grace, who was the shortest. She was just able to peer over the top edge of the flag, as it was proudly displayed by the five women.

<u>V.E. Day in Trafalgar Square</u>

The large throng of people gathered the six girls in their wake, as the tight formation of excited people, almost rolled down The Mall. On reaching Buckingham Palace the King's Flag was fluttering in a stiff breeze, on its mast. The Queen Victoria Memorial statue stood proud, in its enclosed lake, appearing to guard the Palace. Many people were now splashing in the water surrounding the statue. Others had climbed the statue, to be hanging from its peak, with champagne bottles exploding further into the air. Grace and her friends negotiated their way to the front of the Memorial. Crowds of people were jammed tight against the closed Palace gates.

The chant then began. The sound was quite frightening, as the people gathered tightly towards the gates. The Palace Sentry guards held their positions without hardly blinking an eye.

"We want the King. We want the king. We want the king" The chant went on, without a break. Many of the crowds were jostling for position, to be as close to the railings as possible. The Union flag held by Peggy disappeared. It was last seen being waved high in the air by some Sailors, about half way up the Queen Victoria Monument.

The chant went on and on. At last the balcony doors of the Palace opened, and there they were. The King, in full military uniform, and the Queen, waving her right hand, in a side to side vertical motion. The smiles on their faces told a thousand words. The two Princesses were there as well. Princess Elizabeth was in Army uniform, and Princess Margaret just waved to the crowd below.

When the balcony doors were opened, the crowd went wild with excitement. Grace was pushed from one place to another by the swelling throng of people. She had lost her friends. Grace was not a tall person, and so she struggled to see the King and Queen, by looking between other people. All of a sudden, her world of vision changed, for she was lifted high onto the shoulders of two large sailors, standing side by side, and waving a drink bottle in the other hands. The view was wonderful. The Sovereign was in full sight. Grace took a moment to look down at the host of shouting people below her raised vantage point. This is something never to forget, she thought. Betty and Peggy saw Grace on her raised viewpoint, and waved frantically at her.

Then they were gone.

The Royal Family re-entered the Palace, and the balcony doors were closed.

Some chanting continued, but mostly now, it was party time. The sailors gently returned Grace to the ground, and disappeared into the singing crowd before she could thank them. The other girls found Grace easily, for now they knew where she was. The subject flashed through Grace's mind for a moment, that Albert would have loved to have been here.

Many of the crowds started to move away from the Palace, and disperse into the City. The noise of the masses of people was still overpowering, as groups of open-air parties found their own spaces.

Back to Trafalgar Square was perhaps the best thing to do, as the mass of people, made their way back along the Mall. To try to catch a train back to base now would be almost impossible, with the large amount of people wanting transport. The girls sat on the edge of the pool wall in Trafalgar Square watching the people enjoying the freedom of not being at war. The threat of bombs was gone. No more killing, or the chance of being killed, gave an air of euphoria.

The Square now had many less people than earlier. The pigeons returned to finding the odd morsel of food on the paving slabs. Bus's made their way on the roads around the Square, carrying so many people that they were hanging onto the rear platform. Taxi's, and Hackney cabs, were full of people, jammed into the vehicles.

> On Tuesday, 8th May, 1945, the Prime Minister, Mr. Winston Churchill, formally announced the end of the European War in the House of Commons, and a similar announcement was made in the House of Lords.
>
> After the announcement had been made, Mr. Speaker invited M.P.s to follow him in procession to St. Margaret's, Westminster, for a Thanksgiving Service. The Serjeant-at-Arms, carrying the mace, walked in front of the Speaker at the head of the procession followed by Privy Councillors. Walking four abreast, Junior Ministers and the rank and file M.P.s followed. After the service the procession returned to the House of Commons.
>
> **Prominent Buildings Illuminated**
>
> BIG BEN
> THE HOUSES OF PARLIAMENT
> BUCKINGHAM PALACE
> ST. PAUL'S CATHEDRAL
> NELSON'S COLUMN
> AND
> ALL TOWN HALLS IN LONDON.
>
> **Searchlight Display**
>
> London Region H.Q. will give a searchlight display over Central London, to-night from 11.45 p.m. to 12.15 a.m. and again to-morrow night during the same hour.

Time for some peace thought Grace. She told the others, that she was going to the Church Saint Martins-in-The -Fields, located on the side of Trafalgar Square. The other girls joined Grace, up the stone steps, and into the huge open doors.

How cool it was inside. Hundreds of wooden chairs faced the Alter, deep inside the East end of the Church. The quietness of the building was very peaceful. Several people were sitting quietly in the chairs. Grace and Betty each sat in a chair, near the back of the Church. The other girls wandered around the Church, looking at the plaques on the walls, describing the bodies in the underground vault's below.

Quietness was a relief from the sound of the milling crowds outside. Just sitting in the tranquil place had Grace, again thinking of Leslie. Did he know of the peace? Was he still safe? Where was he? When will he return home?

12 Met, Squadron, Q section noticed a marked difference in RADAR detection since the eighth of May. Air traffic was minimal, and sea vessels detected had less movement. The high-level vapour trails from bombers no longer existed. Information on traffic movements were still important, but now British and Allied aircraft could be told directly of other air traffic in the vicinity, and not by coded messages. The RADAR stations had now become the beginnings of Air Traffic Control. The systems became a very successful operation. Great care had to be taken, as the War with Japan was still raging, so every aircraft detected must be identified.

Leslie was told that at some time in the near future, his Squadron will be replaced, to allow them some well-deserved home leave. The firm instructions, were that their location must still, for the moment, remain a secret.

A new Airfield landing strip was being constructed at Saint Antoine, about five miles from the Squadrons RADAR camp, near the coast. A dedicated RADAR station for the airfield was included in the new construction. When it is completed, then the existing temporary camp could be removed.

Occasionally Leslie would visit the new airfield, just to see how the construction was developing. The Royal Engineers were doing very well, supported by a large contingent of local Corsicans. Paid work for the locals, was a new experience for many of the men.

Some aircraft were monitored on Leslies tubes, coming and going from the new airstrip.

Late August, and the work on the airfield was complete. Leslie and several other RADAR operators assisted with the change-over to the new permanent system, How the technology had changed since the last upgrade that 12 Met had been given.

The new operators had been very glad of the help given by the 12 Met men.

One early morning the Group Captain arrived at the camp with a lorry full of men. The day had arrived. Jed, the camp donkey, was given to a local family. He never did produce milk, or eggs, but plenty of fertilizer.

The changeover was complete. The men who had arrived on the truck, started to dismantle the camp. It was like losing a good friend. Almost three years of Leslie and his team in the camp, had made the place like home. However, the real home will not be far away. Many goodbye's to Corsican friends had taken place over the previous days, and the boat was given to Petra and his family.

The kit was packed and loaded onto the trusty Bedford trucks. The men of 12 Met stood for a few moments, just looking at the camp area. What a time had been experienced here. Happiness, unhappiness, fear, adventure. All of the emotions came rushing back into the memories of the men. What will the future now bring?

The men of 12 Met, boarded the Bedford trucks and headed down the uneven track to the mountain road, for the last time. The winding road was so familiar, with every corner, and every bump in the road known as a mental map. A man pushing a bicycle loaded with peaches, stopped pushing his bike and waved his arms as if to stop the trucks. The trucks drew to a halt, covered by a cloud of dust from the road surface, almost obliterating the view of the local man.

The men of 12 Met Squadron

The peach seller passed huge bunches of his load of peaches onto the back of one of the trucks, with welcoming arms retrieving the fruit. The seller waited for a moment, as Leslie took a photograph. A wave of a goodbye from the peach seller, and the trucks move off towards the airfield.

The trucks were parked in a tarmac area beside the new airfield's reception building. The men of the Squadron filed into the building, with each of them carrying a very full kit-bag. A Douglas D.C.10 aircraft was boarded on the tarmac apron. Engines roared, and they were off. As the aircraft climbed in the cloudless blue sky, the small size of the Island of Corsica became very evident. Some of the men could identify the location below of their camp.

The aircraft continued to climb into the blue sky. It changed its heading to the North East. Seating in the military D.C. 10 was very basic, with seats located on each side of the fuselage. The men of 12 Met Squadron looked concerned at each other, for they thought that the aircraft was going to England, on a different heading. A Squadron Leader was sat opposite Leslie, so Leslie asked him if he knew where they were going?

"Northern Italy, to Lavarino reconnaissance Squadron," the Officer replied. "You have got to assist with the work in that region for a while. Did you lot think that you were going home? Sorry chaps, thought you might have been told."

What a disappointment. The 12 MET boys continued the flight without further discussion, with all were feeling very unhappy that they had not been informed of the plans.

After landing at an airfield in Italy, the Squadron was moved to a base near the Austrian border. They were told to go to a meeting in a rather dirty room. It had long tables and wooden bench seats. The Commanding Officer apologised for the condition of the room. He addressed the men, informing them, that they will be working at Lavarino in support of the reconnaissance Lysander aircraft Flight. He explained that even though the War in Europe was now over, such work must still continue. The task was to assist with RADAR in the North of Italy, and South Austria.

The sleeping arrangements were awful, the mess that had been left behind when the Germans ran away was unbelievable. Rubbish was strewn everywhere. The bedding was dirty, and the washing and toilet area was disgusting.

The men of 12 MET settled into the work quickly, with the equipment in a permeant building, and not under canvas. New bedding arrived, along with a contingent of cleaners, from a nearby camp. Living and working conditions gradually improved. Working life became boring, but acceptable. Leslie, continued his regular letters to Grace. He was delighted to receive a letter from her indicating that her release from the Army, was drawing near.

Grace had now received information regarding her release from the Army. Betty and Peggy had already been released, and were now home. Betty had returned to her parent's home, and Peggy to her new husband Jack. The question was, would Grace be released in time for a wedding in December? And would Leslie be granted home leave for the event? Life at Mill Hill all of a sudden, began to become hard. Grace knew that her escape from the Army was imminent. One morning the Commander told Grace to report to the medical officer for an examination. The Medical Officer was a very portly lady, in a long white overall coat. The examination was very brief. Grace wondered how could the M.O. discover anything by just looking into her mouth, taking blood pressure, and asking if she felt all right. The results never-the-less, were good. The written certificate said, that she was perfectly healthy.

Two days later an Army lorry took Grace, and fifteen other women, back to the camp at Wrexham. Things were happening very quickly now. On arrival at Wrexham, the women had to produce their pay books, and medical certificates.

The pay books were stamped by a senior Army officer with a stamp that said, "Released from Duty", and it was signed by the officer. Then it was all over. Uniform clothing was returned, and Civvy Street clothes were issued, along with railway train passes to return home.

Nobody said thank you, and nobody said goodbye. It was a very cold, unfeeling exercise. The train ride to Birmingham, Bristol, and the small branch line to the home town, was forgetful. To Grace it all seemed like a dream. From the train windows the countryside flew past at great speed. Her mind was empty of thoughts. The excitement of being a civilian, and no longer a soldier, had not yet become a major feature. The events of her release had been very quick, with hardly a moment to absorb the situation. The previous years had been totally based around the Army, the War, and the unwanted disruption to her life.

Grace's final short walk home from the small station was very odd. She remembered, that the many previous walks from the station, had been under different conditions. Somehow this time, the walk was more relaxed. It was a very odd feeling, for all she wanted to be was at home. At last there it was. Her own back door to her beloved family home.

Life at home for Grace began to return to some form of normality. She had been issued with food and clothing coupons from the Army. These became very precious, as they were slightly more generous than those issued to civilians.

Elsie and Jim were delighted that Grace was now out of the Army, and was settling down at home.

"We really think, that some form of work would be good for you," Jim suggested to Grace. "Your Mum and I, are very happy that you are now home and safe but, you must now consider what you are going to do with your life. We are very much aware that you haven't even touched the piano since you came home."

"I cannot touch those piano key's since Albert died. "Grace replied, with tears freely running down her cheeks, and her eyes red, as she continually tried to dry her tears. The death of Albert had affected Grace deeper than she would ever have thought. The cold day at the railway station, when Albert appeared in the freezing waiting room, was the last time she ever saw him. It is a memory that stayed with her to her dying day.

"I do agree that I must find some work to keep me occupied. Leslie doesn't have home leave yet, so the wedding is out of the question for the moment. When I left dressmaking before the War, I do have some contact addresses of ladies, who might be interested if I started my own dressmaking business."

"That is s very good idea," her father agreed. "If you need help and support, we will do all that we can, but you must work from home because we cannot afford to pay for any work premises."

The idea was put into action without delay. Grace wrote to several ladies who had been customers of her previous employer. The lady that Grace had worked for before the War had now retired, so returning to that employment was not now an option. The making of clothes was an easy task for Grace. She had been trained to a very high level before the War, and had completed her apprenticeship in the trade.

The response of Grace's letters from the ladies was very positive. One lady required a new gown urgently. The lady was indeed a 'Lady', being the daughter of a Lord. The information that Grace had received from the Lady, was that she also required Grace to design the Gown. The Lady visited Grace for measurements, and to agree the design created by Grace. The garment was a fine bottle green silk, long, and full gown, with all under skirts, and a tight-fitting bodice, and puff shoulders. Grace worked day and night to complete the project before the required completion date. The customer was delighted. As a result, she provided Grace with several more commissions. Within days of letters being sent, several other ladies also provided Grace with design requirements, and clothing contracts. The business was now under way.

The hinged cover over the piano keys remained firmly shut, and became a very useful surface to support dress making materials. The work room was now in the front room of the house.

The end of the Summer, and the beginning of Autumn, was starting to show its face. The Apples on the Golden Delicious Apple tree were ready to eat. The pips inside the apples were now a dark brown, indicating that they are ripe for picking. Fruit from the tree was an important commodity, and easy to store. Jim had recovered very well from his mining accident, so he was able to pick the apples that had not already fallen to the ground. Elsie wrapped each apple with great care in newspaper. She laid them in shallow wooden fruit boxes, ready for storage in the light reduced cupboard under the stairs. The soft fruit had already been harvested and had been made into jams and jelly. The quince apples from the japonica trees, were boiling away in a very large pan over the fire in the combination fire place. Muslin cloths and jam jars were prepared for the almost ready, japonica jelly.

The kitchen work from the harvest was brought to a halt as Earnest, Elsie's Brother, arrived at the back door of the house.

"I wanted to tell you all first," Earnest announced, looking very excited. "As you know, I have been very unhappy since Alberts mother died. Emmy, from the Salvation Army and I are to be married. Emmy lost her husband a few years ago, so we decided that we both needed good company and friendship, for the rest of our days. So, there we are then. We hope that you all understand, and will be happy for us." He sat heavily in a chair, looking at his sister with eyes that seemed to be begging her to understand.

Elsie threw her arms around Earnest's neck in a warm Sisterly embrace. Jim was standing beside his wife, holding his cap in his hand, clearly forgetting to remove his muddy boots before coming into the house from the garden.

"Of course, we understand and fully support your decision," Elsie said as she released her embrace on Earnest's neck. We know how unhappy you have been since 'D' day. This is truly a wonderful thing, and you have all of our blessings. We know that Albert would also approve.

Grace had entered the living room to hear and witness most of the conversation. She realised that her mother had stopped stirring the boiling fruit, in the pan. Grace resumed the stirring of the fruit, and removed the pan from the fire by swinging the pan supporting arm, away from the heat.

"What good news Uncle Earn," Grace said, checking that all of the fruit had boiled to a liquid. She knew that things would never be the same again. So, she understood that her Uncle needed to be happy, and she was happy for him.

CHAPTER 17

For some reason unknown to the men of 12 MET Squadron, they were moved from one base in Northern Italy to another with very little warning. At one point it became clear that the political situation was changing very fast. Information was very sketchy, but indicated that a variety of agreements were being made between Britain, its Allies, and other Countries, as a result of the cessation of the War.

One evening in an Officers Mess, now used as a canteen, the conversation between the men became very heated.

One man said. "Don't know why we all went through hell, just for them up there to toss us about like paper dolls. If they can't get it right at this stage, what chance will we have? It took a lot to keep 'Gerry' out of England. Now you watch it all fall around our ears. I've had enough. I want to go home. At least I'm alive, and will go home one day, unlike many hundreds of thousands of other poor sods."

All of the men looked at the Airman who had made the profound statement. It was very strange, for this particular man was known for not usually having any conversation or discussions. Obviously, the men's feelings were changing, perhaps everyone has just had enough.

Leslie tried to calm the situation down, as several of the men were now shouting at each other and getting very excited.

"Come on chaps," Leslies said in a loud but controlled way. "We are almost there. Release from the RAF is not far away. We can shout and scream as much as we like, but we cannot do anything from here. When we get home, you can always become a politician, then you might be able to change the World. I think we all know that there will be many people looking for new homes. A small number of people may come to England. Some men from other Countries did help us during the War. Let's try to stay calm just a bit longer."

The men's excitement calmed down, with a few mutterings from some of them. But generally, the dignity was maintained again.

The Squadron was moved yet again. But this time to a small airfield in Southern Austria. The Summer warmth from the sun had changed to the cooler air of early Autumn. Distant mountain tops showed the signs of an early snowfall. Work never really materialised to any great extent, as orders had not yet come through. At least, Leslie was now able to tell Grace where he was in the World, in his very frequent letters.

The Men of 12 MET Squadron were told to pack all belongings yet again. But this time they were flown back to England. The base at Hednesford again became home.

Being back in 'Old blighty' again was a wonderful feeling. Standard RADAR work on brand new systems and equipment was a relief. Leslie was able, at last, to write to Grace with a British postal address. Almost as soon as the men arrived at Hednesford, Len received his release from the RAF. The friendship between Leslie and Len was very secure. Addresses were exchanged, and a promise to stay in contact was never broken.

Letters between Leslie and Grace became more frequent, as the postal service became much more reliable. Written discussions about the wedding, and a date, became more important. Leslie applied for twelve days home leave for the last few days in November, and the first few in December. His request was granted. The date for the wedding could now be set for the first of December.

Grace now set to work arranging the Chapel, Minister, the hall for the reception, Bridesmaids and their dresses, flowers, food at the reception, informing all family members and guests. the printing of an order of service, and someone to take a photograph of the event.

"How on earth do I do all the arranging with Leslie not able to help?" Grace complained to her Mother. "Not only do I have to do everything on the list, but also finish the dresses for the Bridesmaids, and my vail. I also have to complete the dress for Mrs. Smith. I just cannot do miracles."

"Miracles do happen sometimes my dear," Elsie replied. "I will do most of the arranging, if you can do the dressmaking. Your Dad can arrange the hall for the reception with the Caretaker. Just move forward in an organised way, and let things take its own path."

Elsie always was a calming influence to any situation. She looked at things as if a power above her would control and guide her, to a good conclusion. She had a very strong belief in her God, and the Society of Friends, the Quakers, of which she remained a practicing member. Life, to Elsie, had already been planned out, so to follow the planned path ahead will always result in happiness.

The organised work for the wedding arrangements proceeded as Elsie had predicted. The Minister was a little concerned about the very short notice of the wedding, but he had become accustomed to this over the last few years, as home leave for service people could not always be planned a long way ahead.

Grace had chosen Leslie's Brother Don's Fiancée, to be one of her Bridesmaid's. On one meeting for a dress fitting, she told Grace that they were to be married exactly one week after her wedding. What excitement, Grace thought. The two Brothers getting married one week apart from each other.

Mid November. Leslie was now getting very excited. He was to marry the woman of his dreams in two weeks. The men of Met 12 Squadron were being released from the service one by one. Eight men remained from the original fifteen. All further release of personnel had stopped, much to the annoyance of Leslie. He was hoping to be a civilian for the wedding, but that just will not be the case.

At last the day for Leslie to travel home had arrived. His travel documents were signed by the Officer, who said with a twinkle in his eye. "Don't do anything that I wouldn't do young man. I want you to be back here on time after your leave, because things are happening here as well."

For Leslie the train journey home seemed to take for ever. The trains were crowded with people. The platforms were crowded with people, and the new railway coach with a corridor, had only standing room left to Bristol Temple Meads Station. As Leslie disembarked the train onto the platform at Bristol, he was greeted by his Father who was waving his arms above his head, and shouting Leslie's name. What a relief to see his Dad. The kit bag was loaded into the back of the oil van, and Leslie joined his Father in the front seats.

The journey home was without talking. The metallic thunder from the van's engine was very loud, so that conversation became impossible. The engine noise, was joined by the sound of heavy rain on the sheet aluminium roof of the green Jowett Bradford van. The motor of the single blade windscreen wiper was turned on to full speed. The wiper blade occasionally moved across the windscreen, leaving almost as much rain on the window behind it, as in front of it. Leslie did not care, for he was on his way.

At last the home town was ahead of them. The rain had not eased throughout the hour's journey from the station. The High Street was around the corner. Leslie's Dad Charlie stopped the van abruptly. The High Street was flooded with water from the stream that ran along the length of the Street. The flooding was much too deep for the van to pass.

"Dammed rain," Charlie swore as he turned the van around. Home was only on the other side of the High Street, and up the hill overlooking the town. Charlie continued. "Every time it rains, the High Street floods. Dammed nuisance. Got to make a three-mile diversion every time. The Council just won't spend the money. They cannot understand the problems it causes. They are like all committees, they go into a meeting to design a Horse. They come out having designed a Camel. Just can't get anything right."

The van made its way through an adjacent village to avoid the flooding.

As the van arrived outside the rear of the family house, the rain magically stopped. Leslies Mother Edith, was at the open back door of the house, with arms wide open to welcome her long lost Son. Her Motherly hug was long, and delivered with deep love. The tears of happiness streamed down the cheeks of Edith. Almost four years of not knowing if he would return home alive or dead. The fear of War very much took its toll on the families of service personnel, waiting at home. Newspapers were read, and wireless reports listened by thousands of people with deep interest over the years. Much of the emotions were because many families did not know where their children were in the World. Every time a Telegram Boy was seen the fear returned. It often became a very painful time for Edith and Charlie, along with hundreds of thousands of other parents. Now that fear was over. Charlie just stood and watched the emotional reunion.

The kit bag was recovered from the van, and simple gifts given to Edith and Charlie.

"After you have had a good meal inside you, you must go down and see Grace. She knows you are coming home today, so you must see her as soon as you can," Edith insisted as she placed a large dinner plate in front of Leslie, with all of the best ingredients she could obtain, using the food coupons.

Leslie did enjoy his meal. Charlie sat at the table beside Leslie and said. "Nothing like a bit of home cooking. What do you think Son?"

"Blooming lovely," Leslie replied, as he wiped the plate clean with a piece of bread laced with the best butter. "The last time I had a meal like that was the last time that I was here."

"Time to see Grace," Edith insisted, taking the very clean plate to the kitchen for a proper washing up.

Leslie was still wearing his RAF uniform with the tight-fitting battle dress tunic, with the two gold stripes of a Flight Lieutenant, proudly displayed on the shoulder straps. Time was precious, so without changing his clothes he set off to visit his betrothed. Across the road in front of the house, to the footpath that lead to the railway lines that ran across the top of the town. Having to wait a few moments for a long passenger train to pass, and he was on his way again. Down another path and then the hill road to the High Street.

As Leslie approached the High Street, he encountered a marching group of RAF Cadets, from the Air Training Corp. The NCO leading the group was an A.T.C. Flight Sergeant. On seeing Leslie approach the Sergeant immediately halted the marching boys. He stood very much to attention, and gave a very smart salute.

"Good afternoon Sir," the Sergeant said as Leslie approached.

Leslie returned the salute and replied. "Good afternoon Sergeant. A very smart parade you have there."

The Sergeant completed his salute and said. "Thank-you Sir. We are so proud of what you have all done in the War, that we want to show our support. Are you able to tell us a bit about your experiences Sir? We won't take up much of your time. Were you serving at home of overseas?

"I am so sorry, but I am afraid that I am in a bit of a hurry at the moment," Leslie responded, sliding past the smart group of young men. "Sorry Sergeant. Must go."

Leslie almost ran the rest of the way to Graces house. He did feel very sorry at having to leave the parade so abruptly. But he was on a mission, and nothing would stand in his way. As he approached the front path of Graces home, the front door was flung open wide, and Grace ran to throw herself into Leslies open arms. Grace was holding Leslie so tightly that he was unable to move his arms to respond. Eventually Grace did release her tight hold, allowing Leslie at last to hold Grace in his arms. The meeting was very loving and tender, taking place half way along the front garden path from the street.

Mrs. Montgomery who lived in the adjoining house, opened her front door. She took a few steps along her front garden path. Her flower-patterned full apron, was partly hidden by her folded arms across her rotund chest. "Nice to see you home safe and well Leslie," she said, making as if to close her front gate and trying not to look nosey. "I suppose Grace is happy now," she concluded going back inside her house and closing the door.

Grace was indeed happy. She was very happy. Her Man was now in her arms, and she wanted it to stay like that for ever.

At last, Grace invited Leslie into the house to be warmly greeted by her Mother and Father. The kettle was pulled over the roaring fire on the iron swinging arm. Leslie was given the seat beside the fire, usually occupied by Grace's Mother. Grace sat on the floor beside Leslie's legs, and rested her head on his knees, looking at his face as if she had never seen a man before.

"So, come on then Lad. What have you been up to?" Jim asked, leaning forward in his chair, hoping to hear an intriguing tail.

"Bit of a problem in that respect," Leslie responded as he gazed deeply into Grace's eyes. "Most of what I did is covered by the Official Secrets Act, but what I can tell you is that I went to Malta, Tunis in North Africa, Corsica, Italy and Austria, and of course good old England. I saw quite a few things that I wish I hadn't seen. Had to do a few things that I really didn't want to do. Made some very good friends. Had some very uncomfortable times, living for years in tents in the mountains of Corsica, hiding, and operating away from the enemy.

Many of us have got to the stage where all we want to do is to forget. The trouble is, that I have still got to go back, for how long, none of us know."

"Sorry Son," Jim said, shaking his head, knowing exactly what Leslie was feeling. He has seen many things while serving in the Australian Army in the last War. Like most old Soldiers, he had put so much to the back of his mind. The high level of death and destruction was such, that nobody must forget. So many time's Jim found himself quietly pondering on the past. He also knew, that both Leslie and Grace must also have seen, and been, through Hell.

"So, you two," Elsie excitedly announced, desperately wanting to change the subject. "In just three days-time you will be Husband and Wife. Have you decided where you are going to live? Will it be with Leslie's Mum and Dad, or will it be here with us?"

Grace replied to her Mothers question. She stood up, and threw her arms around Elsie. "We would love to live here with you both, if you will have us. My bedroom at the back of the house will be just fine for us. We will be saving our money in a proper savings account, so that one day we will have a home of our own."

"You will be most welcome for as long as you need to be here," Elsie responded, holding Grace's hands. Grace could feel the power of love passing from her Mother to herself.

Grace and Leslie were left alone, to discuss the wedding arrangements. Jim made himself busy in the garden shed. As it was the end of November the garden was very muddy from the recent rain, so it could not be worked on at the moment. Jim enjoyed taking broken things apart. He put wood screws in one box, threaded brass screws and nuts into another box. Bits of copper was collected in a heavy cotton bag, other broken and unimportant items were thrown away. He knew that brass, copper, and iron could be sold to the 'scrap man'. The few shillings made from the sale helped with the meagre income from his disability pension, from the Coal Board. Every money saving and earning opportunity was exploited. Toilet paper was made from strips of old newspaper. Fallen tree branches were collected in the hand cart and used as firewood. The outer lead sheath, of old electric cable was stripped, and the copper conductors save and eventually sold. Chickens provided eggs, and eventually meat. The produce from the garden was a vital source of food throughout the year. Such jobs were very important to Jim. Not just for the financial gain, but also as a means of mental therapy. If things could be used again, they were. Even the bones from the meat joints were ground to a powder, and used on the garden as fertilizer.

Jim took the opportunity to consider the wedding. Grace had known Leslie for many years. They first met at Sunday School when they were both very young. The relationship just developed over the years. It was always assumed that at some time, they would be married. So, now here it is. Three days away. Jim and Elsie always knew where in the Country Grace was, while she was in the Army. But they had been very worried on many occasions. The heavy bombing in London, and Coventry was a constant cause for concern. So many service people never returned home. Thousands of families lost their homes, and all of their possessions, and in many cases their lives as well. Jim was grateful that Grace and Leslie were lucky in returning home as they have. Poor old Earnest, loosing Albert and his mother as he did. Must have been hell in that Army Tank on 'D' day.

Jim's thoughts were halted by Elsie shouting that a cup of tea was ready for him.

After his tea, Elsie asked Jim to carry out a few important tasks. He firstly, wandered along the road to visit Bob, who was the caretaker of the hall to be used for the wedding reception. Bob was always a bit forgetful, so Jim thought it good sense to confirm the booking for the next Saturday.

"Now then, where did I put that booking in book?" Bob said, in a very broad Somerset accent. "I know I put it here somewhere. Ah Hear it is. Under that pile of rubbish, ready to be chucked out. So, let's have a gander. There it is Jim me old mate. Four thirty Saturday afternoon, for four hours, all in yur name Jim."

Jim felt a little more confident having seen the booking in the 'booking in book'. At least one thing had a good chance of happening on the day.

Bob continued to read from the book. "Nine folding tables and thirty folding chairs. Two of the tables by the stage, and all with white table cloths. All grub and cutlery supplied by others. Three-pound fifteen bob and a tanner. The tanner is for me Missus for cleaning up after you all."

The next job for Jim was to visit Mrs. Brown who was making the wedding cake. Jim had always been a little frightened of Mrs Brown. A Widow from the last War, she had always considered that any man was the one for her. She was a good Christian woman, but all of the men were concerned about her advances.

Jim cautiously knocked on Mrs. Browns front door, and took two steps backwards, just in case.

The door was opened wide to reveal a tall, well-built woman. A long white apron covered her body from her chin, to one foot from the ground. Her hair was held in place by a neatly tied scarf around her head, a classic 1920's golden curl emerged from under the front of the scarf. Her sleeves were rolled up well above her elbows. Jim thought her face explained clearly her intentions. A thick layer of powder, rouge, dark eye make-up, and bright red lipstick, expertly applied, completed the look.

"Hello Jim. how lovely to see you?" Mrs. Brown said, inviting Jim to pass her in the doorway, face to face, so that her well-endowed chest had to squeeze between them. "Come into my parlour you lovely man, and see my recent construction."

After squeezing past Mrs Brown, Jim went right through to the kitchen at the rear of the cottage. He saw a three-tier white wedding cake on the kitchen table. An icing piping bag lying beside the cake.

"Is this Grace's cake?" Jim asked, as he made sure that the table came between himself and Mrs. Brown.

"It is. Do you like it?" Mrs. Brown asked, as she walked around the table towards Jim.

"Oh yes, it looks very good. We are looking forward to seeing it finished on Saturday," Jim said, as he made his way towards the front door at some speed.

"Surly you don't have to go so soon Jim? Stay a while and enjoy a little something with me," the Lady shouted as she ran behind Jim, trying to catch him with outstretched arms.

In moments Jim was in the street, making very sure that his jacket was tidy, and without any flour marks. Mrs. Brown was last seen, standing at her front door, making very sure that her golden curl was still in place.

Jim felt a lot safer arriving at home until Elsie started to ask questions. "Did you see Bob?"

"Yep."

"Is the hall booking still fine?"

"Yep."

"Is he going to arrange the tables as we asked?"

"Yep."

"Did you see Mrs. Brown?"

"Yep."

"Did you see the cake?"

"Yep."

"Does she have enough food coupons to buy all of the ingredients? I had to ask several people to contribute some coupons for the eggs, sugar and fruit, because we don't have enough in the family.

"Don't know."

"Did you ask her?"

"Nop."

"Did you stay long enough to ask her? I know what a reputation she has with men. So, did you leave quickly?"

"Yep."

"Oh, dear Jim. That means I must go and see her myself. Will you come with me this afternoon?"

"Nop. Sorry, got other important things to do this afternoon," Jim replied, rapidly leaving the house by the back door. Jim made his escape telling himself under his breath, that he never wants to see Mrs. Brown on his own, ever again.

Elsie put on her winter coat and shoes, and pined her felt winter hat using a long hat pin, to her hair. She left the house by the back door, to visit Mrs. Brown, but there was no sign of Jim.

Friday the thirtieth of November. The day before the wedding. Leslie had emptied the contents of his RAF kit bag. He had been very careful to bring his dress uniform jacket to wear at the wedding, unfortunately, the jacket was very creased from being jammed into the kit bag.

Leslie held the jacket in front of his Mum. "Any chance of an Iron please?"

Edith took the jacket from Leslie, with a view to run a hot iron over the garment. Her actions were stopped abruptly as another of her sons, Don, came through the back door, with his kit bag on his shoulder. The jacket no longer was important, as she threw her arms around the neck of her eldest Son.

"Hello all," Don said, as he threw his kit bag into an empty arm chair. "Got here in time for your wedding Boy. And in plenty of time for mine next week."

Eventually the Jacket did get ironed, along with a uniform shirt, and trousers.

The two boys and their parents spent the rest of the afternoon and the evening talking about where the boys had been during their RAF service. Don, was able to talk about his service, firstly working on Spitfire Merlin engines, and then as an instructor on the engines. Leslie was only able to explain where he had been, but not what he had been doing.

Bed time arrived, but Leslie was unable to sleep. The excitement of seeing Grace after such a long time, along with the expectations of tomorrow, overpowered his mind. Eventually the morning arrived with a frost so deep, that ice had formed on the inside of the bedroom window. It had created a variety of fragile patterns. Charlie, had already lit the fire in the living room, and was chatting to Don, with cups of tea in their hands.

Edith was in the kitchen cooking breakfast. Leslie arrived in the room, looking as if sleep had escaped him.

"For goodness sake go back to bed Leslie," Charlie said, looking at his sleepy son. "As long as you are ready by eleven o'clock, go and get some sleep. Anyone would think that you stayed awake to see Santa Clause all night."

Leslie did sleep until a quarter past ten. He was ready as instructed, by eleven o'clock. Don also looked very smart in his RAF uniform, as he was to be Leslie's Best Man.

The family was driven to the Chapel by Charlie in the big Austin car recently bought by Charlie from an elderly friend. Not a seat was left available in the Chapel, except for the Groom, Best Man, and the Groom's parents. Elsie looked very smart in the front left pew of the Chapel. The heating boiler must have been lit many hours earlier, as the Chapel was very warm. The ends of the pew's had been decorated with evergreen branches, and a vase on a tall wooden stand contained a group of large headed Chrysanthemums.

The organ started to play Mendelssohn's Wedding March. The organist Mr. Jones, looking in his strategically placed mirror as he played, occasionally touching a wrong organ key, resulting in a few winces from the congregation. All stood to acknowledge the entrance of the Bride.

Leslie was determined not to turn around to look, but his curiosity became overpowering. Grace looked divine. Her long vail covered her pretty face. She was carrying a bouquet of wonderful large headed Chrysanthemums, partly covering her white wedding dress, with broderie anglaise stitched to enhance the garment.

After the ceremony the single photograph was taken outside the main door of the Chapel. The sun was bright, but the air was cold, so, Charlie drove the newly married couple, the five hundred yards, to the reception hall. At the hall all was as agreed with Bob the Caretaker, and his 'booking-in' book. Bob's Wife, for her extra tanner had installed two large glass vases' full of beautiful Dahlia's cut from the garden. The hall looked wonderful, much to the relief of Jim. The wedding cake took pride of place on a white clothed table, located to one side of the hall. The cake was being tended by Mrs. Brown, who was winking and smiling at several men.

The food was eaten, the cake was cut, the speeches had been delivered, and the small children raced around the hall at great speed, getting in the way of the adults. More photographs were taken of the couple, Brides Maid's, Best Man, Mother of the Bride, and Groom's parents, by Jim, using his folding Kodak camera.

The allotted time for the vacation of the hall came all too quickly. Charlie disappeared to collect the Austin car. The doors to the hall were opened. to reveal, that a fall of fresh white snow had covered the World like a blanket. A nearby gas streetlight, illuminated the snow with a yellow glow, making the covering look almost warm.

Charlie drove the happy couple back to Grace's home, that was now also Leslie's home. Elsie had arrived at the house earlier, having walked the few hundred yards from the hall. The kettle as boiling away over the warming fire, and two cups of steaming coco greeted the couple. Elsie, had obtained the coco many months earlier, to be used only on a special occasion.

CHAPTER 18

Married life was not only a new experience, but also one of deep love. The time is now here for both Grace and Leslie to live life in a different way. Each of them started to understand the other person in a way that neither of them had done before. The small, and large feelings and thoughts, were being learned by both about the other. Many mistakes were made, as were apologies for misunderstanding the 'learning curve'.

One week later, it was the turn for Don to marry Olive. The ceremony took place in a Methodist Chapel in the Village where Olive was brought up, and had lived. Olive had been a nurse in the Army, however, now she was the Village Postwoman. Don was very smart in his RAF uniform. Leslie was his Best Man, and was also in RAF uniform. Charlie and Edith had a second opportunity, to be very proud parents.

All too soon the leave time for Leslie was over. The return train ride, to RAF Hednesford seemed to be a bit of a blur. His thoughts were still hovering over the memories of the last few days. How life had changed. He now has a different responsibility from just looking after himself, to now also considering his Wife. That is a new aspect for Leslie to deal with. No longer is he 'one of the boy's', he is now a married man. Did all married men feel like this? he asked himself. Did all married men think more of their Wives than themselves, as he did? He noticed that even boarding and disembarking the train, was done more carefully. What odd feelings he was having.

The guard house at RAF Hednesford again loomed in front of Leslie. At least he was back before his leave time was up, by just four hours. After changing into a more relaxing uniform in his billet, he made his way to the officers Mess. On entering the Mess, it was as though nothing had changed. He made his way to the canteen area, and helped himself to a piece of Victoria sponge cake, and a mug of tea.

"Hello Skipper," a voice came from a table. It had several Airmen huddled over their mugs of tea. "See that you went through with it, with that shiny gold band on your finger. Don't know if you have heard yet? but we are to be released soon, but the delivery of release books hasn't arrived yet. Going to be another month before the next batch arrives." The voice came from Stan who had always been the quiet one in the Squadron. "Better come and join us, and tell us what married life is like."

Leslie sat next to Stan with cake in one hand, and tea in the other. The moment Leslie sat down, everybody stood up, and to attention. "It's the G.C.," Stan whispered out of the side of his mouth.

Leslie turned to face the Officer who was standing just inside the door. It was the Group Captain. Leslie smartly saluted the Officer, as he was the most senior in the room.

The Group Captain returned the salute and said. "Very Good. Stand down please. Gentlemen, I have some good news and some bad news. The bad news is that release documents will not be at this base for another two months, due to problems with the printers. I know that many of you are over due for release, but there has been a major cock-up. Sorry about that. The good news is, that you will remain operational at this base for the foreseeable future. At least you will get good food, good accommodation and good beer. You will be given new duties by your C.O. Thank you for your attention," the Officer saluted, turned, and walked out of the room.

"So, there you have it straight from the horse's mouth," Stan said, slamming his tea mug down hard onto the white clothed table.

Leslie returned to his billet with the cake and half cold tea. He sat on the chair next to his bed, and wrote a long and detailed letter to Grace. He expressed his deep love for her, before telling her that he will be in the RAF for at least another two months. Leslie also wrote a letter to the employer, that he had worked for before his service. The company were Electricians and had a base about half a mile from his now marital home. He formally applied for the job that he had been promised, would be kept open for him, upon completion of his military service. Hopefully he will have a job when he is released.

The Wing Commander did issue new orders to the remaining men of 12 MET. The task was now to teach new recruits about the RADAR, and reconnaissance systems. The conscription system had drawn in a variety of people into the RAF. All National Service personnel had to complete a service of at least eighteen months. As a result, most of the new recruits had little or no interest in the subject. All they wanted to do was to complete the eighteen months, as easily as possible, and without having to work for it. The threat of War and staying alive under difficult conditions, did not come into the new recruit's minds. The people who were interested, were the people who joined the RAF as regular volunteer servicemen and women. Leslie often thought that the lack of interest shown, by conscripted people, would have killed many, and perhaps themselves in the War. This situation was quickly addressed by the H.Q. Only regular volunteers were placed on RADAR and recognisance. Training became much easier as those who were being trained, wanted to be trained.

The letters to Grace from Leslie were almost daily, with letters from Grace in return, being almost as frequent. One important letter did arrive for Leslie. It was an offer of a job as an Electrician with his former employer. This was wonderful, he would now be able to support his new Wife, and the child that she told him she was expecting in August.

Early February, and Leslie had a forty-eight-hour pass. The journey to home seemed to take for ever. All he wanted was to be at home. It had been snowing heavily, so this added to the slow journey. The last walk home from the station in the deep snow, was the same route that Grace had taken on many occasions previously. The thought passed through Leslies mind about the last time that Grace saw her cousin Albert, in that cold, snow covered station waiting room. He could just imagine that meeting, for he also had to pull the deep collar of his great coat, high above his ears to keep the cold icy wind away. He had to follow the route of the road, as the track across the fields was now too deep in snow for it to be a safe route.

Leslie approached the house by the side path, with a view to going to the back door. The path was blocked by a snow drift about five feet deep. The North Easterly cold snowy wind had caused the drift. The path to the front door was quite clear, so he entered the front door to a very warm welcome from Grace.

Jim and Elsie were listening to a wireless program with Tommy Trinder and Ted Ray, entertainers and comedians. It was good to hear laughter in the house. It was even better, that the coal fire had warmed the room with a welcoming glow. As the wireless program ended, Elsie asked Leslie if he would like a bath. She said that the others would go into the front room to give him the privacy he required. As Leslie had not had a bath for a long time, he agreed. He had usually only had showers in the billet, that were of luke-warm water.

The tin bath was brought into the living room and placed in front of the fire. The bath had been hanging on an outside wall in the back yard. The steel of the bath was freezing due to the weather conditions. The bath was turned from side-to-side, and end-to-end to ensure it was well warmed in front of the fire. Several very large saucepans full of water, were put onto the swinging arms over the roaring fire, as the tin bath was being warmed. Eventually the bath was warm, and the water boiled. The bath was placed on the hearth rug in front of the fire. Jim and Elsie disappeared into the front room. Cold water first, then the hot water added to the right temperature. It was wonderful. Grace made an excuse to join her parents. Leslie slipped deep into the welcoming hot water. What luxury. A white tin enamelled tall tapered jug, with the wide end at the bottom, was provided for washing hair.

Warm towels completed the exercise. The next task was to empty the bath. Grace returned to scoop the water from the bath, using the large saucepans. Leslie stopped her. She was expecting their first child. She was not to lift heavy saucepans of water. Leslie was now fully dressed, so, as he had the bath, it was now up to him to empty it. He filled the large saucepan with water from the bath, opened the back door with a view to tip the water down the outside kitchen drain. One step outside onto the now icy floor. His legs flew from under him, his arms went high in the sky, including the one, holding the saucepan. Leslie arrived onto the icy floor, with the full saucepan raining down on him from above, upside down. What a mess. The saucepan was unhurt, the floor was unhurt, Leslie's pride was very badly hurt, as was the base of his spine. His clothes were now very wet, so a change of clothes was now in order. The bath was eventually emptied by Jim.

Later the family sat around the fire laughing at the recent events, as Leslie was now sitting on a very soft cushion, protecting his coccyx.

Grace was not showing any growth in her figure yet, but had been feeling very unwell on occasions. Her mother told her that it was normal, and it was called morning sickness. Grace wondered if pregnancy was really the thing for her. But if that is what had to be overcome, then she would overcome it, somehow.

Leslie was a lot cleaner when he left the house for his return journey, than when he arrived, having had a bath, and a second dousing in the back yard. The base of his spine was still very tender, but improving. More snow had arrived, so the walk to the station was taken very cautiously as he had no intentions of falling again.

The railway lines were now covered in snow, but the small black six-wheeled locomotive approached on time, hauling two coaches.

The steam escaping from the locomotive, and covering the platform like a fluffy blanket, had a strange comforting feeling as it caused the station buildings and beyond to be obscured. The strange effect was that Leslie felt enclosed and safe. In moments the cloud of steam disappeared, and reality returned.

Work at RAF Hednesford became very mundane. The days dragged by, as the routines became endless. Letters to and from Grace, continued on an almost daily basis. The time for Leslie's medical tests arrived. This being the beginning of the process to be released from the service. He passed with flying colours. The ration coupons were issued, so surly release was imminent.

As last, Leslie was called to the release office. A civilian suit of clothes was provided, in exchange for all of his RAF uniform. He did manage to retain his folding cap and badge. The Officer filled in the release book. It indicated the length of his service, the countries in the World where he had served and the medals available to him. This included the Italian Star. The book also included a synopsis on how he had performed, and his full-service record. This was to provide a basic reference for any future employer. A signature by the Officer, and a date stamp, concluded the exercise.

That was it. All those years of work, discomfort, fear, and worry was over, without anybody saying thank-you, or goodbye. The feeling was one of disappointment, and relief, all at the same time. He had seen and done things, that would not have been normal in any other environment but War. And now, it was all over.

The journey home was much cheaper than previous journey's, for Leslie had been given travel vouchers. As he watched the countryside dash past from the railway carriage, he asked himself a question. Did any part of his RAF service make any difference to anybody else, except his family, himself and Grace? He reflected that in the First World War, the enemy did not invade Britain, in this conflict again, the enemy did not invade, so will that always be the case in the future? On that journey home he decided that he will put the War behind him in his mind, and never to discuss it again.

Being home for Leslie was now a different way of life. No longer did he have to worry about getting back to the base in time, or the discipline of military life. He felt that it was for time being, a well-earned holiday. At some point the holiday must end. A visit to the electrician's Company who had promised him work, resulted in immediate employment. Skilled electricians were hard to come-by after the War, so Leslie was asked to start work on the following Monday.

Grace began to grow steadily with her unborn, who was occasionally moving about inside of her. The local Midwife, Nurse DeBocsier, was a frequent visitor, as she was also a close friend with her Mother Elsie. All was well with the pregnancy, so it was decided, that, if there was no change over the next few months, then a home delivery would be fine.

Leslie enjoyed his work as an electrician. He had been provided with a works Ford van. After only a few months with the company, the Government bought many large electrical businesses. The Company changed to one of several sections. One section dealt with the supply cables, and systems to properties, and the one that Leslie worked for installed and repaired electrical systems in homes, and other buildings. It was known as 'The Electricity Board'.

Leslie knew that working for a large company was not for him. A large company, in his mind, tended to treat employed people as numbers, and not people. This reminded him of the RAF, and the military life that he had left behind. Grace and Leslie discussed the matter at length with both Grace's and Leslies parents. The decision was made. It was time for Leslie to start business on his own, and to be his own boss.

Work for electricians was always in demand. A small Ford five hundredweight van was purchased, for twenty pounds. The spare wheel that usually was attached to the outside of the passenger door was missing, as was one windscreen wiper blade, but the van did work well. The side valve engine was quiet, and did not use oil, this being a general problem with that type of engine. The business was set-up. Leslie was to carry out the work, and Grace would do the book-work as she had the skills from her Army days. Grace also continued with her highly requested dressmaking business, although, getting close to the sewing machine became more difficult each day.

Jim was also now very happy. As Leslie removed old electrical items from re-wires and alterations, he dismantled, and sorted the brass and copper for his recycling.

Charlie knew that the business was right for Leslie and Grace. Don, was now also a civilian, having left the RAF only a few weeks after Leslie. The time was approaching for Charlie to consider retirement from the oil delivery business. His service with the Home Guard had ended soon after V.E. day, as the home defence requirement was no longer required. Don worked at a nearby car and bicycle repair garage using his mechanical knowledge, obtained in the RAF. Charlie sold the Bradford van and the Austin car, and bought a 1936 Wolseley Hornet Six, car. The twelve-horsepower car, was blue at the bottom, and black at the top. Edith loved to travel around in the car, going to areas that she had never seen before. Towns that she had heard of, now became a reality.

One day Charlie was chatting to the man who lived in the house next door. Charlie was explaining to the man how Edith loved to see other places when travelling in the car. "Never been out of the town but once in my life," the man told Charlie. "I went to the next town, down the road once, a few years ago. Couldn't understand a damn thing they were saying with that accent they have. So, I come home again, and never been there since."

Life for all was settled, and at last set in some sort of pattern. Bob the Hall caretaker had died, so the caretaking of the hall was passed to his Wife. Mrs. Brown at last found a willing man. She married him, and changed colour by becoming Mrs. Green. The High Street had been closed for several months, as work to divert the river through an underground culvert was carried out, to relieve the flooding. The dance hall opened its doors on Saturday mornings for roller skating for the young ones, and the Cinema showed Micky Mouse films on Saturday afternoons.

All was peaceful until the Midwife, who was attending Grace on the due date, responded to the loud cry from Grace's just born child, announcing. 'It's a boy'.

~~THE END~~

or is it

THE BEGINNING?

Printed in Great Britain
by Amazon